C000231153

FIND YOUR

To the runway farmer!!

All the best.

Rohan

# Also by
# Rohan West

*Broken Vows*

# FIND YOUR NORTH STAR

A NOVEL, BASED ON A TRUE STORY, BY

ROHAN WEST

Matador
Unit E2 Airfield Business Park,
Harrison Road, Market Harborough,
Leicestershire. LE16 7UL
Tel: 0116 2792299
Email: books@troubador.co.uk
Web: www.troubador.co.uk/matador
Twitter: @matadorbooks

ISBN 978 1803135 526

British Library Cataloguing in Publication Data.
A catalogue record for this book is available from the British Library.

Printed and bound in Great Britain by 4edge Limited
Typeset in 11pt Minion Pro by Troubador Publishing Ltd, Leicester, UK

Matador is an imprint of Troubador Publishing Ltd

To Jim, Daphne, Ray and Lyneve

# PREFACE

Four and a half years have passed since Father Albert Robertson left his life as a Catholic Priest, and married the love of his life, Abigail McCarthy. Defrocked and excommunicated by the Church, and shunned by both families, Albert and Abigail begin a life together in Auckland, New Zealand. Neither family has contacted them since 1937.

These events cut Albert's younger brother, William Robertson, to the core. It was William who'd broken the news of Albert's elopement, setting off the chain of events tearing their family apart.

With the flames of World War II now engulfing the world, William is a volunteer in the Royal New Zealand Air Force. After completing training as a navigator, William is assigned to 75 New Zealand Squadron, within RAF Bomber Command, based at RAF Feltwell, Norfolk, Great Britain.

With a casualty rate of forty percent, William's chances of survival are amongst the lowest in the Allied Armed Forces. It's little wonder then that his first tour of operations is off to a bad start.

# CHAPTER ONE

*Date – 27 December 1941*
*Tour of Operations Count – Operation 1*
*Target Location – Brest, France*
*Assigned Aircraft – Wellington Mk.Ic Z.8971 AA-E*
*Take-off – 16:30*

'Dear, merciful Lord. Let me live. Don't take me. Not on my first op.' William Robertson crossed himself and kissed his St Christopher's medal then stuffed it back under his thick, brown leather flight jacket. He continued throwing out the last of any materials and supplies they didn't need, making the aircraft as light as possible; anything to give them an extra few feet of altitude.

Gordon Bolshaw, the wireless operator, heard his prayer. 'Not to fear Robbie. We'll be fine. We're bailing out but we'll be back over Blighty when we jump,' he said in a clipped, matter of fact, English accent, raising his voice to be heard over the screams and moans of the dying aircraft. 'Don't worry, old boy. Keep doing your job.' He winked and returned to his instrument panel, alternating between tapping out a Mayday and current coordinates, and making calls on the radio. Bolshaw let out a heavy sigh and crossed himself.

'"Don't worry, old boy?" The bloody plane's going to crash,' William whispered to himself. Returning to his position, he looked at his charts and tried to concentrate. Next to impossible with the cold night air rushing through the plane. He looked back at the two by one-foot hole in the fuselage where they had taken some flak. The anti-aircraft shell had knocked out the port side engine, causing them to limp back across the Channel on half power.

William's first operation nerves oscillated between mild to severe. His hands shook for minutes at a time, throughout the flight. He'd been surprised the actual bombing part of the raid was when he was at his most calm and focussed. It was running the gauntlet of anti-aircraft flak that raised his stress exponentially. The flashes of light, noise and aircraft shuddering as each shell exploded around them, made him jump and twitch at every vibration and unexpected sound. When shell fragments ripped into their aircraft, he was compelled to set aside his fear to survey the damage and report back to the pilot. They'd got halfway across the Channel before one engine coughed, spluttered and finally petered out.

According to the instruments and William's calculations, they were only a handful of miles from the Devon coast. He'd told the pilot to fly in a direct line from France after a bombing raid on Brest. He calculated they would cross land almost directly over Salcombe, then follow the Kingsbridge Estuary directly north.

The pilot, Harry Machin, boomed over the radio and jolted William away from his charts. 'Lads, we've passed over the coastline. Give it another five minutes before you bailout, so you don't get blown back out to sea. Top effort, chaps. Great work bringing her home. See you all on the ground. Over.'

William let out a large sigh, dropped his head, crossed himself twice, then went back to his charts.

'Stay on task, young man. Plot the course so I can tell the lads where we are when we jump,' yelled Bolshaw.

William estimated they should pass four miles west of Totnes, on a heading north towards Ashburton. Exeter to the northeast and Plymouth to the southwest are the biggest towns, with plenty of military presence. 'We should be OK', he said to himself. He heard the remaining good engine power down and felt the aircraft start its descent. Cold beads of sweat trickled down his back. He checked the instruments again; the altitude was two thousand feet when they crossed the coastline, but was now seventeen hundred and dropping. William turned his focus back to his charts; ground around Ashburton was six hundred feet, but a steep and quick rise to eighteen hundred feet.

He looked at his watch; seven minutes had passed, yet there was no word from the cockpit. 'Skip, what's going on? Time to bail?' No answer. 'Skip. You there? We'll hit the hills soon.' Still nothing. He turned to Gordon, who was frozen, wide-eyed. William fumbled to unclip himself and clambered up to the cockpit, only to find it empty. 'Jesus, Mary and Holy Saint Joseph. They've all bloody bailed,' William shouted. 'Bugger me! I'm not sticking around.' Moving back to his position, he yelled to Gordon, 'They've all gone. We gotta go.'

The angle of descent made their shuffle to the crew door more like rock climbing. Each step took a couple of seconds, time he knew they didn't have. This, combined with the near hurricane swirling through the plane, sapped almost all his energy. William was running on fumes of adrenaline. As he reached the open door, he shouted, 'Bloody hell.' Even in the blackness of night, he estimated the plane's altitude was now no more than one thousand feet off the deck.

Gordon was standing by the door, 'You jump first, old chap.'

'Go!' shouted William. There's no time for politeness.'

'Oh no, I insist,' added Gordon.

'If you don't jump now, you'll get my size eight planted up your jacksie. Get out!' yelled William.

Surprise flashed across Gordon's face. He nodded, and then was gone. William pulled himself to the door. He could make out the trees and contours of the ground. 'Stuff it. Let's go boy,' he shouted, and jumped.

His descent to the ground only took a minute, but his mind spun with visions of his family; his parents playing piano in the living room, his brothers, Gary and Howard, kicking a rugby ball in the backyard. Only a few feet off the ground, an image of his eldest brother, Albert, in his clerical robes with a massive crucifix behind him, exploded into his mind.

'What the hell?' William said out loud, distracting him from the landing. The ground met William before he was ready. He hit it at an awkward angle and felt a pop in his right ankle. Sharp pain shot up his leg as he rolled down a slope. After four or five rotations, he came to rest and winced. 'Bugger you, Albert. Still causing me grief, half a world away.'

He dragged himself up onto his knees, took off the parachute harness, and then hauled the chute towards him. He attempted to stand up, placing some weight on his right ankle. There was some pain, but not as much as he expected. Years of sprained ankles from rugby had left him reasonably immune to all but the worst injuries. He dropped the parachute at the base of a nearby oak tree, and then started up the slope he'd rolled down. William heard the drone of the plane during the last seconds of its ghost flight across Dartmoor. As he reached the ridgeline, there was a flash of light and flame illuminating the night for a couple of seconds. He spotted a large building two or three miles to the south. A church? It could be the sanctuary he needed. Seconds later came the sound of the crash. An explosive force hit his trembling body.

The high-pitched crack of a rifle shot pierced the night air. William realised his silhouette must be easily visible; 'Bloody Home Guard. Probably thinks I'm a German.' He hobbled off the high ground, back into the blackness of the valley, cursing Albert's name with each bolt of pain that ran up his leg. 'Why the hell did he come into my mind? Bloody bad timing. Typical, makes an appearance just to mess things up.' He racked his brain to think of the last time he had given Albert the simplest passing thought. It must have been around Christmas of 1939, when he had sent a Christmas card, saying he and Abigail had produced a daughter, with another child on the way. Usually becoming an uncle would be wonderful news, but not in this case. The shock of a man who, only two years previously had been a Catholic Priest and was now a parent, shamed the family. William had then tried to put Albert out of his mind, in line with the family decision enforced by their mother, to blacklist Albert and Abigail.

Distracted by his thoughts, William was surprised to come upon a village so quickly. He hoped it was the hamlet with the church he'd seen from the hill. He found a gate out of the farmers' field onto the road, grateful to have a flat surface to walk on. It didn't appear to be a big village, only a scattering of about ten houses; no pub or shop. The row of houses came to a sudden end, replaced by a tall stone wall. A further hundred yards on, an archway some twenty feet high, opened up the solid stone façade. There was no gate, so he entered to find well-manicured gardens and lawns. It would be an interesting place to explore in daylight. When he rounded a corner, he stopped dead in his tracks. He'd found the church, but this was no simple church, it was more like a Cathedral or Abbey. What on earth was a church this size doing in the middle of the Devon countryside? In the faint moonlight, William could make out its main tower. It stretched close to three hundred feet into the air, with four mini-turrets on each corner. The front of the building was framed by two towers, with two large stained glass windows and a rose window positioned between them.

He made his way down the path to the front door. He found the handle, and as he lifted it, a deep thud emanated from the mechanism. The heavy door opened and a wave of incense laced air wafted around him; a reassuring aroma, taking him back to so many Sundays at Mass with his family. A low glow of candlelight come from all directions, illuminating the bowl of Holy Water in the entrance alcove. William dipped his fingers in the liquid and crossed himself. His knees buckled, exhaustion throwing him to the floor. He took a couple of deep breaths, and hauled himself to the closest pew. Stretching out, he fell into a deep sleep within seconds.

*

William woke to the familiar sounds of a full Latin Mass. It must be a Catholic church, he thought. He swung his legs down to the floor; his ankle felt swollen, pressing hard against his boot, throbbing with every heartbeat. As he emerged from the pews, the assembled Clergy stopped the Mass and stared, wide-eyed.

Another vision of Albert invaded William's mind. This time of Albert at his Final Profession ceremony in Wellington, some ten years before. William shook his head, expelling the memory. 'Sorry Brothers, I didn't mean to scare you,' he said quickly. 'Flight Sergeant William Robertson, RAF 75 Squadron. We bailed out nearby last night. This was the first place I found open.' He stood up, but buckled and stumbled forward, yelping in pain. He caught his fall and sat back down. 'Rolled my ankle on landing. Think it's knackered,' he added, as a couple of the Brothers ran over to him.

'Come, my son. Let's get you to the infirmary,' one said.

They helped him to a small building next to the Abbey, propping him up on a padded table. Releasing his right boot, his ankle expanded to at least three times its normal size.

'That's a good sprain. It'll keep you off your feet for a week or two,' said the first Brother. 'We'll bandage you up and get you a cane, so at least you can be mobile. Brother Peter, can you go to stores and get us a walking stick?'

'Thank you, Brother. I didn't get your name,' replied William.

'Brother Benjamin. We'll get you patched up, have some breakfast, then we'll take you to the local constabulary. They usually coordinate rescues of airmen,' said the clergyman.

Bandaged up and with a black, lacquered walking stick, William was treated to a breakfast of bacon and eggs, a pint of fresh milk and pot of tea.

'What is this place?' he asked.

'Buckfast Abbey. We're a Benedictine monastery. Been here since 1018,' replied Brother Benjamin.

'The Abbey is that old? Goodness gracious,' replied William.

'Oh no. The church is new. We only finished it three years ago. The original was destroyed during the disillusionment of the monasteries under Henry VIII.'

'Amazing. There's been a church here eight hundred years before we were colonised. Incredible,' said William.

'Australia or New Zealand?' asked Brother Benjamin.

'New Zealand. 75 Squadron is mostly made up of us. Got a scattering of others. Have to say, it was reassuring waking up to Mass,' replied William.

'You're Catholic?' William nodded to the question. 'I'm glad we could provide you sanctuary in your hour of need. Finished?' Brother Benjamin looked at William's empty plate. 'Best we get you down to the Police Station and link you up with your crew mates.'

*

'The lucky last. We were wondering when you might turn up,' the Police Constable's voice boomed across the counter with a thick southwest accent. 'We've accounted for the whole crew now. Most of you got knocked about a bit; two with broken ankles and two with busted ribs. They've been taken to the Totnes hospital already. How are you?' the policeman asked.

'A bad sprain. Can put a bit of weight on it. The Brothers looked after me,' replied William.

'Good. There's a truck coming down from RAF Exeter for the rest of you. Should be here around lunchtime. The only other fit member of your crew is down at The Valiant Soldier. I'll take you there.'

*

They were only a couple of steps inside the pub when a deep voice with a drawling southern American accent filled the room, 'Billy-Bob. Y'all made it. Praise be.' Reginald Dubois jumped out of his seat and enveloped William in a deep hug. With his arms extended, he resembled a bear, about to ensnare its prey. At six-foot-one, he was five inches taller than William and easily three stone heavier.

'Steady on Reggie, ya big lug. Good to see you too, mate. You in one piece?' asked William.

'Darn tooting, me boy. Take more than a little 'ol bailout to break Reginald Louis Dubois the third. Tough as 'ol boots, us Cajun's. Y'all OK?' replied Reggie, as he pulled out a packet of Lucky Strike, popped a couple of cigarettes out and offered one to William.

'Thanks, mate. Yeah, fine. Rolled my ankle on landing. Nothing major. Thanks for asking,' replied William. Reggie helped William to the table and chair where he'd been sitting, gave his Zippo lighter a flick and lit William's and his own smoke, then ordered a pot of tea.

'What happened with the bailout? We were left in an empty plane,' asked William.

'What? When Skip said we'll go after five minutes, that's exactly what I did. I went straight outta the back. Used the door next to me turret. When Skip gives y'all a time check like dat, take it as Gospel,' said Reggie.

'Good to know. Major piece of knowledge to take from my first op. Where did you end up?' asked William.

'Coupla mile south. Smooth descent and a soft landing. Lucky nuff to hit flat ground. Found a farmhouse pretty quick. They was great. Gave me a coupla beers and a bowl of lamb stew. Y'all?'

'I came down on a hill, rolled my ankle. Saw the plane come down. Couldn't have been more than three or four miles from where I bailed. Ended up at a Benedictine Monastery in the next village,' replied William.

They continued to swap stories of their experiences until the RAF truck arrived.

At RAF Exeter, the first stop for both of them was the base hospital. Reggie was in and out quickly, getting a clean bill of health. William was sent for an X-ray to check there wasn't a break. He was propped up on a bed, in the Accident and Emergency ward, when the curtains to his cubicle were pulled back forcefully making William sit bolt upright. In strode a Nurse carrying a clipboard and a large envelope. Closing the curtain behind her, she addressed William without looking up from the notes.

'Flight Sergeant William Robertson,' she stated, not giving him a chance to reply, 'Your X-ray has come back negative for breaks, so it appears to be only a bad sprain. That's the good news. Bad news, depending on how bad it is, you'll be signed off for at least a week. Now let's take a look.'

She was already starting to look at his ankle when William finally replied. 'South African, right?' he asked, picking up her accent.

'Excuse me, Flight Sergeant?' she looked up for the first time. Her radiant, pale green eyes mesmerised William.

'You're from South Africa?' he stumbled over his reply. 'English, though. Not Afrikaans.'

'Very perceptive. Half and half. Not many can pick the difference. You have a good ear.' She tucked a loose strand of her black hair back into her hat. She continued to inspect his swollen ankle. 'It's reasonably big, but not the worst I've seen. Let me know the level of pain you feel,' she said as she started to manipulate his foot with one hand and supported his ankle with the other.

'Fine. So is that,' he replied as she pushed his foot back towards him, then pulled it forward. 'A bit sore, there,' he said when she turned it outwards. 'Hell's bells,' he yelled as it was manipulated inwards.

'As I suspected. It's the ligament on the outside of your ankle. You'll be off for a week. Nothing more.' She started to wrap a bandage around the ankle. 'So, how do you know the difference between the South African accents?'

'We have a few on base, both English and Boks. When you get one of each together, it's quite pronounced.' He was at last able to concentrate on her; on top of a forthright bedside manner, she had warm hands, and was probably five-foot-four or five, with pronounced cheeks and dimples. In spite of the unflattering Nurses' uniform, he could tell she had a nice figure.

'You say you are half and half?' William asked.

'Mum is English, from Bristol, and Dad is South African. Where's your base?' she asked.

"RAF Feltwell. Up in Norfolk,' replied William

'The New Zealanders are there. Thought I picked your accent. You're a long way from base. What happened? If you can say.'

'Yeah, no worries. Bombing raid down in Brittany. Got hit by flak, managed to limp back but had to bailout over Dartmoor. I hit a hill on landing,' William replied.

'You all made it?' she asked.

'Yes, thank God. A few got dusted up on landing, but nothing serious, so I heard.'

'There you go. All set.' She put his sock on over the bandage. 'You should be eligible for a weeks' sick leave from your Squadron's Medical Officer, and we'll issue you a pair of crutches. Keep the weight off it for two or three days, then start to do some stretches once the swelling goes down.'

'What sort of stretches? Can you show me?' William started thinking of questions to keep her in the cubicle.

'Initially, move the foot and ankle all directions, like I just did, without any resistance. Maybe five to ten stretches, three times a day. As it gets stronger, do the same but with some resistance. Mainly to ensure the ligaments don't heal with scar-tissue or have long-term restricted movement. OK?' She stood in front of him, with her hands on her hips.

'Yes, thank you. Sorry I didn't get your name,' William enquired.

'Staff Nurse Darlene du Toit. Pleasure to meet you, Flight Sergeant.' She broke out into a broad smile that lit up the cubicle. 'Now, I really must go. Can't leave our other patients waiting.' She turned and was gone as quickly as she entered. William slumped back onto the bed, with a slight frown, but it soon vanished and was replaced with an intrigued smile.

# CHAPTER TWO

'What on earth was in the vodka those Poles gave us?' William's voice was raspy and an octave or two lower than normal.

'Some sorta Polish firewater. Never drunk so much straight liquor in one sitting in me life. Sweet Jesus, dem boys are some buncha hard units,' said Reggie. He rubbed his face and his mouth stayed open, his lower lip jutted out.

'I need tea and something to eat. Breakfast in the Sergeants' Mess is a fading memory. Want to come to the buffet car?'

Reggie shook his head, with too much vigour, and put his hands on his temples.

'I'll bring you a cuppa,' William added. He staggered down the train, having to hold on to the sides of the narrow walkway of the carriage, nursing his swollen ankle, he lost his balance a couple of times as the train shuddered along the tracks. He tried to remember how many drinks he'd consumed last night; there were four pints, each with a vodka shot, then another four straight vodkas. The Polish fighter pilots had somehow adopted them after dinner and proceeded to educate Reggie and William on the fineries of Polish drinking culture.

'Here you go Reggie. Got you a scone as well. Going to be a long trip back. You need to eat, mate.'

'Thanks buddy. Feel like a couillon for hitting it so hard last night.' Reggie lit two cigarettes, and gave one to William.

'Couillon? You got to translate your Cajun sayings for me.' said William, accepting the smoke.

'Fool, dope, idiot. I'll try. Although today ain't gonna be a good day for thinking,' replied Reggie.

'You're not wrong. They'd cracked open another bottle as we left. Never seen anything like it.' William took a long pull on his tea and looked pensively at Reggie, 'You know they'll break us up now. With the rest of the boys out of action for a fair while, they'll need to slot us into other crews.'

'Yup, a bit crap, buddy. We were gettin' sharp as a crew,' replied Reggie.

'Been meaning to ask you for a while. Why did you come over?' asked William.

Reggie leaned back on the triple bench seat, extended his arms out across the top of the seat-back, so his palms flopped over the ends.

'I read a lot about what was happening in de war and thought y'all need all de help ye can get. I was pissed off we was on de side-lines, doing nothing. Dem Nazi bastards are evil. Dey want de whole world and won't stop till dey get it. I wanna kill me some Nazis. Plain and simple. I'm talking Old Testament wrath and vengeance.' William eyes widened and his eyebrows rose at Reggie's reply. 'Before I started working on de shrimp boats, I joined de US Army Air Corp, after I finished school. Trained as a gunner on the Keystone B-5A's, but didn't make it through training. From Christmas '39 I saved up to get my ticket to England. Got here in summer of '41 and joined the RAF Volunteer Reserve.'

'How'd you get here? Thought before Pearl Harbour there were laws against joining other countries military. We've heard stories of Yanks getting arrested trying to get to Canada,' said William.

'Had ta be sneaky. Looked at going up to Montreal, use me French to pretend ta be a Québécois and join de Canadian Airforce, or at least get to Britain. Like ya say, too many boys getting arrested.' Reggie broke off a piece of scone and scoffed it down, before continuing. 'Used me fishing contacts to get to Nassau, in da Bahamas. Went by Key West, nice 'n quiet there. No Feds. In Nassau, I told dem I was from Haiti. Me French come in handy.'

'Good Lord, man. I doff my cap to you. That's some effort to get into the fight. It's a fair old distance on a fishing boat,' replied William.

'A bit over three days to Key West. Had to do a bit of fishing along de way, so we had a catch to land and sell, so we didn't look suspicious. Found a Bahamas flagged boat which took me to Nassau in another day'n a half. Then I walked into de first recruitment office I saw, 'n signed up. Simple as dat. Spoke in broken English 'n French. Told 'em I was from Port-au-Prince, 'n said I wanted to stop de Nazis,' explained Reggie.

'The Germans do seem hell-bent on taking over the whole of Europe. Darn near did it in less than a year. We're the last line in the west now. Scary when you think about it.' William took another drink of his tea, stared out the window and took a final drag on his cigarette. 'The Japanese are doing the same in Asia and the Pacific. We're all bit worried being here. Reckon us and the Aussies are in their plans. Why haven't you gone back or transferred to a Yank squadron?'

'Can't deny Pearl Harbour got me thinking about going back. I've heard there's chat about establishing a full US Air Force wing here next year. But ya know, I'm kinda attached to you crazy Kiwis now. Y'all took me in, no questions asked. Didn't want to know about me past, you accepted me for who I am. Y'all are good people, and keen for the fight. Couldn't ask for more,' replied Reggie.

William gave a slow and deliberate nod, 'And there's a lot of fight to be had.'

Both men stared out the window for a few miles; the odd green field and flock of sheep broke up the brown and grey dominant colours of the winter countryside. When William turned back to Reggie, he was asleep; the train's gentle oscillation swaying the big man back-and-forth.

As William continued to take in the rolling hills, farms, woodland and villages, he chuckled at some of the odd station names – Whimple and Templecombe amused him most. His booze-addled mind drifted off to peculiar memories; playing street cricket with his mates and his brother Gary, riding their Indian motorcycle in the paddocks behind their house, and strangest of all, seeing his brother Albert go through the Final Profession ceremony back in 1931.Why this, he thought? What could possibly connect the memory to his current situation? Was it the long train journey they took, from Wanganui to Wellington; the bizarre nature of the ceremony; or seeing Albert in a wheelchair only a couple of days after he was injured in the Napier Earthquake?

Albert kept invading his thoughts at regular intervals over the last three days. He'd banished Albert from conscious thought since Christmas 1939. Their mother, Margaret, was constantly wearing black since it was confirmed Albert had been defrocked and excommunicated for eloping with Abigail. They received a Christmas card from Albert saying he and Abigail were parents, with one child and another on the way. Margaret then banned the utterance of Albert's name around her and instructed all the extended family there was to be no further contact with the couple.

William's mind drifted back to that day in 1931, when his then beloved older brother brought such joy to their mother. Committing his life to God and the Catholic Church had Margaret brimming with pride. Being only fourteen at the time, William remembered he was confused by the ceremony and what it meant, but he was excited to watch his eldest brother. Someone he'd loved and admired. He did recall trepidation, or at least some distance, in Albert's eyes. William had put it down to still being in a bad way after the quake, but with what he knew now, was Albert experiencing something deeper? A sense of making the wrong decision, hurtling down a path he didn't want to be on. The biggest question to gnaw away at William, was if being in the clergy wasn't the life Albert wanted, then why had he gone through with the final step of becoming ordained less than two years later?

William had replayed this discussion with himself many times since the night in 1937 when he broke the news to his parents that Albert had eloped, yet he was still no closer to an answer. Oh, what a night; how it was seared into his memory. As he walked into his parents' house, he felt like a thief, or an arsonist; come to destroy a peaceful existence. The visceral sobs and wailing of his mother were unforgettable. The running away together smacked of selfishness and self-indulgence. Surely, Albert must have known the impact their actions would have on the family, especially Mother. Wasn't resistance of temptation one of the key personal characteristics of the clergy? If he'd met Abigail during the earthquake and loved her so much, he had the best part of two years to extricate himself from the Church before he was ordained.

The whole episode had created a lot of gossip in the town. In the first couple of years, he'd batted off a fair number of questions. Not so much at church of a Sunday morning, much too sensitive to be brought up in the house of the Lord himself. In the pub, at the shops, or on the street; this is where he faced a constant barrage of queries. He was thankful an absence of details and background allowed him to plead ignorance more often than not. One night at the local pub, near his parent's house, came to mind.

He'd gone in for drink with Gary while they were home over the Easter weekend in 1938. It'd been less than a year since Albert had eloped with Abigail, with still not many facts revealed and more questions than answers. Halfway through their first jug of beer, a man neither of them recognised, sitting a couple of tables away raised his voice, 'Still, ain't like running away from the Church to shack up with your piece of skirt.'

Both William and Gary's eyes narrowed as they turned to look at the man, and he continued, 'I've heard it's straight to hell for priests who break their vows. Couldn't think of anything more embarrassing than to be related to such a disgrace of a human being.'

William shot up out of his chair, 'Excuse me mate, but who are you? You got something to say to us, say it to our faces,' he said pointing at the man, but there was no response. 'Yeah, thought as much,' William added as the man said nothing, and slowly sat down.

'It's the parents I blame. Looks like they raised a lying, cheating bastard with no morals. Whole family's probably the same,' the man continued.

Gary was ready for the reaction. He was a half-step ahead of his younger brother and got in front of William as he flew out of his seat and launched himself at the man.

'You want to step outside and continue your yap?' William spat at the man, as Gary held him back. 'Come on, mate. Put up or shut up. Let me go, Gary. He deserves a slap.'

'Oi, you two. Best you leave,' said the bartender. 'Trev, shut up. You're out of order,' he added, turning to the mouthy man. 'Sorry fellas. Yeah, he's a prick, and for a church-going man, he's got some acid in his heart. News of your brother started to do the rounds here a couple of months ago. It's a hot topic for some. Hate to say it, but probably wise to give this place a wide berth for a while.'

'Where the hell did that come from?' asked Gary as they walked home.

His own reaction had surprised William. He was fully prepared to get into a scrap with the man. 'I'm not about to take any rubbish from a stranger about Albert, especially insulting the family. It's bad enough what it's done to Mother, so I don't want anyone else piling on.'

'Yeah, fair enough, but you're only five-foot-eight and eleven stone soaking wet. The bloke had a good two stone on you, maybe more. You've got to pick your battles, William,' added Gary.

'So, we capitulate whenever someone abuses our family? No thanks. I'd rather stand up for our honour,' said William.

'Turn the other cheek?' said Gary.

'Eye for an eye?' William snapped back.

Within the family, once Mother had laid down her edict, there wasn't much discussion about the issue. In quiet times, alone with Gary, the two of them barely mentioned Albert's name. Gary had kept the 1939 Christmas card, and had contemplated writing back, but the guilt of going against Mother's instructions had got the better of him. Gary had taken the whole thing hard, and as Albert had conducted his wedding to Sarah, he wondered if their marriage was still valid in the eyes of the Church. He had visions of it being annulled and them being branded as living in sin. More ammunition for Mother, as if she needed anything extra.

*

'What a state of affairs when I can't talk to my brother about something so serious in the family,' William whispered, so he wouldn't wake up Reggie.

Suddenly the blurred views from the window came into focus; the countryside had given way to the endless urban landscape of London. As the train pulled out of Wimbledon station, he nudged Reggie awake to get him ready to disembark and cross town to get a train to Ely.

*

*6 January 1942*
*RAF Feltwell, Norfolk*

After a week of sick leave, William was given the all-clear to start operations again. He went to the Flight Operations hut to get allocated a crew. As they expected, Reggie had got his new crew assignment the day after they got back from Devon, and had already clocked up two training flights with them. The upside of their old crew being broken up was the rooming allocation had been updated and Reggie was now William's roommate.

As he entered the room, he stopped as if ordered to attention; a queue of men about a dozen long greeted him. 'A fresh intake,' he thought to himself. In front of him were two tall, broad-shouldered blokes; one dark-haired, and one with sandy-coloured hair. They were sharing jokes, as if they knew each other well.

'You lads fresh off the boat from back home?' asked William.

Both men turned to William and shook their heads. The dark-haired one replied, 'No, mate. Transferred down from Maritime Surveillance up in Scotland. Wanted a bit more excitement. You?'

'Been with 75 Squadron for a few weeks, but my old plane crashed in Devon and most of the lads are still in hospital, so I'm here to get a new crew,' said William.

'You've been in a scrape already?' asked the other man.

William nodded, 'Was my first ever combat operation too. Took a hit to our port engine but managed to limp back to Blighty before we had to bail. Interesting introduction to the war. William Robertson is the name.' He offered his hand to one man, then the other.

'Gordon Newdick. Good to meet ya,' replied the dark-haired man.

'Ray Trengrove. Pleasure,' said the other.

'We've been over since late 1940. Racked up a few operations, but not been shot at too many times. What do ya reckon, Ray? asked Gordon.

'Two. Maybe three. Long-range stuff from German ships. Nothing to get us flustered. This sounds like she's going be a bit hairy here,' replied Ray.

'Lads, you're up,' said William as the queue moved.

All three picked up their papers, opened them up and started reading out their assignments.

'Pilot Officer Fraser, A.A.' said Ray.

'Pilot Officer Leggett, R.' said Gordon.

William looked at Gordon and smiled, 'Me too. I've got Leggett. How about that?' You'll do me, Mr Newdick, he thought. You're a good egg; experienced, friendly, strong.

'Right. Time to find our crews,' said Gordon.

In the flight crew hut, they went their separate ways. William and Gordon tracked down their pilot in a corner of the lounge and introduced themselves.

'Terrific. The new boys. Splendid. Pilot Officer Rufus Leggett, but everyone calls me Pruno,' said Rufus. His face broke out in a wide smile, his cheeks puffed up into little balloons, giving him a warm and friendly air.

'Norwich?' asked Gordon, picking up the thick Norfolk accent.

'Well spotted. King's Lynn, actually. Not far away, but I go to see Norwich City play as much as I can. Well, used to, before the war. Come and met the lads,' Pruno motioned them over to three other men. 'Lads. Here are our new crew members.' Pointing out the existing crew, he continued, 'Second Pilot Sergeant Arthur Osborne; Wireless Operator Sergeant James Mayall; and Gunner Sergeant Cyril Green. I'll leave you to get acquainted. Now we are back to a full complement, I need to report in and get our training flight instructions. Be back soon.'

Handshakes ensued and the obligatory swapping of nicknames; Ossie for Arthur, Slim for James, Cy for Cyril, Gordo for Gordon and Robbie for William. Standard procedure for New Zealanders, Australians, and Brits – must shorten, or change someone's name to either make it easier to say or match their personality. All the nicknames were straightforward, except for "Slim" Mayall, which had William wondering, but then Slim stood up to shake hands with William. Towering over him by at least four inches, and as wide a barn door, the reason for the name Slim was apparent; the opposite of his physical stature. He would give Reggie a run for his money in terms of size.

*

*12 February 1942*
*RAF Exeter, Devon*

An ear-piercing screech rose from the chair being dragged on the floor. Darlene gritted and bared her teeth, with an apologetic nod to the Librarian, then lifted the chair out from under the desk. She slid into the chair and tried to pull the chair in, without any further commotion. The Librarian stared at Darlene from over her eyeglasses, forehead lined and mouth turned down in a hard frown.

Her favourite place on base, she came to the library as often as she could. It was her sanctuary from the trials of treating the servicemen and their horrendous wounds. When she wasn't brushing up on her medical knowledge, she loved to dive into the fiction section. She was partial to some of Agatha Christie's work. She liked Christie's general mysteries, but had already tired of Hercule Poirot's character. Since meeting William, she'd started reading Katherine Mansfield's work. She wondered if William was a reader, and if so, whether he liked Mansfield? However, her favourites were the Brontë sisters' novels, Charlotte's "Jane Eyre" and Emily's "Wuthering Heights". She had her own copies of both and re-read them at least once a year.

She slid the UK Ordinance Survey Atlas of Britain and Ireland across the desk to sit in front of her. As she flipped the book over onto its front, it landed with a loud thud, causing her to sheepishly look around for any response. She flipped through the index and quickly found the "F's", her finger tracing down the list of names: Farnborough, Farnham, Farringdon – then Feltwell. She made a mental note of the page number and grid reference, then thumbed through the book to the right page. She found the town within a couple of seconds, in the southwest corner of Norfolk; close to the borders of Suffolk and Cambridgeshire. 'Cambridge? Should be a nice place to live,' she whispered.

She undid the buckles of her leather satchel and rummaged around between the pockets and compartments then pulled out her copy of the War Office listing of military and general hospitals, along with a letter (still in its original envelope), a pencil and writing pad.

She ran her fingers around the edges of the envelope, then picked it up; the same warm sensation danced through her body as it did the day she received it. She recalled the tingles in her fingertips when she turned it over to read the return address – Flight Sergeant William Robertson, RAF Feltwell, Norfolk. She re-read the letter, for at least the twentieth time, with a broad smile:

*5th February 1942*
*Dear Darlene,*

*I do hope this letter finds you in good health. This is a short note to let you know I am safely back at base.*

*I must ask for your forgiveness on two fronts. First, at the presumptuous nature of writing to you without your express approval. Second, the tardy timing of the letter, given it's the best part of six weeks since we met in Exeter.*

*It is late, but Happy New Year. Did you have a fun evening? Was there a good party on base? We had a decent knees up in the Mess. I certainly had a fuzzy head the next morning. Thankfully, I was still officially in recuperation, so wasn't expected to do any flying. Some of the lads had training flights and came back green around the gills.*

*I've been with my new crew for a month now. Cracking bunch of lads. No operational runs yet, just lots of training flights. No complaints though, but it doesn't get you any closer to completing your tour, so we'd rather be doing operations and giving Jerry a bloody nose.*

*I've definitely noticed the days getting longer and the light changing. It will be spring soon enough, which will be fabulous. In fact, only yesterday, I saw the first snowdrops of the year. Shouldn't be too long before the daffodils are out. I'm still getting used to the seasons being six months behind. I assume it's the same for you. Having my first winter Christmas was a shock to the system. I imagine the local countryside is picturesque at the height of spring. What's the Devon countryside like? We got a taste on the train ride back up to London, but it probably isn't at its best in the middle of winter.*

*I hope you haven't been too busy with patients, but given the current situation with the war, I imagine it's a false hope. Perhaps more appropriate is there isn't too much stress for you.*

*If it isn't too forward, would you be interested in meeting me if I was to come back to Exeter for my next leave? Not sure when that might be, but we do get leave every four or six weeks. I'll wait for your reply, hoping you do write back, before I organise anything.*

*Yours faithfully and warmest regards,*
*William Robertson*

Darlene folded the letter with great care and placed it back its envelope. She opened the War Office booklet of hospitals to Cambridgeshire; the list was short – Cambridge, Ely and Huntingdon. Careful analysis of the map determined Ely was closest to Feltwell. Using her pencil as a guide against the distance key, she estimated it was only about fifteen miles, as the crow flies. She gnawed on the end of the pencil, adding new bite marks to the already pock-marked wood. Then made her decision.

*

After her shift, Darlene went in search of Matron. She opened the double doors of the corridor housing the administrative offices.

The cloud-diffused winter sunlight didn't provide significant illumination; sporadic, low wattage bulbs did little to lift the gloom. Add to the murky light, the echo of the "clip-clop" of her heels hitting the tiled floor, the walk to Matron's office took on an ominous air. Two-thirds the way down the hallway, Darlene found the office. She patted down the front of her uniform, straightened her hat, pushed her shoulders back, and filled her lungs before she knocked on the door.

'Ely? In Cambridgeshire?' Matron cocked her head at Darlene's request for a transfer. Darlene nodded. 'You know it's slap-bang in the middle of the Bomber Command bases? Those poor lads are taking a hammering. Many more serious wounds and deaths than we're getting here. We've got it much easier in comparison.'

Despite after knowing Matron for some eighteen months, her strong West Country accent forced Darlene to concentrate on every word.

'Yes, Ma'am. I know it's in the heart of it. That's one of the main reasons. I want to give more to the war effort. It's so quiet here at times,' replied Darlene.

'I read the medical updates and some raids have seen casualties and wounds from up to eighty percent of their aircraft. Ranging from odd moderate wounds, through to dozens of aircraft lost over Germany and the occupied countries. Remember the Wellington crew we had in here after Christmas?' Darlene gave a sheepish, quick nod. 'Well, crashes on take-off and returns are prevalent. I can't sugar-coat it for you Nurse du Toit, the operation nights are absolute carnage amongst those squadrons,' continued Matron, leaning closer to Darlene; her cool green eyes holding the young Nurse in a stern, yet sympathetic gaze. 'Have you seen a crewman's guts explode when you take his flight suit off?'

Darlene sat back in her chair and took a deep breath. Although she'd been on duty for nearly two years, the worst she's seen was a Polish fighter pilot, whose Hurricane was badly shot up in a dogfight with a Messerschmitt 109, and a couple of crew members of a Beaufort maritime reconnaissance plane which had been hit by anti-aircraft fire from a German destroyer. None of the crew died or lost limbs. In addition, both incidents were at least a couple of months apart, not a daily occurrence. Had she thought deep enough about this move? Was she really going to pack up and leave her life here for the chance to start seeing a man she'd only spent barely an hour with and received one letter from? With those numbers, William could be dead before she got to Ely. She drew in another lungful of air, closed her eyes and bit the inside of her lower lip, calling on her inner strength for clarity of thought. In this world torn apart by death and despair, with no end in sight, she had to do more for the overall effort and give herself a chance to find love.

'Yes, Matron, I'm sure I want to go. I want to officially request a transfer to the Ely RAF Hospital. As quickly as possible, please.' The hair on her forearms stood up and a flash of heat ran up her spine.

*

Her room in the Nurse's Barracks appeared larger and cosier than yesterday; the light from her bedside lamp had a softer hue. Tonight, in the depths of Devon mid-winter, the twelve by seven-foot room appeared more spacious, the oak furniture glowing. Matron told her earlier in the day the transfer was well underway.

'I spoke to my counterpart at Ely, and she is eager to get you there pronto. She said they are preparing for the Yanks to arrive. Their squadrons will start operations this summer, so they're expecting casualty rates to go up and the hospital needs more staff. I'm finishing off the paperwork this week and if it's approved sharpish, you could be on your way by the end of the month, or early March. I know that sounds fast, I thought it might take two or three months, but as I said, they need people there now. Springtime in Cambridgeshire? It'll be a nice distraction from the work.' Matron gave Darlene a tight smile.

Darlene floated back to her room; her feet gliding though the hallways, carried along by the euphoria she could be in Ely in less than ten days. She took out her writing pad and started to compose a letter.

*

*27 February 1942*
*RAF Feltwell, Norfolk*

A smile broke across William's face as he saw his favourite armchair in the Sergeants' Mess was free. He quickened his pace to make sure he didn't miss out on getting what he thought was the most comfortable piece of furniture on base. Not much to look at, the light brown art deco chair was showing the wear and tear of many users; patches on the arms were threadbare, where elbows and fingers dug into them and there was a heavy indentation on the seat cushion, but its high back and deep seat always enveloped William in a warm and relaxed embrace.

He placed his armful of maps and charts on the chair to reserve it and went to get a cup of tea. He placed the mug and a couple of biscuits on the small side table and settled in, dunking a biscuit into the tea before biting it. However, it was still firm; he'd lose a tooth if he didn't soak them. He unfurled the first of his charts and started studying the pre-set flight paths for a range of target cities in Nazi Germany and the occupied countries of Western Europe. Familiar names jumped out at him; Paris, Dunkirk, Hamburg and Cologne, and he placed his ruler and compass on the chart, taking notes. Unknown locations he'd never heard of soon outnumbered the known sites; Lübeck, Essen, Rostock, Emden, Kiel, Bremen, St Nazaire. He'd know them all by the end of his tour.

'Morning, Robbie. Mail call,' said Jack Mayall as he dropped an envelope onto one of the arms of William's chair. 'What ya studying?' he asked, a bundle of letters in his hand.

'G'day, Slim. Thanks for the letter. Brushing up on target flight paths. Want to join me? Grab a seat,' replied William.

'Cheers, mate. That'd be bonza. I'll get a cuppa first. You want another?' Slim asked, nodding at William's mug.

'I'm good as gold. Still going on this one,' said William, picking up the envelope, a quizzical look on his face. His eyes grew wide, and a tingle of excitement flashed through his body as he read the sender's details:

Staff Nurse Darlene du Toit
RAF Base Hospital Exeter
Exeter, Devon

William looked at Slim as he was preparing his tea, his back to William. He brought the envelope up to his face and drew in its aroma; English Rose, the fragrance he remembered Darlene wore when she cared for him at the hospital. He smiled.

'Nice receiving a letter to give you a lift, eh?' said Slim, returning with his mug and pulling a chair up close to William. 'I'll do the rounds to the other lads soon. Now, let's have a look at those charts. Let me tell ya, I'm sick of these training flights. Want to get into the real action. Where do you reckon we'll head first?' He leaned over the map and William tucked Darlene's letter into his tunic pocket.

While he was examining the charts and maps with Slim, William's mind was constantly pulled away to visions of Darlene and thoughts of what was in her letter. The thirty-odd minutes he and Slim spent studying flight paths, radio transmitter and beacon locations and potential targets, dragged on. Now he was back in his room, he hungrily dug out Darlene's letter and opened it with a single flick of his index finger.

*19th February 1942*
*Dear William,*

*What a delight it was to receive your letter last week. I have re-read it multiple times and it always gives me a warm feeling and leaves me with a smile.*

*What a wonderful thought of spending time with you here in Devon. I would say yes, absolutely come down, but life has taken some interesting twists and turns in the last couple of weeks.*

*To cut a long story short, RAF Hospital Ely is looking for additional Nurses and I have asked to be transferred up to Cambridgeshire. My request has been approved today and they expect to move me up to Ely within the next month.*

*Obviously, it is a big move for me, but I want to do more for the war effort and being in the middle of all the bases there should give me the opportunity to contribute. It would be wonderful to reconnect with you too. Getting our schedules to coordinate may take some work, but I will make contact as soon as I get settled. The thought of seeing you again fills me with immense joy and has me counting down the days until I'm in Ely.*

*Until I see you again, love and best wishes,*
*Darlene*

He dropped the letter into his lap, 'You bloody beauty,' he whispered, smiling like the proverbial Cheshire Cat.

# CHAPTER THREE

*3 March 1942*
*Ely, Cambridgeshire*

A young woman in an Army Auxiliary Territorial Service uniform approached Darlene at the Ely train station.

'Staff Nurse du Toit? Lance Corporal Cartwright. I'm your lift to the hospital. Pleasure to meet you. That all you got?' She looked down at the two small suitcases Darlene was carrying.

'Pleasure to meet you too. Oh no, I have a footlocker trunk. They'll be unloading it from the baggage carriage. Please call me Darlene,' she replied as she regarded the ATS NCO. She was shorter than Darlene, maybe five-foot-three, and heavier set than herself, not chunky, but athletic and strong. A common bob haircut displayed her copper hair under her ATS cap and her cheeks were lightly freckled. What caught Darlene's eye was that Lance Corporal Cartwright was wearing trousers and only a shirt with rolled up sleeves; no tunic.

'Thanks Darlene. My name is Miriam, but most people call me Mer. Let's go find your footlocker,' she shot Darlene a warm smile as she spoke.

A train station porter helped Miriam get the locker into the back seat of the Army-green coloured Austin 8. Darlene was impressed with Miriam's strength, as she took the "heavy end" and the porter positioned the front of luggage into the car. 'Cheers Stan. See ya down the pub Friday?' Miriam asked. The porter nodded and touched his cap as he turned away. 'Right, Darlene. Let's get you to the hospital.'

'You know him?' asked Darlene, noticing Miriam's muscular forearms as she strained to turn the steering wheel to pull out of the station courtyard.

'Oh, Stan. Yeah. Went to primary school with him. Nice lad. Failed the Army physical because he had rickets as a kid, but he's in the Home Guard. He's bloody busy here with all the military personnel movements, especially recently. Tell ya what, you've arrived at a good time. Them Yanks are starting to pour in. I hear they'll be ready for ops in June. Early July at the latest. My word, they are fine young things. You got a fella?' Darlene gave a quick, sharp shake of her head. 'Oh darling, they're going to be buzzing round you, like bees to a honey pot. Unless of course, you don't like boys,' Miriam gave her a quick wink and a cheeky grin.

'Would be nice to step out with some dashing airmen.' Darlene tried to change the subject, without being too blatant, 'You're the first ATS I've seen wearing trousers. Where'd you get them from?'

'With the amount of lugging stuff around I do, those bloody skirts are ridiculous. The women's combat trousers are a different colour and material, so I managed to get a couple of pairs of men's dress trousers and altered them for my little legs. Only wear the skirts for formal occasions now. Funny thing is, no one bats an eyelid now,' replied Miriam.

'Yeah, I noticed you're pretty handy with the physical work too.' The car rattled and bounced on the narrow street, forcing Darlene to raise her voice.

'I'm a farm girl and I played a lot of netball at school, so I'm not afraid of getting stuck in. You play any sport?' asked Miriam.

'Hockey's my sport, and a bit of tennis in summer,' replied Darlene. 'I'm from Capetown, so the weather is pretty good and we swim often too. Oh, my word. What a stunning church,' Darlene exclaimed. They had turned a corner and the grand Gothic tower of the Ely Cathedral came into view. Darlene's eyes grew wider and her mouth remained open.

'It's our Cathedral. A beauty, isn't she? About eight hundred and fifty years old. We're proud of it,' Miriam pulled her shoulders back and broke into a small smile as she spoke.

With an appearance more like a castle than a traditional church, its tower was topped off by ramparts around a flat roof, rather than a spire. Four turrets stood guard at the corners. The street ran alongside, so Miriam slowed down to give Darlene more time to take it all in. Agog, she leaned across Miriam so she could look out the driver's-side window.

'Over two hundred feet high, and it's stunning inside. I'll take you in for a good look round when you've settled in. I have a mate who works there. He can give a tour, if you're keen?'

Darlene nodded vigorously to Miriam's offer. 'Crikey. It's stunning. Exeter Cathedral is beautiful too, but this one is different. I'd like a tour. Thanks,' replied Darlene, now craning her neck to look out the back window.

A comfortable silence settled in the car, both women smiling contentedly.

Then Darlene saw a signpost for the hospital, 'How's it going at the moment?' she asked, pointing to the sign.

'Thankfully, been quieter since the start of the year. Weather's been a bit shit, so there haven't been many operations. Fully expect them to fire up again now it's spring. Plus, with the Yanks starting training flights, it'll be busy again in no time,' Miriam gripped the steering wheel tightly as she spoke; her knuckles turning white under the pressure. 'Righty-ho, here we are.' Miriam swung the car into the main hospital driveway and stopped outside the main entrance. 'Welcome to RAF Hospital Ely. Let's go find Matron and get you sorted. I'll drop your stuff off at the Nurses' quarters. It'll be in your room once you're finished up. I'll take you to the pub on Friday night. Get you started on your Ely social life.'

Her room in the Nurses' Home was reassuringly familiar, with few differences to her place in Exeter. Miriam had expertly placed the footlocker at the end of the bed and the suitcases on the bed. Shunning the immediate task of unpacking, Darlene found her writing pad and started to pen a new letter to William. A broad smile lit her face as she wrote.

*

Darlene opened up her wardrobe to survey her options for her first night on the town in Ely; even if it was only a few drinks at a pub with Miriam and her friends.

Gun-metal grey pant suit? No, too "look at me" this early in her stay. A green dress with open neck and wide collars? No, too much green around with all the uniforms around town. Her three floral patterned summer dresses? No, not the weather for them yet. Powder blue, tailored skirt suit? No, it was a goodbye gift from her grandmother in Capetown, only for special occasions. She remembered her grandmother giving it to her, presented inside a garment box, 'Something special to keep for best. Maybe to impress a nice young soldier. Be careful with your heart, too,' she'd said.

The visions of her family drifted away and Darlene's attention swung back to her wardrobe. The last option it was then; the burgundy dress with the high neck, along with a wool cardigan and her trusty tweed coat. Shoes? Nice and simple, dark brown flats with the single strap. It wasn't too cold out, so no hat tonight. Happy with the ensemble, she got dressed then went downstairs.

Miriam strode confidently into the foyer, as Darlene reached the bottom step. Her trouser motif extended to after work; dark blue wool, high waisted pants with a double pleat down the front, a white blouse, and charcoal jacket. 'How about that for timing? Nice outfit. Love the colour,' said Miriam.

'Thanks, Mer. You too. Am a big fan of pleated trousers. I'm ready to go if you are,' replied Darlene.

'Fabulous, let's crack on. How's the first few days been?' Miriam opened the door for Darlene as they walked to the car.

'Busy, straight away. First day was paperwork and meeting the rest of the Nurses on my ward. Today and yesterday, I was on the ward, looking after patients. We're half-full at the moment, with a few due for discharge soon. Like you said, not many operations recently, but talk going round is they expect spring and summer to be hectic. A bit chilling when you realise what it actually means.' Darlene let out a heavy sigh as she ended the last sentence.

'You hear a lot of stuff in my job. Much of it is rubbish, but once in a while I get some gold. Heard at least three times they are gearing up for a big increase in raids over summer. Gonna pull all the operative bombers they can get their hands on to hit the Nazis as often as they can. My guess, you lot will be full to the brim from June onwards. Time to get your socialising in before the shit hits the fan,' replied Miriam.

Darlene knew she wasn't doing a good job of hiding her shock. 'In my briefing, they said we have a catchment of nine RAF bases and two for the Americans, when they get set up. That'll be hundreds of planes and thousands of aircrew going up.' The words of her Matron back in Exeter rang in her ears, "… operation nights are absolute carnage …"

'Sorry, Darlene. Didn't mean to wind you up. Hopefully you'll have enough time to get up to speed. Let's not worry about it tonight. We're almost at the pub now. Time to relax and have a couple of drinks.' Miriam reached out and gave Darlene's hand a light squeeze.

Although it was past sunset, the glow of dusk illuminated The Prince Albert pub well enough for Darlene to see it presented itself in a fine fashion. Its façade of bright white paint shone as the light faded. A simple two-storey early Georgian era building, with three large sash windows on the upper level and two at ground level. There was a passageway on the left of the building, leading to the back, a relic of an earlier era when it would have been a coaching inn. Colour was provided by a bright red front door and a matching red sash separating the levels, with the pub's name painted in gold.

'Come and meet the gang,' Miriam held the door for Darlene. Against the dimming light outside, Darlene's eyes struggled to adjust to the murky indoor environs. Heavy curtains shrouded the two windows and apart from a partially lit bar, there were few operational lights.

'We're always in the far corner,' Miriam pointed to a table of three people. 'Evening Bob. How ye doing? This is Darlene. She's arrived from Exeter to work at the hospital. My usual and for you, Dee?'

'Gin and tonic, thanks. Lovely to meet you, Bob,' replied Darlene.

'Pint of Bass and a G 'n T. That ain't a West Country accent.' The bartender's thick, meaty hands made the glass look half-sized as he pulled Miriam's drink.

'No, I'm South African. Came over to help out eighteen months ago,' replied Darlene.

'Doff me cap to ya, Darlene. Loads of you colonial types here. Appreciate what you're doing. First one's on me,' Bob placed the two drinks on the bar and gave them a one-finger salute.

'Very kind. You don't need to,' Darlene replied, as she pulled out her purse and rummaged around for coins.

'Put that away, Love. Our treat and a thank you.' A small smile broke across his face. In spite of the dim light, Darlene could see the light in his eyes.

'Right folks, meet Darlene. You know Stan, this is Betty, and Harold,' Miriam pointed to each person as she spoke.

'Nice to see you again,' said Stan.

'Lovely to meet you. Mer's been talking about you all week,' said Betty. Miriam shot a withering look across the table at Betty.

'Pleasure,' said Harold.

'Great to meet you all. Thanks for letting me into your Friday drinks group,' replied Darlene. 'What do you both do?'

'I'm a WAAF at Mildenhall,' said Betty.

'I'm a carpenter and handyman at the Cathedral,' said Harold

'Harold's going to give us a behind the scenes look around,' Miriam added, nodding at Harold.

'Oh, yes, that would be wonderful. It looks stunning. Does the Cathedral job keep you out of the war?' asked Darlene.

'Oh no. I was over in Europe at the start, when we tried to hold Jerry back in Belgium and France. Was a bit like sandcastles up against the incoming tide. Not a hope. Took some shrapnel at Dunkirk. Lost a chunk out of my leg and still can't raise my left arm past here,' Harold lifted his left arm up to horizontal as he spoke. 'Got a medical discharge, but Stan and me are in the Home Guard.'

'Betty always has loads of juicy gossip. Dee and I were chatting about a jump in raids soon. You got any news for us?' asked Miriam.

'Crikey, there's loads of chat buzzing around. The factories are pumping out bombers like billy-o. There'll be hundreds of new planes ready in late spring and all the squadrons are being pressured to increase their operational crews.' Betty took a sip on her glass of sherry, surveyed the group to ensure she had all their attention, then leant into the middle of table, 'Heard from good sources all the crews flying Wellingtons will be permanently reduced to five airmen, losing their second pilots sometime in April, to create more crews for the new planes,' she explained. Nodding of heads and raising of drinks greeted her.

'We alright talking about this stuff here?' asked Darlene, looking around the table.

'Considering you are the only new person I've seen in this pub since New Year, I think we're OK. Unless one of us has turned.' Harold narrowed his gaze at the others.

'Shut up, Harry, ya dickhead,' snorted Stan.

'I've heard about a German spy who was arrested in a pub down in Essex,' added Darlene.

'Yeah, read about it. Kent, I think it was. Romney Marsh area. Still, good to be careful. Loose lips and all that. We're OK here. Out on the street we watch what we say. Like Harry said, any new face here would stand out,' added Miriam. 'What's been going on at the station, Stan?'

'The Yanks are pouring in. Heard there's going to be more of them soon. There're dozens of them coming and going every week now. Cocksure of themselves, no doubt. Mind you, they ain't shy about tipping us when we help with their luggage. Making a few extra bob, so I won't complain,' said Stan.

'Bloody hell, Stan. Your round then. Pint of Newcastle for me. Betty looks like she's ready for another sherry,' interjected Harold. Stan's face fell as he hauled himself up and shuffled off to the bar.

'Lovely, thanks, Stan,' Betty called after him. 'Wait until the Yanks start bringing in their planes. Place will be over-run with them,' said Betty.

'I've heard they're going to run daytime raids. Bloody crazy. We took a hammering when we bombed in daylight. Suppose it'll mean we can smash Germany around the clock,' added Miriam.

Stan plonked down the three drinks in the middle of the table, then slid them to Betty, Harold and himself.

'Thanks, lad,' said Harold, 'Cheers and welcome to our new friend,' he added holding up his pint, inviting the others to join the toast.

'Thanks, Harry. What do you and Stan do in the Home Guard?' asked Darlene.

'Lots of training and manoeuvres, to help the regular Army slow a Nazi invasion, but it's looking less likely. We do some roadblocks and airfield security. We've worked at Lakenheath, Mildenhall, Methwold and Feltwell,' said Stan.

Darlene sat up at the mention of William's base. 'We talked about those bases in my briefing. Do you meet the airmen?'

'Not really. We either man the entrances or patrol the perimeter fences at night, so the crews are either on raids or sleeping,' said Stan.

'Main interaction is checking their papers at the entry gates,' added Harold.

Darlene's shoulders slumped; another possible avenue of contact with William closed off. She took a long pull on her drink; she knew she'd have to rely on her letters, or maybe a phone call to the base. She knew she wouldn't be able to get through security to get on base. A wait now seemed unavoidable, but for how long? Her mind wandered back to the hospital in Exeter; talking to William while treating him and the almost immediate attraction she felt for him. What was it, specifically? She couldn't say, but something more esoteric, ethereal. The mysterious spark that comes by only once-in-while.

'What do ya reckon, Dee? Hello, Darlene,' Miriam nudged Darlene on her elbow to pull her back out of her daydream.

'What? Sorry, was a thousand miles away,' Darlene shook her head as she replied.

'Another round? You want a G and T again?' asked Miriam.

'Oh, yes. Absolutely. Here, let me get them,' Darlene stood up, grabbed her and Miriam's glasses and went to the bar. 'Same again, thanks Bob. This time I'm paying.'

'Good as gold, Love. How are you getting on with them?' he asked.

'They're fun. Lots of great chat,' said Darlene, and she gave him a warm smile.

'You'll get loads of banter with them. No doubt. Harry can be a bit gruff, but he don't mean no harm. Still trying to get over his war wounds. Betty loves a gossip. Maybe too much so with what she does. She needs to be more careful. There you go. One and ten, thanks,' said Bob as he handed over the two drinks.

'Thanks, Bob. Appreciate the advice.' Darlene took the drinks back to the table, 'Pint of Bass, madam.'

'Oh, before I forget, there's another new Nurse coming in next week. I'm due to pick her up on Friday, so might be a bit late for drinks,' said Miriam.

'Exciting. Where's she from?' asked Darlene.

'Not sure exactly. Only know she's coming in from London. Got to meet her off the 15:30 train from Kings Cross. Will give her the once-over and see if she's up to snuff to join our group. Can't let any old bird in. Got to keep our standards up,' Miriam winked and smiled at Darlene as she spoke.

Darlene looked away and felt a rush of blood to her face; she grabbed her drink and took a gulp.

*

*Date – 13 March 1942*
*Tour of Operations Count – Operation 2*
*Target Location – Dunkirk, France*
*Assigned Aircraft – Wellington Mk.III X.3359 AA-H*
*Take-off – 20:50*

The Leggett crew sat in the briefing room of the Flight Operations hut, listening to the Squadron Leader outline the operation; a small contingent of only four aircraft from the squadron were assigned to join a strike on the docks at Dunkirk. William studied the map and aerial photographs of the target zone. A quick calculation of flight time resulted in less than two hours. Apart from a mine-laying operation, he couldn't have hoped for a better operation as the first with a new crew in a new plane.

'Righto lads. Listen up,' Pruno said to the crew as they circled their chairs. 'Straight forward operation tonight; Dunkirk docks, engine start at 20:30, only a small battery of AA, so flak should be light, weather forecast to be fair. There's only four of us from 75 going up. Hopefully we don't get a lot of attention from fighters. A good run to help us get acquainted. Questions?' There was a communal shake of the crew's heads. 'Finish your own preparations and see you back here at 19:30. Dismissed.'

William thought the fillings in his back teeth would pop out; the entire aircraft rattled and shook as it charged down the runway. Pruno pulled the nose up and took the plane through a smooth climb to cruising altitude. As per the forecast, it was a smooth run south to Dunkirk.

On cue, Pruno come onto the radio to tell the crew it was five minutes to the target. William shuffled down the narrow gap to the bomb aimer's area, wiggled into a comfortable position lying on his front on the small mattress, and started his preparations. Almost as if it was pre-planned, when Pruno dropped the plane to the bombing altitude, the anti-aircraft flak fired up. Having a good number of raids under his belt, Pruno appeared to pick his way expertly through the field and kept an altitude above the lower blanket of flak. Being in the position most exposed and vulnerable to the flak, William was grateful for Pruno's proficiency, but his heart was still going at near a hundred beats per minute. Each pop, flash of light and black cloud of the flak shells increased the intensity of his heartbeats.

'One minute to target. Ready to go Navigator?' asked Pruno.

'Affirmative, Skip. All set,' replied William. The target approach landmarks of railway lines and fuel tanks passed through his aiming sights; their target was the docks, with previous raids aimed at the other strategic infrastructure. As the last of fuel tanks came into view, he checked the wind speed one last time, and as his hand hovered over the release lever a shell exploded close to the plane, fragments of shrapnel battered the fuselage. Pruno took evasive action then corrected the aircraft. 'Bugger. Where's my target?' asked William, frantically searching the ground thorough the aiming mechanism. 'I can still get it.' He released the bomb bay's cargo. 'Bombs gone. Doors closing. Taking target area photographs,' William reached over and activated the camera to get evidence of the success of the operation, then dropped his head to the floor.

*

*13 March 1942*

Miriam joined the group for Friday night drinks after they had started their second round. Two empty packets of pork scratchings and a quarter of a pork pie and a half scotch egg, sat in the middle of the table. Crumbs of the snacks were scattered across the table.

'What's the story with the new Nurse?' asked Harold.

'Exciting, let me tell you,' Miriam's voice was up a couple of octaves as she spoke. 'She's Czechoslovakian. Name is Milena something. One of those unpronounceable European names. Lives in London and was at St Mary's in Paddington. Speaks perfect English, in fact sounds a bit posh. Her parents were diplomats here in the Twenties, so she went to school here. Pretty much about all I got out of her.'

'Sounds a bit exotic,' said Darlene.

'What do ya reckon about her joining us? Not sure about a toff coming in,' mused Betty.

'Well, she's not technically a toff. She's Czech. Do they have Lords, Ladies, Earls, Viscounts, and Duchesses?' asked Stan.

'Ya don't need a title to be a toff. Just money and like to look down on us working types,' hissed Harold.

'Ease up on her lads. We don't know her and she seemed normal, apart from the posh voice,' pleaded Miriam.

'You met her, Dee? You given her the once over?' asked Betty.

'Not yet. I've seen the name Milena Dvořáček pop up on the new staff roster, but she's assigned to a different ward. Haven't heard she's in the Nurses' Home,' said Darlene.

'Oh no. She's in digs. Boarding with an old lady on Prickwillow Road. I dropped her off there,' replied Miriam.

'I'll introduce myself next week. We'll spend lunchtime together and I'll report back,' said Darlene to nods around the table. 'What else is new folks?'

'Me first,' Stan sat up bolt straight and put his hands on his hips. 'Air Vice Marshall Cochrane and his entourage came through the station during the week. Must have been visiting some of the squadrons. He had some hangers on.' He sat back with a broad smile on his face.

'Must have been what all the commotion was about on Tuesday. I finished my shift before he arrived on base, but there was lots of scuttling around by the Officers during the morning,' said Betty. 'Not much from me. Been a quiet enough week ops-wise. No more news on when the thousand bomber raids might start,' she added.

'Not much happening at the Cathedral. The heavy rain during the week had us worried about the roof, but it held up. Repaired a couple of pews. Nothing else,' said Harold.

'Personal question. Any of you stepping out with someone?' asked Darlene. 'Betty, you must have loads of lovely RAF types doting on you.'

'Airmen? Bloody hell, no. Maybe the non-flying Officers, but they aren't much interested in us lowly WAAF's,' replied Betty, dismissively.

'Why not aircrew?' asked Darlene, trying to belie her inner worry over Betty's reply.

'Don't want to be heartbroken. Casualty rate is bloody high, plus all the ones that end up as POWs. Operation nights we're up at the flight board writing "crashed on take-off, crashed on landing or FTR".'

'FTR?' asked Darlene.

'Failed to Return. You'd think we'd be numb to it by now, but it doesn't get any easier. On the bad nights, we still have a little cry.' Betty drained her sherry. 'Stan, Pet. Be a sport,' she pushed her empty glass over to him and nodded her head towards the bar.

'I'm so sorry, Betty. I didn't mean to upset you,' Darlene reached across the table and held her hand. Betty squeezed hard in return. 'We only see a fraction of those boys come through. Can't imagine seeing so many crews go up and not come back.' Betty nodded gently and bit her lower lip at Darlene's reply.

'So many new faces come and go when we're on gate guard duty,' added Harold, as he rolled his pint in his right hand. 'Main familiar faces are those senior Officer's and the ground crew lads. Most of the aircrew get through their tours get out straight away. They don't hang around. If they do stay in, it's usually as instructors, but that is bloody dangerous, too. Flying beaten up old planes, with green crews. Don't know which is more dangerous; live ops or going up with raw recruits. There was huge difference between the older blokes and the kids when we were over in France. Throw in a thirty thousand pound, barely airworthy aircraft. Not for me.'

Darlene's mind started spinning; what was she doing thinking about stepping out with William? He'd only started his tour; he only had a fifty-fifty chance of surviving. Would he make it through the coming week, to meet her next Saturday, let alone over thirty raids? What on earth was she thinking, turning her world upside down for no more than a half-chance at love?

*

Reggie charged into their room, 'Come on Billy-Bob. Saddle up. I wants ta go ta midday Mass at St Etheldreda's. I've organised a car for us.' The big man cast a shadow over William as he stood next to him.

William looked up from the book he was reading, his face etched with scepticism.

'Don't be like dat now. Been a couple of months since we've been. Got me a hankering for communion. Won't be taking no for an answer,' added Reggie.

Closing his book, William swung his legs around, exhaling forcefully as he got off the bed. He knew Reggie wouldn't change his mind now. There would be nothing gained by arguing with the big fella.

Taking a pew near the back of the small church, William searched his memory for the last time he attended Mass. There had been one visit since Christmas, but exactly when was coming back blank. Given there'd been less than a handful of Masses since he arrived in Britain, it shouldn't be this tough to remember.

The sweet aroma of incense, the murmur of chatting parishioners and the stations of the cross wrapped him like a familiar and comfortable blanket. Memories of Mass with his family filled his thoughts; his first Communion, their last Mass at St Mary of the Angels in Wellington, before they moved to Wanganui. Then came the vision of his brother's wedding, when Albert was the presiding priest at Gary and Sarah's nuptials.

William shook his head to jettison the memory. Reggie's gaze narrowed. The image of Albert at the altar started to fade, but as St Etheldreda's priest emerged from the sacristy, Albert's face superimposed on the priest.

'Kick me,' William whispered to Reggie.

'You what?' replied Reggie, his usual smile replaced with a frown.

'Don't ask, just do it. Not too hard, mind,' demanded William.

Reggie flicked a sharp nudge to William's ankle, causing the smaller man to wince and grit his teeth. Even a light kick from the big man packed some force. The pain inflicted had the required impact; Albert's face vanished from William's vision. He settled back into the pew and gave himself over to the rituals of Mass.

*

*21 March 1942*

The spring sunlight filled Darlene's room with a warm, golden glow. She closed her eyes, spread her arms and let the sun heat her skin. She was only in her camisole and knickers. She had three different outfits assembled on her bed, but still hadn't decided which one to go with. Given today was what she would say was her first date with William, she wanted to make an impression. All the options were nice and would turn his head, but one kept screaming at her "pick me". A bold choice, but she decided to go with her gun metal grey pant suit with a white silk blouse and her coat, to take the edge off the mid-spring chill.

She positioned herself in the sunny corner of the main doorway to wait for William. A light breeze brushed her skin but didn't take too much warmth out of the sun's rays. It was a good day to step out with a lovely man, she thought. Halfway down the street she saw a familiar face walking towards her. The man was a smidge shorter than she remembered from Exeter, but definitely more dashing in his day uniform than his flight suit. A few yards away, a broad and warm smile broke across his face, the smile that had magnetically drawn her to him back in December.

'Well, hello, Darlene. Wonderful to see you again. My word, you look stunning,' William took her hand and lightly kissed it.

A pulse of energy shot up her arm from the touch of his lips on her skin. She felt her ears warm and any chill of the breeze was quickly swamped.

'What a delight. These three months seems like a lifetime. So much to catch up on,' she said, letting her hand linger in his.

'Any ideas on where should we go? I haven't been able to spend much time in Ely so far. Only a couple of trips in for Mass of a Sunday,' replied William.

'There's a couple of nice parks in town, near the Cathedral. They should be close to full bloom with flowers and blossoms. Worth a look. It's a fair walk into town from here. We can take the bus,' said Darlene as she pointed down the street to the bus stop.

They settled into the back row seats on the next bus, and William spoke first, 'I have to admit, your letter took me by surprise. What on earth brought you up here?'

'With the Americans due here soon, the hospital hierarchy know they'll get busier. So, they asked for volunteers. Exeter was a bit quiet, and I knew there were a number of Bomber Command airfields around here and where the Americans would be based. I wanted to do more, felt a bit stuck out on a limb down in the southwest. And there is the added bonus of being able to see you again.'

'Yes, the Yanks coming in has caused a bit of chat amongst the lads. It's fortuitous the hospital needed more Nurses so soon after we met. Serendipitous, one might say,' William gave her another of his warm smiles.

Darlene sighed softly as the same rush of energy from his earlier kiss of her hand, surged through her body again.

# Chapter Four

*27 March 1942*

Miriam, Darlene and Milena strode into the Prince Albert; Miriam and Darlene exhibited the confidence which comes with being regular customers, known and liked by the landlord. With an unwritten reservation in the establishment, they went over to the group's table; Darlene took the lead, 'Evening all. Milena, here's the gang we told you about; Stan, Harold and Betty.'

'An absolute pleasure to meet you,' said Milena in an impeccable, Home Counties accent, as she shook all their hands, and fixed them with her warm eyes and smile. Both Harold and Stan stumbled over their replies, but Betty was decisive.

'Mer and Dee reckon you'll fit in OK with us, so welcome,' said Betty.

'I'm thankful for their vote of confidence,' replied Milena, flashing a broad smile at Betty.

'Milena, what would you like to drink,' Darlene interjected.

'Could I please have a scotch and water? Thank you.' Stan and Harold raised their eyebrows at each other. Milena kept her hands crossed on her lap, with no motion towards her pockets or to grab her purse; the corners of Betty's mouth turned down and she gave small nod of her head.

'You fitting in to Ely, OK?' asked Stan.

'Lovely little town, to be honest. First time I've been here and I have to say I like it a lot. I have been to Cambridge a number of times, however, I hadn't ever gone the extra few miles to Ely,' replied Milena.

Darlene and Miriam returned from the bar, placing the drinks down on the table. Miriam quickly sat down next to Milena, leaving Darlene to hunt for an extra chair. 'Scoot over your two,' she said as she tried to get some space between Betty and Stan. 'Cheers all. To our new friend. Welcome Milena,' she added, lifting her glass, urging the rest to touch glasses.

'We hear you've got an interesting background,' said Harold.

'Miriam's been sharing our chats, I see,' Milena tilted her head to Miriam, who quickly grabbed her pint to shield her now flushed face. 'I suppose it is out of the ordinary. My father was a Czechoslovakian diplomat and was assigned to our London Embassy in the summer of 1926. I was nearly ten when we came to England and I went to a nice school. I stayed on and went to boarding school when my parents went back, then trained as a Nurse,' said Milena.

'You never went back home?' asked Darlene.

'Oh no, I had many trips back to Czechoslovakia. Mainly Christmas and summer holidays with my grandparents in Reichenberg. As you can understand, I haven't been back since Christmas 1938. Sad not being able to see family,' she said.

'You don't have a European accent at all,' commented Stan.

'When I was young, we moved to Prague for Father's work, and my English teacher there was from Windsor, so learned English with her accent. I came here so early and stayed so long, I feel more English than Czech,' she gave a warm smile to Stan and Harold.

Betty pursed her lips then crunched up one side of her face and sighed, 'What's been happening at the hospital, Dee?'

'We've definitely been busier. There were a couple of raids on the twenty-fifth, and we had a few wounded aircrew from those,' replied Darlene.

'Yeah, we lost a couple of planes on the run to Essen.' Betty thought she saw a physical tic from Milena, a quick scratching of the back of her neck. 'You two better get ready for more patients if they concentrate on Happy Valley.'

'Happy Valley?' asked Milena.

'It's what the aircrew call the Rhine and Ruhr River valleys. A bit of gallows humour, 'cause there's nothing happy about the bloody place,' explained Miriam.

'Do we lose a lot of planes there?' asked Milena.

'If not the highest loss rate of any place, damn close to it. But it's the industrial heart of Germany, so we gotta go after it. Double edged sword,' replied Betty.

'You are a WAAF, correct? Which base are you assigned to?' asked Milena.

'Yep, Mildenhall. One of the largest around here. I'm a wireless operator mainly, but help out with the flight operations too,' replied Betty.

'You must know a bit about what's going on?' continued Milena.

'I keep my ear to the ground, but we all have different perspectives. When we put it all together, we think we have a decent idea of what's happening. Then again, it could all be windbag gossip. Right team?' Betty nodded to the rest of the table.

'I ain't gotta clue what's going on. Just keeps me head down and does me job,' added Stan.

'It's the best we can do. Have to trust the top brass know what they're doing and have the plan to defeat the Nazis,' said Miriam.

'First-hand knowledge tells me not to put too much confidence in them,' snorted Harold, then took a deep swig of his pint. Milena looked at him quizzically. 'I was at Dunkirk. Right stuff up from go to whoa. If it wasn't for the fishing and sailing fleet, most of us would be in graves or Nazi POW camps,' he said, answering her unasked question.

'Come on folks, all a bit morbid for the first night with a new friend. Any nice or funny news?' asked Darlene.

'I heard the ENSA will be doing a tour around the bases later this Spring,' said Miriam.

'Jesus. Every Night Something Awful. Hopefully, I'll be rostered on to do guard duty somewhere far away from them,' quipped Harold.

'Don't be such a sad sack. They have some halfway decent performers. I'm going to go,' replied Miriam.

'Who are they?' asked Milena

'The Entertainments National Service Association. Basically, a bunch of performers who put on shows for the troops. They can be hit and miss. I've seen a couple of good shows, but also one absolute howler,' said Darlene.

'I'd be keen to take a look. Miriam, you, Darlene and I can make a night of it. Keep us posted on details,' replied Milena.

'Right, you lot. Sorry to be first to leave, but I'm rostered on tomorrow morning. Good chance the bus will be running tomorrow night. Better get home for a decent night's kip. Nice to meet you, Milena. Next Friday good for ye, lads?' asked Betty, as she sipped the last of her sherry and stood up to leave. Nods came from around the table.

'Good as gold, girl. Hope it's a smooth night. No FTR's for you. See you next week,' replied Miriam.

'I'll head away too. I'm working on Sunday. Don't worry about a lift, Mer. I'll grab the bus. Night all,' said Darlene as she followed Betty out the door.

As the two women crossed the street to the bus stop, Betty turned to Darlene, 'Can't put my finger on it, but there's something odd about Milena.'

'I'm sure you said the same about me when you first met me. She might have lived here for sixteen years, but she's still got a European air about her. She's certainly not your typical Cambridgeshire girl,' replied Darlene.

'Nah, not it. I've met plenty of continental types over the years, but there's something that doesn't sit right. Maybe I'm dreaming it. Anyway, here's your bus, Dee. Hope tomorrow night is a good run and you won't be busy on Sunday. See you next week.' They embraced before Darlene hopped onto the bus.

*

*Date – 28 March 1942*
*Tour of Operations Count – Operation 4*
*Target Location – Lübeck, Germany*
*Assigned Aircraft – Wellington Mk.III X.3597 AA-C*
*Take-off – 19:50*

'Alright, lads. This is our first target in Germany itself.' Pruno addressed the crew in a corner of the briefing hall. The five other men were seated in a circle in front of him. 'Last couple of runs didn't have us go over Germany, so we need to be ready for a hell of a lot more flak, searchlights and night fighters. The Dunkirk and St Nazaire runs were easy enough compared to what we should expect tonight. Robbie, you've got our flight plans?' Pruno nodded to William.

'Thanks, Skip.' The room echoed with the rustling of paper as William unrolled his charters and opened his notepad. 'Going out is straight forward. Head northeast to our first beacon at Cromer on the Norfolk coast, turn east-northeast out over the North Sea. Between the West and East Frisian Islands, we'll turn directly east, then passing the end of the East Frisian's turn east-southeast for virtually a direct run to Lübeck. We'll pass over the German coast at Büsum. Return home is further south, closer to the Frisian's, so we might pick up some night fighters from their bases in the Netherlands. We'll be over Germany itself for less than ninety miles. Straightforward. From a flight perspective, no concerns for me,' he closed his book as he concluded.

'Excellent, thanks Robbie. The run into Lübeck is along the Elbe River valley, halfway between Hamburg and Kiel, so a high concentration of defences. We need to be ready for anything. Cyril and Gordon, you could be busy. Stay sharp. Ossie will be another pair of eyes for you. Any questions, lads?' There was a collective shake of heads to Pruno's question, 'Top stuff. Get some rest. See you at dinner.'

As the crew walked out of the building, Cyril broke away from the line of men and ran over to the wall. His body convulsed violently as he brought up a small stream of vomit. With one arm propping himself up against the building, he gulped down large, heavy breaths.

'Jesus, Cy. You alright, mate?' asked Gordo.

He held out an open palm with his other arm, 'No worries, lads. Got a few nerves. We'll be right.' He stood up, pulled out his handkerchief and wiped his mouth, 'Phew. Usually happens after the briefings. Should be right as rain from here on.'

Ossie raised his eyebrows and frowned at William and Gordo.

*

The night sky was illuminated by dozens of searchlights. The light pouring through the bomb aimer's windows into the aircraft was so bright, it reminded William of the sunniest summer's day back in New Zealand. He had to shield his eyes to be able to read the aiming equipment.

As soon as they hit the bank of lights, Pruno took major evasive action, 'Buckle up, lads. This could get rough,' he said over the radio.

William continued his procedures; first away was two 1,000-pound bombs, then three 500s, one 250-pounder, and finally a dozen bundles of flares to act as pathfinders. All was going smoothly; he pulled the trigger to release the last bundle of flares, but before he could announce "Bombs gone", there was a sound of an explosion, a thud and reverberation. 'We've been hit?' William queried out loud. A strong smell of fire assaulted his nostrils as rushed back to his navigator's table. A bright light and smoke pulled his attention to the rear. 'Jesus Christ,' he yelled.

Ossie was at the astrodome observation hatch, 'We've taken a flare. We're on fire.' He was clear and calm on the radio. Pruno immediately put the plane into a dive, to direct the flames away from the fuel tanks and the bomb bay. Ossie pulled himself towards the back of the plane to join Gordo, who was closest to the fire from the rear gunner's position. Ossie pointed the fire extinguisher at the blaze and pulled the trigger. Nothing. He shook it a couple of times, then tried again. Still nothing. 'Oh, bugger me,' he said.

'Hands, Ossie. We gotta use our hands,' yelled Gordo.

Both men started to beat the flames with their flight gloves. After half dozen swats, they had to pull back and slap their gloves together, putting out the flames that had taken hold on them. After a minute, there was no discernible decrease in the flames.

'Get ready to bail, chaps' Pruno said over the radio.

'We're over water, Skip,' replied William. 'Best we get over land. We won't stand a chance if we go into the sea. I'd rather take on the Germans than the Baltic. Bear one hundred and eighty degrees to port. Get us over land.'

Pruno turned the aircraft around and headed back to Germany. It didn't seem right, but he knew Robbie was correct; at this time of the year, they'd all likely be dead inside ten minutes after going into the Baltic Sea. At least this way they'd get a fighting chance of survival and perhaps make the border and contact with the Danish resistance.

Their beating of the flare still wasn't making any dent in its fiery intensity, but they had managed to push it back towards the outside of the aircraft, but was now wedged in the geodesic frame, out of reach of their hands. Three minutes had passed, although it seemed like seconds. Pruno repeated his order to bailout.

'It's no good, Ossie. We can't get at it. We gotta go,' shouted Gordo.

'Not if I can help it,' replied Ossie. He started stamping at the flare. Two, three, four attacks with his boot, but it was still wedged in place.

'Come on Ossie,' William yelled from near the hatch.

'A couple more,' replied Ossie. He pulled his leg up, so his knee was up near his chest, and thrust down with every ounce of energy he had. Terror came over Gordo's face as Ossie's leg went through the framework, forcing the flare out of the aircraft, but trapping Ossie himself. Half in and half out, the force of the air sucked him closer to oblivion. Gordo grabbed him underneath the arm pits and wedged his feet in the framework on either side of the aircraft. William turned away from the hatch and dived at Gordo, grabbing him around the waist.

Slim got on the intercom, 'Flare's gone; fire out. Level off, Skip.' Pruno pulled the plane's nose up and turned back to the sea, away from any searchlights and flak batteries.

Gordo and William started to drag Ossie back into the plane with all the care and control they could muster; the jagged, ruptured geodesic frame could have sliced Ossie's leg open. Inch by inch they brought him back in. Slim came over and closed the hatch, cutting off one source of frigid air pouring into the plane.

'Almost there,' said Gordo. 'Couple more inches.' One more heave and all three men fell back onto the floor of the plane.

'They're in. They're in. Let's get out of here,' said Slim to Pruno. Almost instantly, the plane started to climb as Pruno took them to a decent altitude for their return.

'You got him?' William asked Gordo, who nodded. 'I gotta get some coordinates for Skip.' He jumped up to the observation hatch to check their current location; with the next full moon in four days' and minimal cloud cover, the moonlight illuminated the night. Ahead, the sea glistened, and to the starboard side, the moonlight allowed him to make out some land. Port side, the lights of a small town twinkled. He returned to his table to find all his charts and equipment strewn across the floor. He frantically flicked through the papers and found the Northern Germany chart at the bottom of the pile. He put it on the table, placed the map plotting arm on it, then checked the compass reading and got on the intercom.

'Skip, we're heading directly northeast. Looks like we are in the Lübecker Bucht. Pretty sure Neustadt is on our port side. Turn one hundred and thirty-five degrees to port, head directly west. That will take us halfway between Neumünster and Keil, and then pass over Heide. We'll be back on our planned flight path then.' He pushed himself back into his seat, let out a heavy sigh, then placed his head on his desk.

Slim came onto the intercom, 'Jesus, lads. That was some dodgy do. Incredible effort boys. Skip, get us the home, there's a good lad.'

'Roger, Wireless. Will give it my best shot,' replied Pruno.

Ossie re-took his position next to Pruno. He looked at the charred palms of his gloves and flexed his fingers a few times. Pruno took one hand off the control yolk, grabbed Ossie's left hand and squeezed it tight.

Frigid air from the hole in the fuselage whistled through the plane; drowning out the engine noise. William pulled the collar of his flight jacket up higher to stop his neck getting colder. He jiggled his legs and tapped his feet to ward off the frozen air. It was going to be a long trip back.

*

'Navigator. Passing a small town on our starboard and the coast is three minutes away. Presuming it's Heide,' Pruno's calm voice broke the tension in the aircraft.

'Roger Skip. In twenty minutes, turn fifty-five degrees to port, then fifteen minutes after later, turn thirty degrees to starboard. It should then be a straight run to Cromer, on the Norfolk coast,' William instructed Pruno.

'Don't think I've ever been as eager to get back to Blighty. I'll be bloody glad to see the back of this run,' said Gordo.

Murmurs of agreement came from all the crew.

# Chapter Five

*28 April 1942*

Pruno and Ossie sat at the front of the room, neither man making a great deal of eye contact with the crew as they sat down in the Flight Operations hut. The lads had been buzzing with chat and rumours about the reason for the briefing; were they about to announce a new major offensive, was the squadron was being merged with another, or were they going to be moved to another base.

Whatever it was going to be, William knew it wouldn't be great news; flexibility and adaptability were key aspects to their existence. Since the flare fire in March, the crew had been pretty stable, only saying goodbye to Cyril and Slim, as they completed their tours of duty. They'd seen them off with big nights at the Sergeants' Mess, with a mixture of relief for them, and frustration that most of the remaining crew still had twenty-odd ops to go before they could get home.

Their replacements, Paul Bosson (Boss) and Kerrison Morris (Tas), had slotted seamlessly into the Leggett crew. William knew the results the squadron had achieved kept the top brass happy, so there was no need for big changes.

'Effective immediately, Ossie has been assigned to a new crew, and I will become sole pilot for us,' said Pruno to the sullen men.

'To say it's been a pleasure, privilege and an honour to be your Second Pilot over these past few months, is a horrendous understatement. Day after day, night after night and raid after raid, you've proven yourselves to be professional, courageous, and resilient. Along with being an outstanding flight crew, you're also terrific men. If my new crew are half as good as you, they'll still be bloody good,' said Ossie

A morbid silence hung in the air for a few seconds. 'Well, this is shit. What's the bloody story?' asked Tas, as subtle as ever.

Pruno stepped in to help Ossie out, 'As you know, ever since Bomber Harris became top dog of the RAF, they've been increasing the number of aircraft and operations. He's got a target of having "a thousand bomber" raids by the summer. They've got to the point where they are producing new aircraft and needing more crews faster than they can train pilots. So, to get more planes in the air, they are cutting Wellington crews from six to five, putting pilots into new aircraft and building crews around them. They hope to have twenty to fifty percent more aircraft by the middle of summer.'

'A thousand aircraft in a single raid? Bugger me, that's some firepower,' said Gordo

'What are these new crews going to be hitting? We're already smashing the hell out of the German factories, railways and ports. Not much more to target within our range,' said William.

'It's for the top brass to know and to tell us in due course,' replied Pruno, 'But if I was to hazard a guess, I think we all know what the future may hold target-wise.'

'We know the Luftwaffe were all over the place with their bombing. Christ, look at what they did to Coventry. What, over five hundred civilians dead or wounded. I know we can't be pin-point with our bombing either, so more blanket bombing in the general area of the targets. It doesn't sit right,' added Boss.

'Look lads, I'd rather not hit anything except pure military and industrial targets, but those days are over. You're right Boss, Coventry was brutal, as were all the raids on London and Bristol. Hell, some small mining towns up north have been smashed. The Nazis have given no quarter wherever they go. As for innocent civilians? Maybe in the occupied countries, but in Germany itself, to me they're all complicit. A kid who's in the Hitler Youth today will be on the front line tomorrow, trying to kill us by war's end.' Gordon said.

'Moot point, I suppose. We go to where they tell us, and we know Robbie is one of the most accurate bomb aimers around. Anyway, Ossie, you're a bloody good bugger. Gonna miss ya,' added Tas.

'Sad and pissed off,' Gordo added. 'I've been over here around two years, been in at least three type of aircraft and multiple pilots, and you're brilliant. That crew will be in great hands with you Ossie, but it's gonna be bloody strange not having you suit up with us. Thank you for being a great pilot and a top egg.' All the crew nodded their approval at Gordo's words.

'Right lads, we're done. We have night flight training tonight and given the frequency of ops this month, we should expect another run in the next couple of nights. Make sure we're focussed for the briefings. Ossie starts training his crew tomorrow and we wish him well and thank him for everything he's done for us. Three cheers, lads.' Pruno led the crew.

*

*Date – 29 April 1942*
*Tour of Operations Count – Operation 17*
*Target Location – Gennevilliers, France*
*Assigned Aircraft – Wellington Mk.III X.3720 AA-U*
*Take-off – 21:25*

William couldn't stop looking up at the vacant Second Pilot's flip down seat, still in its retracted position. No Ossie; first time without him since the Dunkirk run back in mid-March. Close to half of his entire tour always had the reassuring presence of Arthur Osborne as Second Pilot. Now they were permanently down to five; no more groan inducing jokes and constant updates on the weather and cloud formations from Ossie. William noticed the whole crew was much more subdued; there was no running commentary from Gordo in the rear turret on the formation and flying prowess (or lack-thereof) of the aircraft around them; no bravado from Tas about how many German fighters he'd hit tonight; and the bare minimum of orders and instructions from Pruno. On one hand William was thankful it had been an uneventful run to the target, a northern suburb of Paris. On the other, a bit of flak or occasional night-fighter would have broken up the long periods of crew silence. Then, William was jolted back to the task at hand.

'Twenty minutes to target. Prepare for our run in.' Pruno's voice was crisp and clear over the intercom.

William read his instruments one last time to confirm their position, then worked his way down into the bomb aimer's position. As he looked out of the viewing bubble, he was surprised at the lack of searchlights and flak so close to the French capital. This was their first raid on Paris, and he was expecting more defences. 'Could be a smooth op,' he whispered as he crossed himself.

'Passed Rouen, turning east and descending to bombing altitude,' Pruno's voice sharpened William's preparations.

A direct southeasterly run over the docklands of the Paris suburb of Gennevilliers, targeting the docks themselves, an aircraft engine factory and a power station; all contained on a tight horseshoe bend of the Seine. Their primary target was the power station, barely a half-mile east of the aircraft engine factory.

As Pruno levelled out from his descent, William could see the first few aircraft in the stream had done a good job of prepping the targets, with all three well lit up with flares and incendiary bombs. 'Thanks, lads,' William said to himself.

'Over to you, Robbie,' said Pruno.

'Thanks, Skip. All set. Hold her steady and this should be a good drop,' William replied to Pruno. Looking through the viewfinder, the ships and barges on the Seine gave him a good line to the target near the main docks area. 'Hold, hold, hold,' he whispered, then as the aircraft engine factory hit his viewfinder, he pushed the bomb release. 'Bombs gone. Checking for impact.' He announced over the intercom. Looking back to the target, clearly visible explosions came up from the power station, illuminating the docks, cranes and oil tanks. 'Target hit confirmed. Photographs taken.'

'Affirmative. Target strike successful. Let's go home, Skip,' Gordo added from the rear turret.

*

A couple of minutes after they passed Rouen, Gordo came onto the radio, 'We've got company, Skip. Junkers 88 on our tail. Seems he's only got eyes for us.'

'Thanks, Gunner. Can you get rid of…' Pruno's reply was cut short by the blast of Gordo's guns as he engaged the Ju 88. Pruno started weaving the plane left to right, with moderate climbs and dives.

'No good, Skip. He's sticking to us like a fly round a sheep's bum. He's not bad, this Jerry,' reported Gordo.

'Hold on, lads.' Pruno had barely finished the instruction when he threw the plan into multiple corkscrew turns. William held tightly onto his table, but couldn't save his charts; they flew through the cabin as the aircraft dove.

'Bastard's still on our tail. Can't fix him in my sights,' shouted Gordo.

William felt bile rising in his throat, being tossed left to right, forward and backward, plus the intermittent vibrations from the sporadic burst of gunfire from Gordo's turret. As suddenly as the dive started, the plane levelled out. William pulled himself closer to his instruments.

'Now only three-hundred feet off the deck, Skip. No room for error now,' he reported.

'Easy, Skip. Any lower and we'll be pruning the trees.' An unusually tense voice of Tas updated the rest of the crew on how low they were.

'Thanks, lads. Good as gold. If we can't shake him, we'll scare the shit out of him,' added Pruno, as he pushed the throttles to their limit, sending a surge of noise and vibrations through the plane.

'Coastline coming up. Skip. Will be over the Channel in few seconds,' said Tas.

The distinctive pops and zings of bullets hitting the fuselage echoed through the aircraft, then Pruno dropped the plane even further.

'Seventy-five feet, Skip,' William shouted.

'Christ Almighty, we're low. Should have brought me fishing rod,' added Tas.

'He's climbing. Might be trying to come at us from above. You should see him, Tas,' said Grodo.

'Got him. He'll try for our blind-spot, between our gun arcs. He's a cunning prick,' replied Tas.

'Tell me when he's diving, then hold on,' said Pruno.

'Steady, steady. Here he comes,' replied Gordo.

Pruno pulled the plane up and banked to starboard. 'You got a shot, Tas?' he asked.

'Almost. A bit more, Skip. Yes, got him.' Tas then opened up a prolonged salvo at the Ju 88.

Pruno reversed the manoeuvre to dive and bank to port. This time, Gordo shot at the German. Pruno levelled out the plane at the previous low altitude, 'Anyone see him?'

'He's pulling away to port. Looks like he's disengaging. Great work, Skip,' Gordo reported.

Pruno eased the plane up to a cruising altitude as silence fell over the crew.

*

A low-key reaction greeted touchdown, thanks to Pruno and congratulations drifted through the crew from Tas in the nose to Gordo in the tail. In the truck on the drive back to base, cigarettes were lit, long drags taken in and lots of nods and smiles shared between the crew. Pruno spoke up, 'Tremendous work tonight lads. We got into a tight spot, but a remarkable response. Top stuff. Was strange with Ossie, no doubt, but we've come through it. I knew we would do it; now you should know we'll be alright. If we continue to do our jobs the best we can, it's all I can ask. I'll get the first round at the bar.' The truck erupted with cheers and the smiles grew wider. The truck driver turned his head and gave them a quizzical look through the cab's back window.

*

*Date – 6 May 1942*
*Tour of Operations Count – Operation 20*
*Target Location – Stuttgart, Germany*
*Assigned Aircraft – Wellington Mk.III X.3586 AA-A*
*Take-off – 21:55*

A collective groan came from the crew when the curtain was pulled back in the briefing room and the night's target was revealed; Stuttgart – a range of Daimler factories.

'Again? Two ops in a row deep into the south. Bugger,' said Boss.

'Was getting used to those French runs and gardening ops. Knew it was too good to last,' added Gordo.

'Alright lads. We got off lightly on the last run with the icing problem cutting it short. We take what they give us, no moaning,' Pruno cut in. Boss and Gordo gave each other a nod and a smirk.

*

William estimated they were close to Baden-Baden; a few miles over the French-German border when the pops and booms of exploding flak fired up. It brought their smooth run to a dangerous and potentially deadly end. He jumped up to the Second Pilot seat to take a look. 'How is it, Skip?' he asked.

'Light enough now, but expect it to get heavier closer to the target. Twenty minutes to go, Robbie. Let's make sure these ones count. Be nice to hit Hitler's favourite company hard.' Pruno gave William a wink and a thumbs up.

William started his bombing run preparations; took an updated position reading then squeezed down into the bomb aimer's position. The glass-enclosed area was illuminated by the searchlights, flashes from the flak explosions and the glow from flares and incendiaries. Almost on cue, as Pruno predicted, the flak field got thicker as they passed over the western outskirts of the city. William crossed himself, said a Hail Mary, and added his usual request to the Lord to help Pruno get them through. Looking through the viewfinder, key landmarks appeared; the Stuttgart Central Train Station, the Unterer Schlossgarten city park, then the River Neckar, which is the last key site before the main Daimler factory. They were in the second half of the wave of aircraft to hit Stuttgart, so William found many of the factory buildings and surrounding residential areas well ablaze as they reached their drop zone. The thick smoke and a light blanket of mist made accurate targeting difficult for William. 'Just hit the factory. Don't mess up,' he whispered to himself. He delayed the release by a couple of seconds to make sure they were only over the factory. 'Bombs gone. Check impact Gordo? Difficult to confirm from my spot, but will take photos anyway.'

'Impact confirmed. Significant explosions sighted. Great stuff, Robbie. Bloody hell. We're giving this place a right going over tonight.' The orange light of fires across the city filled Gordo's gun turret. Erupting fireballs surged into the night sky and reflected in the glass panels on his left and right. He exhaled deeply and used the back of his thick glove to wipe away a tear. 'Get us home quick as you can, Skip,' he added.

*

*16th May 1942*

As soon he heard there wouldn't be a raid, William prepared himself to go into Ely to see Darlene. They now had a standing agreement to meet on the Saturday afternoons whenever there wasn't a bombing operation. This would be their fourth Saturday together since Darlene had started at the hospital. Not as many as he'd wanted, but with the thirteen ops in April, they'd had far fewer chances to meet than he had hoped. Those numbers and the raids ran through his head; thirteen runs in thirty days, including three sets of back-to-backs and six sets of runs with only one day between. If they hadn't had a four-day break after the run to Hamburg on the seventeenth of April, they might have snapped. He remembered waking up with uncontrollable shakes in the middle of the night on the eighteenth and Tas stayed in bed all day on the nineteenth. As he walked to the special bus service to Ely, the bright spring sun warmed his skin; today would be a good day, he thought.

William and Darlene jumped off the bus a couple of streets before the train station and made their way down to the River Great Ouse to get on their usual route along the river towpath. Walking arm-in-arm, they followed the path downstream for about fifteen minutes before the town ended and they got into open countryside. Vibrant tulips in full bloom and remnants of dried-up daffodils added to the luxuriousness of the green fields and close to peak foliage on the trees.

'I do love spring. I think it's my favourite season,' said William. He filled his lungs with a deep breath and broke into a smile.

'It's beautiful here. Definitely a more dramatic change in seasons than South Africa. It goes from barren to bursting to life in a few weeks. What's that plant there?' Darlene looked across the river, to a shimmering sea of yellow, which rose and fell in the gentle breeze.

'Rapeseed. It's turned into a cooking oil, but it's also good to eat as a garnish. I think it's one of the most beautiful crops you'll find. Oh, look. Some lambs.' They came to a gap in the hedgerow and surveyed the field. William added, 'Reminds me of home. An eruption of new life all over the place. After all the carnage we've seen, it's nice to see something positive.'

Darlene pulled herself into William and placed her head on his shoulder. 'You doing alright? You don't need to tell me about the ops, but are you managing?'

'The pressure. It's relentless. We've had nineteen runs in the last thirty-nine days, basically one every two days. We try to put the bad thoughts to the back of our heads, but it grinds you down. Days like this are tonic for the soul,' William kissed Darlene's forehead.

'I can't imagine it. Some of our patients get so scared when they are about to be discharged back to their squadrons. I've had a couple throw up as they walked out of the ward. It's so sad. You're not having those sorts of problems?' Darlene asked.

'Not yet, thank God. A couple of the lads have their moments but seem to bounce back,' replied William

'You'll talk to me if ever things get too bad, won't you?' She squeezed his arm, and William nodded. 'You think we've gone far enough? Let's turn around.'

'How about we head to The Cutter Inn? I'm starting to work up a thirst,' said William.

Back in town, they stopped outside the pub to take in the view. The strategic position of The Cutter Inn on a bend of the Great Ouse gave them a broad view of the upstream and downstream stretches of the river; from Ely Gardens to their left through to the railway bridge on their right. The late spring sun lit up the Cathedral's tower as it set over the back of the pub, making it glow and sparkle. A couple of narrowboats floated by, their skippers preparing to take a mooring for the night. One was forest green with brown trim, the other fire red with blue trim. The first boat had a collection of pots on its roof with a range of plants; mint, parsley, and carrots. The second boat owner had gone for a more colourful motif, with a mass of blue, purple, red and orange begonias, fuchsias and petunias. A teenage girl was wandering close to the moored river craft, taking photographs with a box camera.

They had settled onto the low wall between the pub and the river, when the girl approached them, 'Excuse me Ma'am, Sir. Would you mind if I took your picture with the boats in the background?' she asked.

'Oh, lovely. Please do.' Darlene was quick with an enthusiastic reply. 'Come on, snuggle up,' she grabbed William's arm and pulled herself close to him.

'What have you got there? A Kodak Brownie?' asked William.

'Yes, Sir. It's a Six-20. Got it for Christmas last year,' replied the girl. 'Steady now. That looks great. Sun is perfect. And smile in three, two, one. Bang. Got you.'

'Can we get a copy? Here's a couple of bob to cover the cost.' William handed the girl some coins.

'Crikey. Thank you so much. I'll do two for you. Where can I find you?' she asked.

'Drop it off at the hospital for Nurse Darlene du Toit. Here, I'll write it down for you,' said Darlene. She dug into her handbag and pulled out a notepad and pencil.

'Right-o. Might be next week before I get them developed.' The girl beamed a wide smile at the couple.

'Good as gold. Wonderful to see you enjoying your hobby,' said

Darlene as the girl skipped away. 'What a dote of a child. It'll be lovely to have a photograph of us. Let's go in for a drink.'

They set themselves up at a table next to one of the front windows, which gave them a view upstream, towards the railway bridge.

'She was right about the sun. The Cathedral was stunning,' said William. He snuggled closer to Darlene, took her hand and gently let them rest on their touching legs.

'It's absolutely beautiful. I've had a personal tour of it. My friends Miriam and Harold showed me round. I can sort out with Harold for us to have a look, if you'd like. We haven't talked about religion. Can be a bit of a taboo for some. I take it you're Catholic?' Darlene squeezed William's hand as she spoke.

'Yes. I come from an Irish Catholic family. Both my parents were born in County Antrim. You?'

'A relaxed Anglican,' she replied, to which William raised an eyebrow. 'Mum is Anglican and still goes to church regularly. Dad is completely lapsed Dutch Reform. My sister and I were brought up Anglican, but I don't think I've been to a service more than twice since I left South Africa, so class myself as relaxed, rather than lapsed.'

'Have to say I'm the same. If it wasn't for my roommate, Reggie, I wouldn't have been to Mass more than twice. You will have to meet Reggie. Reginald Louis Dubois the third. Top bloke, but mad as a hatter,' a smile broke across William's face.

'That's some name. He a Kiwi?' asked Darlene.

'Good Lord, no. He's American, from New Orleans. Calls himself Cajun. You should hear him speak. Between the accent and his slang, it's tough to understand him sometimes.' Darlene suddenly straightened her posture as she looked out the window and down the river path; William felt her tense up, 'What's the story?' he asked.

'Looks like a Nurse friend of mine. Well, acquaintance more than a friend. Only met her twice,' said Darlene.

'The woman standing by the wee stone bridge? Who is she?' asked William.

'Her name is Milena Dvořáček. She's Czechoslovakian. Moved up from London a couple of weeks after me. She's been to our Friday night drinks a couple of times. She was there last night. She's on a different ward, and she's in digs, not the Nurse's Home, so I don't see her that much.'

'Czech? I've met a few of their airmen. Good lads,' added William.

'It's getting dark, but I'm sure it's her. There aren't many women in Ely who dress as elegantly as she does. If she stays there longer, we should say hello on our way out.' Darlene leaned forward to bring Milena into sharper focus, as the latter looked left and right, then lifted up a loose rock in the bridge, and appeared to place something in the hole. Milena then replaced the rock, bent down and picked up an empty flowerpot by her feet, and flipped it over it from an upside down to a right-side-up position. She looked left and right again, scratched the back of her neck, and started to walked back towards town. 'Hmm, that's a bit odd,' said Darlene.

'Yeah, I saw it too. Strange,' added William, 'What do you reckon?'

'Not sure. She is a bit of a perfectionist. Maybe the rock was out of place and she didn't like an upside down flowerpot. Still, looked out of place. Pity Milena left, but you'll probably meet her at the dance next weekend. You and your crew going?'

'Absolutely. The lads have been talking about nothing else for days,' replied William.

Darlene leaned into William and they fell into a deep, prolonged kiss.

*

Darlene stood in front of her open wardrobe, hands on her hips, and exhaled with force. Her eyes darted along the clothes for the twentieth time, yet she seemed no closer to deciding what to wear. She turned to look out the window; a clear blue sky was going to make for a lovely, mild late spring evening. Back at her wardrobe, she flicked through the hangers one more time. Nearly two-thirds of the way through, the right option struck her. She took out the turquoise pleated dress. It had a small black polka dot pattern on it, with a high neckline. Holding it before her body, it fell about an inch below her knees. She then took a thin black belt and held it across her waist. She gave a small nod then placed the dress and belt on her bed. Now for shoes and a top. Rummaging through her shoes on the floor of the wardrobe, she picked out a black pair with a two-inch heel. Too high for dancing, she thought. No, they'll be fine. She grabbed a cream wool cardigan, light enough so she wouldn't overheat, but warm enough to take the edge off the late evening chill. Makeup and accessories? Easy, she thought; blood red lipstick, small turquoise stud earrings, a couple of dabs of English Rose perfume and her small burgundy handbag.

Happy with her ensemble, she quickly dressed and skipped downstairs to meet Betty, Miriam and Milena.

*

The five men stood in the doorway of the Mildenhall village hall; all in freshly laundered and pressed uniforms, all sharp creases, polished buttons and shiny shoes. Almost as one, they put their caps under the epaulettes on their jackets. The surveyed the scene before them. The dance floor was about half-full, not heaving with bodies yet, but it was still early in the evening. The bar on the left of the hall was doing brisk business; servicemen were three deep already. A light haze of blue smoke hung below the ceiling, a product of the swirls coming off dozens of lit cigarettes. As had become standard procedure at social events, Tas and Boss went straight to the bar, Reggie headed off to do a lap of the hall, leaving

Gordo and William to find a few seats for the gang.

'Looks like the Lakenheath mob aren't here yet. Should be able to grab five seats somewhere,' said Gordo, scanning the hall.

'Don't think we need to worry about one for Reggie. Looks like he's made contact already,' replied William, nodding in the direction of Reggie on the far side of the hall, talking to three women, with one foot up on a chair, his forearms resting on his knee.

'Bloody hell. Fast work. No messing with Sergeant Dubois III,' said Gordo, shaking his head.

'Don't worry. They won't be able to understand a word he says with his Louisiana accent,' William replied, with a cheeky smirk.

They'd secured seats as Tas and Boss returned with five pints. 'Reggie?' asked Boss.

Gordo pointed over to Reggie, now leading one of the women to the dance floor. 'The Ragin' Cajun. No stopping him. Already engaged with targets. As a fellow gunner, I commend his tactics,' said Tas, who had already finished off a third of his pint. 'I'll have his pint, then,' he added without breaking a smile.

William wasn't paying attention to the conversation, as he scanned the edge of the hall for Darlene. He hoped she'd arrive early, as he wanted to spend most of the evening with her. He stood up to look at the other side of the hall when Gordo poked him in the ribs.

'You looking for that Sarfie Nurse you been making time with?' Gordo asked.

'Making time with? Don't know what you're on about, Gordo,' replied William, as he switched his gaze to his friend.

'Christ. Pull the other one, Robbie. You've been into Ely on four Saturdays in the past two months. What have you been doing when you go there? Visiting the Cathedral?'

'What? Our wee Robbie doting on a Nurse. You sly dog,' said Boss.

'Always gotta watch the quiet ones. Sneaky as shithouse rats,' added Tas, finishing off his pint and picking up Reggie's untouched drink.

'Knock it off you lot. We met down in Devon when I bailed out. I already knew her,' William tried to defend himself. The other three men nodded, smiled and took a sip of their beers simultaneously.

William finally found her amongst the whirling couples. She looked back at him, and she gave a quick smile, then returned her attention to her dance partner. William studied Darlene closely; this was one of the few times he'd seen her in civvies with her hair down. She had it in a side part, with a heavy wave in the bottom half, finishing below her shoulders. She reminded him of a brunette Veronica Lake. She was a flash of colour in her turquoise dress. Cute outfit with the black polka dots, he thought. Her dance partner seemed ill-matched for her; he was too tall and his dancing was laboured, slightly off beat. He knew he would be a far better match. He told himself to wait until the end of the song, then go over and talk to her when she returned to her seat. The current song dutifully finished, but the band immediately started on the next, and the lump she was dancing with didn't let her go. She looked back over to William with raised eyebrows.

'Is that her, Robbie? She gave you the signal. Oh, for the love of God, man. Are you going to sit here like a stunned mullet or are you go over there and cut in?' asked Gordo.

'I, um, well. Soon,' replied William.

'Am I going to have to drag you? Don't worry about the big lug with her. I've got you covered if he gives you any gyp.' His mate stood up and motioned William to the dance floor.

Tapping the larger man on the shoulder, William asked if he could cut in. He was about to turn his back on William, the man saw Gordo standing close by giving a flick of his head to motion the man to accept the request.

'I see you have a minder. Is he your friend, Gordon? Good to have friends like him,' said Darlene.

'Yes, Gordo's our rear gunner, always looking after us. You look fabulous. The first time I've seen you with your hair down. How are you?' Now close to Darlene, he could make out finer details; blood red lipstick, small turquoise stud earrings, two gold buttons on the high neckline of her dress, and the heady aroma of English Rose perfume. William took in a deep breath to immerse himself in her scent. Her whole ensemble accentuated her mesmerising green eyes.

'Thank you, William. Like you, wonderful now. I was concerned you didn't see me, then wouldn't come up to get on my dance card. You look dashing in your uniform. Much better than a hospital smock or your tatty flight jacket.' She squeezed his hand and drew herself into him.

'Excuse me Nurse du Toit, that tatty old jacket is a prized possession. It might save my life one day.' He gave her a grin. He felt her breasts nestle against his chest and their thighs come together on the second or third steps. The movement, contact, the heat between them and her aroma put him in a near trance. She was filling virtually all his senses with pleasure. As he expected, their movement on the dance floor was much more flowing and graceful, than with her pervious partner.

Although transfixed by her eyes, he was snapped back to his surroundings by a deep, baritone American voice, 'Billy-Bob. Who da little lady? Is this your Darlene?' asked Reggie. 'This is Betty. She's from the Women's Auxiliary. Betty, this is Billy Robertson.' He twirled his partner towards William and Darlene.

'G'day Reggie. Hello Betty. Pleasure to meet you. Yes, this is Darlene du Toit. From the hospital over at Ely. This is Reginald Louis Dubois III,' replied William.

Betty and Darlene exchanged knowing looks and smiles.

'Delighted to make ya'll acquaintance, Darlene. Charmed.' He reached over, took Darlene's hand and kissed it. Then gave William an unsubtle wink, and spun away back into the dance floor.

'That's Reggie?' Darlene raised her eyebrows at William.

'Yep. My American roommate I told you about. He was our rear gunner on my first raid, when we bailed out in Devon' Darlene nodded. 'He came over here in early '41. To say he's larger than life doesn't do him justice.'

'So, it appears. Poor Betty will have her hands full there,' replied Darlene.

'I've wanted to ask you about why you came up here all the way from Devon. From what I saw of the place, it was extremely pleasant, and if it was quiet, not a bad way to see out the war,' said William.

'Yes, it's gorgeous there. I did like it, no doubt about it. As I said, I needed to do more. With all the bomber and fighter squadrons around here, I knew I'd be busy. Oh sorry, that must sound horrible.'

'It's true. A fact of life. No need to apologise,' said William.

'It's not the whole story,' added Darlene. William raised his eyebrows at her. 'Like I said in my first letter to you, I did hope I would run into you again.' He pulled her closer. She nuzzled into his neck and gave him a light kiss. He felt goosebumps break out all over his arms and a tingle of exhilaration shot down his back.

'On ye bike, little one. Time for my dance,' the thick Belfast accent and the heavy hand on his shoulder shocked William out of his haze. He turned to see a man, with two supporters staring at him.

'You heard, ya scrawny maggot. Jog along,' hissed another.

Reggie let go of Betty and stepped forward, 'Not nice language, especially in front of da femmes. These two is an item. Y'all need to learn you some manners.' Reggie appeared taller and broader than usual.

'And who's gonna teach us? You, ya big dopey Yank?' asked the first man. 'If they're stepping out, they shouldn't have come to a dance.'

'If the Yank doesn't drop some manners on ya, then we'll give it a crack,' said Tas, with Boss and Gordo standing either side of him. His normal dour demeanour was even darker. 'Take your pea-brains and fuck off.'

The second man lurched towards Tas, raising a fist, but hit the floor with a dull thud as Reggie stepped forward and landed a lightning fast, right-hander on the man's jaw. His two friends jumped back with panic on their faces.

'You two couillons want some a dat? I can frapper y'all as well. No, then pick up your man and piss off,' bellowed Reggie. The other two Ulstermen grabbed their mate under his armpits and dragged his limp body off the dance floor.

'Bloody hell, Reggie. You move quick for a big fella,' said Boss.

'Cheers Reggie. Nice punch, but I think I would have taken him myself,' said Tas, giving Reggie a wink. 'Let me get you pint.'

William turned back to Darlene and pulled her close. He could feel her heart racing and quivers shoot through her body. 'It's alright Honey. The lads and I wouldn't let anything happen to you.'

'Who were they?' asked Darlene.

'A bunch of quarter-wits. Not even half-wits. RAF lads from here at Mildenhall, by the looks.'

'Can you take me back to the Nurses' Home?' Darlene looked into William's eyes, and he could see her anxiety, but also her affection for him.

'Absolutely. Let's see if there's a cab out the front,' replied William.

'Thank you. I'll say goodbye to the girls I came with and meet you at the main door in a couple minutes,' said Darlene. She found Betty and Reggie still on the dance floor, 'William is going to take me back to Ely. You'll be OK to stay?'

'Absolutely. Reggie and I are having a grand time. Good-looking chap, your William,' Betty winked at Darlene.

'What about your rule on aircrew?' asked Darlene.

'Might have to make an exception for this one,' Betty exhaled.

'You haven't seen Mer and Milena?' asked Darlene.

'Not since Reggie and I have been dancing. They said they might head out back for a smoke. Have fun, Hon,' Betty turned her attention back to Reggie and continued their dance.

Darlene battled to get to the back door, dodging the throng of bodies as they heaved, twirled and gyrated. A wave of cool spring evening air hit her as soon as she opened the door. She filled her lungs with its freshness. Her eyes struggled for a few seconds to adjust to the darkness. As soon as she could identify shapes and details, she looked around for Miriam. Beside the long wall of the hall, there were about a dozen couples of airmen and their WAAF, Auxiliary or Nurse partners in various stages of courting; some sharing a cigarette, some kissing, and some in more intimate embraces. She scanned the bodies but couldn't see the two women. There were murmurings from the far end of the building, so she went to investigate. A large oak tree was about five yards away from the building; an outside bulb threw a dull light onto the tree, creating some hazy and grotesque shadows. Through the obscurities, Darlene saw Miriam, who was leaning back onto the tree trunk facing Darlene with another person enwrapping her. Miriam's jacket was unbuttoned and her blouse was untucked, her eyes were closed and she wore a satisfied grin. Looking closer, Darlene noted the other person, whose back was to her, checking their clothes and frame, as the person's hands kneaded and squeezed Miriam's breasts. Darlene's mouth dropped open and her eyes widened; 'Milena,' she whispered. Miriam opened her eyes, saw Darlene and her face instantly changed from ecstasy to shock. She mouthed 'No' and shook her head. Darlene quickly turned away and returned to the hall.

'You alright? Looks like you've seen a ghost,' said William, as he opened one of the taxi's back doors.

'Um, I, argh, yes, yes. The fight got me flustered. Thanks for sorting this,' replied Darlene. She gave William a kiss on his cheek as she climbed into the car.

As the taxi snaked through the country roads to Ely, Darlene stared at the blur of the hedgerows rushing by the window. Thoughts and visions swirled around her head; Miriam is a lesbian, not a great surprise; she'd had thoughts along those lines from the first day they met. Was Milena also a lesbian, or merely manipulating Miriam? Given her suspicions about Milena, she was tilting towards the latter, but to what end? To get more detailed information out of Miriam, to put her in a compromised position for additional leverage? A wave of tingles shot through her body as William touched her hand and she rocked back into the seat.

'Sorry Hon, didn't mean to scare you,' said William.

'Was a thousand miles away. No need to apologise. Tonight threw me a bit. The fight, my friend Betty getting swept up by Reggie. Didn't see either of those coming. Happy for them, though,' replied Darlene.

'They seemed to have hit it off. Difficult to resist the force of nature that is Reggie. She's one of your Friday night pub group, isn't she? William asked. 'Would be nice to meet them all sometime. Didn't you come to the dance with a couple of others? Where are they?'

'Well, um, they were around. I think they got onto the dance floor quickly. Couldn't find them at the end,' Darlene played with her hair as she spoke.

'Coming into Ely now, folks. Let me know where I need to go in the hospital,' the taxi driver interrupted.

Darlene told the driver to park around the back of the Nurses' Home. Leaning into William, she whispered, 'As much as I'd love to invite you in, off-limits to men, sorry. But you'll walk me to the door?' It was more of an instruction than a question.

The inky blue sky still had shafts of light flickering through it, making for a beautiful late spring twilight. As they approached the door, Darlene pulled William into a darkened corner. Without a word, they fell into a deep embrace, kissing with a passion which surprised both of them. They pulled back but their foreheads were still touching.

'I've wanted to kiss you since the first time I saw you in Devon,' said William.

'Me too,' whispered Darlene.

Raw passion enveloped them both as they pulled at the other's clothes. The craving that coursed through their bodies and the cool late-spring air struck their skin as it was exposed as each piece of clothing was loosened or removed, made their nerve endings dance. The moonlight illuminated the soft, white skin of Darlene's breasts as William kissed and caressed them.

'Do you have condoms?' she asked. William nodded as he fumbled at the button of his tunic's left breast pocket. Darlene undid his belt and zipper and they quickly became one.

# CHAPTER SIX

*Date – 30 May 1942*
*Tour of Operations Count – Operation 24*
*Target Location – Cologne, Germany*
*Assigned Aircraft – Wellington Mk.III X.3538 AA-N*
*Take-off – 23:10*

'Bugger me, Robbie. Something's up. What's going on with all these crews?' Gordo's head darted back and forth at the gathering throng of personnel.

'The first thousand plane op? Gotta be,' replied William. A large stream of aircrew shuffled into the briefing room, slowing down to get through the door. 'Yep, it's all hands-on deck. Look Gordo, no seats. Standing room only.'

Pruno struggled to keep his crew together as the room kept filling up but found a gap near the back for all five of them.

'Aircrew, ATTENTION,' yelled a young officer as a handful of senior officers entered the room.

Wing Commander Buckley addressed the room, 'At ease men. Given the squeeze in here, I'll get straight down to it. You will have noticed the extra crews getting briefed. Tonight, we are putting up twenty-three aircraft as part of Operation Millennium, which is the culmination of Bomber Command's Commander-in-Chief Harris's vision to see one thousand and forty-seven aircraft strike at one of the largest cities in Nazi Germany.'

He nodded to the two junior officers standing by the map wall. When they pulled the curtain back, exposing the map, there was a loud groan from the experienced crews.

'Cologne. Bloody tough.'

'Back to the Rhine. Fucking brilliant.'

The younger faces looked around with worried faces and whispered; 'What do they mean?' and 'This sounds bad.'

'Settle down men.' Buckley raised his voice above the din. 'Target city is indeed Cologne. Primary military, industrial and infrastructure targets are flak posts across the city, the central train station, the Hohenzollern and Deutzer bridges, the main rail shunting yards, and the docks.' His pointer gave off a loud dint as he touched each one of the targets. 'Secondary targets are administrative and commercial buildings across the central city area. As per the Area Bombing Directive, no specific targets for any crew and you are authorised to drop once inside the Volksgarten,' he motioned to the arched green-belt ringing the western side of the city. 'ETD is twenty-three hundred hours. Pilots and Navigators can collect their briefing papers. Obviously, this is going to be our largest op to date and the first run for many newly formed crews. The briefing from the Group says we'll be in the middle of the back half of the raid. This should give us a bit of cover from both the flak field and night fighters. Be safe out there. Make sure you get home. Go give them hell.'

He was barely two steps out of the briefing hall, before the room exploded with the noise of the crews discussing the raid.

'Lads, let's go over the op plan in the Mess. Robbie, let's get our papers,' said Pruno.

The crew jostled their way into the stream of men as they left the hall. Outside, the stench of vomit assaulted their nostrils. They looked down the side of the building, where two men were propped up against the wall, in heavy convulsions; flies buzzed around at least three other piles of detritus.

Once they were in the Mess, Gordo gave the opening salvo, 'One thousand and forty-seven aircraft. It'll be carnage, on both sides. You know I'm not overly concerned about area bombing, but that's when we're using two or three hundred planes, not a thousand. And for what? To pump up Harris's ego and satisfy his blood lust? Absolute bollocks.'

'What about Ossie? Is he going up into the mincer in a barely airworthy plane with a bunch of kids?' asked William.

'It's three times as many planes as a normal op. I wouldn't put my worst enemy in some of those Mark 1's, let alone crews on their first run. Madness,' added Boss.

'We all know the Rhine is brutal anytime, but so many aircraft? Jerry will know we're coming and will throw everything they have at us. It's not going to be a dodgy do; it's going to be a shitshow,' hissed Tas.

Pruno sat in front of the men, leaning forward, rubbing his hands in short, quick twists, 'Steady on, lads. All valid points, especially on the state of those Mark 1's. As for Ossie, thank God, he's not going up tonight. Good news for us, is we're back in 3538. Our old faithful. If we do our job, she'll look after us. Yeah, the whole op is massive, and it's going to be tough on us and the people of Cologne, but we knew this was coming. It was a matter of when, rather than if. I'll get us in the right position, and we all know Robbie will be as accurate as he can be.' He gave William a wink and one of his warm smiles, and Pruno's cheeks puffed up instantly. 'If you want to have a chat with me one-on-one, come to my room. Alright, lads?' Nods came from around the men. 'Go through your usual pre-flight prep. Make sure it's as normal as possible, don't change anything if you don't have to.' He got up and shook the hands of his crew.

Reggie sat on his bed, back against the wall, his long legs dangling over the side. He looked up from his book when William opened the door. 'Hey now, Billy-Bob. Ain't this op right drigaille. Garbage. We're all spittin' tacks in my crew. What about y'all?'

'G'day Reggie. Same. We're livid. Can't believe they're going put up all those new crews in those Mark 1's. If the flak and the night fighters don't get them, it'll be some mechanical or electrical fault. I hope the ground crew have weaved their magic on those planes. Catching up on some scripture?' he asked, nodding at the Bible in Reggie's hands.

'Yup, brushing up on a few of my favourite verses. Psalm 23 and First Corinthians Chapter 16 Verse 13, for starters. A bit of soothing and motivation. Whadda ya think it's gonna be like?'

'I'm expecting it to be the toughest run we've had. Remember the Essen op on April the sixth? How heavy the flak was?' Reggie nodded to William's questions. 'We got to be ready for that sort of flak field, and worse, plus the most night fighters we've ever encountered. You gunners are going to have your hands full.'

Reggie closed his Bible and stared at the ceiling, 'Makes me think 'bout dat Cologne run in April when Dickie Harris got shot up in the tail of 3487. Top poulain was Dickie. I'll be ready for dem Nazi shits.' William tilted his head and raised eyebrows, a sign Reggie knew well. 'Sorry, Billy-Bob. Poulain means colt, and we use it for a young buck, tough young man.'

William nodded. 'I'm going to write a couple of letters.' He went over to his chest of drawers and took out a pad and a pencil.

*30th May 1942*
*Dear Gary,*

*Warmest best wishes to you, Sarah and the family.*

*If you've got this letter, it means I haven't made it back from tonight's operation. We're about to embark on a raid where there's likely going to be a high casualty count.*

*If you are reading this, we've gone down. Hopefully, I've managed to bailout and am a POW somewhere in Germany. There's plenty of Bomber Command lads as POWs, so always hold out hope.*

*I'm taking it that you got my last regular letter from a couple of weeks ago, so I won't rehash those updates.*

*What's been gnawing at me for a few months is what's happened to Albert. It's nearly five years since he and Abigail ran off, and I've been thinking about where they are, what they are doing, and have we got any nieces and nephews whose lives we aren't involved with. I'm thinking we haven't made the right call in shunning them.*

*Could you start to make some enquiries about where they are? Probably best not to let Mother and Father know. You know how she'll react. If you don't want to, or don't feel able to cross Mother's instructions, it would be sad, but I'd respect your decision. I suppose this is driven from a position that if I have died, I wouldn't want you to have lost two of three brothers in of your life. One harsh lesson of this war for me is life and family are too precious and to willingly lose one side of the family seems to be lunacy.*

*Thank you for being a wonderful brother. What a fantastic life and wonderful memories we have had. Please know you and the rest of the family will have been front of mind as fate metes out its plans for me on this raid.*

*Love now and forever,*
*William*

*30th May 1942*
*Dear Darlene,*

*As I write this, my thoughts go back to our lovely walk along the Ouse a couple of weeks ago. What a tremendous afternoon it was, topped off by a pleasant pint at the Cutter Inn.*

*This is a strange letter to be writing, because if you are reading it, it means I haven't returned from tonight's operation. Hopefully, we've all managed to bailout and are either POWs or on the run with the French or Dutch Resistance. I know you'll be busy dealing with the aftermath of such a massive op. Wishing you and the rest of the staff all the best in coping with our wounded lads.*

*If I haven't returned, I want to say I've fallen in love with you and would have wanted to spend the rest of my life with you. Alas, obviously this may now not happen, but if have survived, please wait for me until the end of the war. I promise you I'll think of you every day and will use all my energy to return. If the worst has happened, I wish you endless happiness and a long, fulfilling life.*

*I go into battle tonight with you close to my heart and in my thoughts.*

*All my love,*
*William*

William folded both letters up, put them in envelopes, addressed them and headed out the door. 'Reggie, I'm going to see the Erks and give them these letters. Hopefully, I'll get them back tomorrow morning and they'll never be sent. Got anything to give to them?'

Reggie shook his head to William's question, 'Gave one for me folks to our ground crew a while ago. Told them to hang on to it until it's needed.'

*

'Scooch up there, Gordo, ya big moose,' Tas growled at his gunner mate. 'Loads of bodies to get in the truck tonight.'

Over a hundred aircrew were lined up and jostling to climb into the transports to take them out to the aircraft stands. An unnerving lack of chat hung over the group; there was twice as many men in the truck as usual, but rarely a word being uttered. The glow of cigarettes and flickering lighter flames illuminated many of the faces. Although he wasn't a big smoker, tonight William asked Boss for one.

'Big night, Robbie boy. Done your letters?' asked Boss. William nodded back at him, exhaling a cloud of smoke to the canvas roof of the truck. 'Done one to Mum and Dad. Praying the post office isn't too busy tomorrow. We'll have our hands full tonight. Force of numbers will keep us safe.' Boss's ashen face belied the confidence of his words.

The truck shuddered to a halt, as ground crew unhooked the tailgate and helped the men down. The senior ground crew NCO greeted Pruno crew, 'Best wishes tonight, lads. She's in great nick. She'll get you home.' Nods and smiles came back from the airmen as they climbed into the plane.

*

Pulling X3538 into the take-off queue, Pruno came onto the intercom, 'We're about to become a part of history, men. A chance to give Jerry a serious bloody nose. Proud and privileged to be going into battle with you all. Stay sharp, be ready for anything they throw at us. Let's get this done.'

At ten past eleven, Pruno hit the throttle controls, and the engines surged into full life; the whole aircraft rattled and strained, itching to soar into the night sky and get into the fight. Pruno released the brakes and they charged down the runway; William crossed himself and kissed his St Christopher medal, for what must have been the sixth time.

*

William estimated they were five miles off the Belgian coast when Tas came on the intercom, 'Fighters engaging the formation from four o'clock. Get ready Gordo.'

'Roger, Tas. Come on Nazis. Get a piece of Newdick hot fire,' Gordo shouted in the intercom.

'Brilliant, Gordo. That's sure to give them the shits,' replied Boss. A wave of nervous laughter rippled through the crew.

'Got a Ju 88 coming in. Engaging,' Tas announced, followed by a short burst from his guns, which reverberated down the length of the plane.

A couple more strafes and exchanges of machine gun fire, they then fell silent. 'They've gone to the back of the formation. Don't seem to be interested in us any more,' said Gordo.

The unmistakable thud of flak shards hitting their fuselage and windows started up. Anti-aircraft fire exploded throughout the formation in the corridor between Bruges and Ghent. It petered out soon after they passed Ghent. William knew it was only a light appetiser before the main course.

Heavy flak greeted them almost immediately as they passed over the German border. The larger 88s laid down a smothering blanket of fire; William struggled to keep his charts on his table as Pruno pulled the plane up and down, left and right, to evade the heaviest fire. The fuselage shuddered with each explosion. William wondered how it could hold together in such a barrage. His vision blurred with the violent vibrations, making chart reading almost impossible.

'First wave of aircraft have already started to drop,' Boss notified the crew. 'Heavy flak at both fourteen and twenty thousand feet. Searchlights working in cones. Moderate fighter engagement,' he added.

William calculated the first aircraft must have been passing over Hürth, a town on the southwest outskirts of Cologne. He estimated they'd hit the flak field in fifteen minutes.

*

'Brace yourselves, lads. The shit's about to get thicker,' said Pruno. Right on cue, William thought to himself.

'Christ, this is heavy. Bugger. There's one hit. Don't think it's one of ours. A bit far up the line.' Tas relayed the horrific vision unfolding in front of him. 'Skip, be careful with those searchlights. They've already locked onto a few planes. I can read my wrist watch clear as day, there so many of them.'

'Roger, Front Gunner. Lads, be ready for quick evasive action. I'll need to do a bit of weaving. It's a tad heavy,' Pruno told the crew. 'Ten minutes to target. Prepare for bombing run.'

William recorded the last positional reading, gave Boss a thumbs-up and crawled down into the bomb aimers position. He froze as the hellish vision of the raid assaulted his eyes. The darkness was lit up but a devilish concoction of searchlights, exploding flak, pathfinder flares, the blasts of the fallen bombs and the resulting fires, tracer bullets from bomber gun turrets and Nazi fighters, and flames from stricken aircraft. The carnage from a raid three-times larger than they had ever been involved with, chilled him to his core. His stomach knotted up and he spat out some bile. He wiped away tears, and settled into his prone position; 'Focus, William. The lads have got us here, so get the job done,' he whispered. He took his thick flight gloves off, exposing his light silk gloves. The bitter cold of the plane stung his fingers. As he got settled and started adjusting the viewfinder, a flash and deafening boom from an exploding flak shell close by made him flinch. Some of the shrapnel tore small holes in the fuselage above him. Another convulsion surged through his body, but he managed to keep it down.

The approach was directly from the southwest, staying on a northeast path. He sighted the rail tracks in the Sülz neighbourhood. There was a thick layer of smoke and many fires along the rail line. 'Looks like the earlier waves dropped here,' he said on the intercom. The Volksgarten then came into his viewfinder; they were now in the greenlight zone, and free to drop whenever they liked. 'Stay on this heading, Pruno. Ready to target the central train station and the Hohenzollern bridge.' The number and intensity of fires increased by the second; crews dropping early to get out of the frenzy as fast as they could. The Deutzer bridge came into the right-hand side of his viewfinder; the indicator landmark for him to release in order to hit their primary target. 'Hold, hold. Bombs gone. Taking target area photographs. Heavy smoke and fire cover. Difficult to confirm target hit. Gordo?'

'Jesus, Robbie. Impossible to say. So many explosions in the last few seconds. Pretty confident we hit or got close but wouldn't put a bob on it. We did our best lads. Get us out of here Skip.' Gordo's voice was up an octave as he reported to the crew.

*

'No more bogies out there, lads?' Boss asked Tas and Gordo, who both acknowledged they were in the clear. 'I'll break out the tea.'

The flak fields of northern Belgium were well past them and there hadn't been any night fighter engagement for at least five minutes. A steady and smooth flight path towards the Suffolk coast gave Boss a window to roll out their tea ritual; he pulled out the thermos and five small stacked cups from his satchel, lined them up on his table and poured four portions. William grabbed two cups and set off down the back to give Gordo his drink, while Boss delivered the warm, soothing elixir to Pruno and Tas.

William took a long pull on his cup, and winced at the shock of warm, sweet tea hitting his throat. Boss was a bit too heavy-handed with the sugar for his liking, but it helped keep the crew awake and energised for the ops, especially the run home. Murmurs of thanks to Boss came over the intercom. William tried to concentrate on his charts and instruments, to make sure they stayed on the right path to Feltwell, but visions of Cologne kept invading his thoughts; the red, orange and purple flames sweeping through all parts of the town; mangled buildings, houses, railway lines and bridges. How many dead tonight on both sides? How many of his Squadron's comrades wouldn't make it back to base? How many German soldiers and airmen, factory workers, railway staff and civilians died? How many families lost their homes, forced to be refugees in their own country? How long would the thousand plane ops continue? All parts of the Nazi machine and infrastructure needed to be smashed or rendered inoperative; that wasn't in question, but crushing the spirit of the German people? Probably, but were there other ways to achieve this? These thoughts and feelings were above his rank and certainly weren't in his head when he volunteered in the fervour of patriotism which swept New Zealand at the start of the war.

'Coastline now visible, Navigator. Is Felixstowe the first town? Got some lights on the port side,' Pruno's voice shocked William back to the present.

'Affirmative, Skip. Felixstowe should be approximately ten miles away, east-northeast. Boss, Bentwaters is another ten miles. Prepare to confirm the ground station transmission,' William updated the crew. Time suspended as they covered those twenty miles; the seconds and minutes dragged out, his watch appearing to grind to a halt. Finally, the GEE navigation unit confirmed they had passed over the RAF base. 'Bentwaters confirmed.' William's voice had a mixture of excitement and relief.

'Back in Blighty, boys,' Boss almost yelled into the intercom. A wave of cheers and shouts reverberated through the plane. Finally, the atmosphere in the plane lifted; the morose cloud hanging over the crew broke up and cleared.

'Lads, I can't tell you how proud I am of you all. It literally was a run into the teeth of Dante's Inferno. Couldn't have asked any more of you and wouldn't have wanted to go through it with anyone else,' said Pruno after the chat died down, and they prepared for landing.

*

William and Gordo stood in front of the operation board in the briefing hall, scanning the aircraft list for updates on Reggie's and Roy's planes. A quick look around the aircrew prep room and questions asked of other crews concluded they weren't back yet. The dim light of the hall was further dimmed by chalk dust as two WAAF's busily recorded the landing times of all the aircraft, the bombing times, altitudes from which the bombs were dropped and any "Remarks"; the code word for any issues with the plane's run, including mechanical or electrical problems, conflict damage, right through to the dreaded FTR – Failed to Return.

'Look, Gordo. Someone got hit. Pilot Officer Jarman. Made it back, though. Know anyone in his crew?' William asked. Gordo shook his head without talking, fixated on finding his mate's plane. Worry lined both their faces as they looked down the list.

'There we go. Ray landed fifteen minutes after us. They should be in the prep room soon enough. What's the story with Reggie?' Relief filled Gordo's voice.

'Nothing listed yet. Take-off time was the same as ours, so they should be back by now.' William was walking over to the WAAF's before he finished his sentence. 'Excuse me Corporal. Any word on Z-1616 D for Dog? It's Sergeant Bertram's plane?'

The WAAF Corporal looked at her clipboard, running her index finger down the page. Her bright red nail polish came as a shock to William's vision in the drab surroundings of the briefing hall. 'Sorry, Flight Sergeant. Not landed yet.' William's shoulders dropped a couple of inches. She noticed his dejection and added 'We did get radio confirmation they passed Knokke about an hour ago. So, at least they got out of Belgium. If they didn't run into any night fighters or mechanical trouble, they should be here within the hour. They'll be alright,' she smiled and gently touched William's upper arm as she finished.

'Story?' asked Gordo.

'They passed Knokke OK. Maybe another hour. I'll stay up for them,' replied William.

As they turned to go back to the aircrew prep room, the other WAAF wrote in the Remarks section for Pilot Officer Johnson's plane – FTR. Both men exhaled and William crossed himself.

*

Shortly before 4:30, the prep room door opened and another couple of crews walked in. William jumped up from the armchair he'd been napping in; he recognised Robert Bertram, Reggie's pilot. 'Robert, so glad you made it back. Reggie with you?'

Before Robert could reply, the six-foot-one frame of Reginald Dubois III burst into the room, 'By the love of God Almighty. I ain't ever been so glad to see the green 'n pleasant land of Blighty. Billy-Bob! What a great sight to greet us,' Reggie shouted. He walked over to William and pulled him in to a deep hug.

*

As soon as they found out there wouldn't be a raid, Tas started to organise a drinking session, 'The bus ain't running tonight, boys. Pints in the NCO's bar straight after dinner. See you there,' he instructed as he poked his head in William and Reggie's room.

'Dunno 'bout you, Billy-Bob, but I'm up for a few beers. Good not to be going back up tonight. Dat was some shit last night. We ended up near the back of the stream. Not much left dat weren't on fire by the time we dropped. As much as I hate dem Nazis, ain't sure laying waste to a whole city is right. Word is we'll be on thousand plane ops for a while,' Reggie's usual upbeat expressiveness was missing.

'Was a tough run, alright. Not much chat in the plane all night. It was nightmarish, no doubt. Not sure about drinks. Want to try and grab a car to go and see Darlene when she finishes her shift. Might not make it back for dinner. I'll let Gordo know. Tas won't take no for an answer,' replied William.

'When y'all gonna make some more formal introductions? Y'all been spending a bit of time stepping out with her. Y'all, her, me and Betty needs to go out one night?' Reggie raised his eyebrows and gave a cheeky grin.

'Sounds like the most dangerous thing we could do for our fledgling romance,' William patted Reggie on the shoulder as he walked out.

William parked the car outside the Nurses' Home and waited for the steady stream of staff to come over at the finish of their shift. The trickle of one's and two's soon gave way to a wave. He wound down his window to scan the faces, eyes darting from person to person, as he looked for Darlene's familiar features. The flow peaked then ebbed away without any sign of her; he gripped the steering wheel hard, turning his knuckles white. A worry line creased his forehead. He craned his neck to the right, checking the Nurses as they entered their dormitory. Turning back to the hospital building, he sat bolt upright in surprise as Darlene appeared in front of the car; smiling broadly, she gave him a small wave and skipped around to the drivers-side window.

'Well now, isn't this a lovely surprise?' She beamed, leaning into the open window, and placing her hand on his forearm. 'Thought I might see you after last night. Thank God they aren't sending you back up tonight.' She rubbed his arm to create a warmth between his skin and her fingertips.

'You want to go for a drink? We can nip down to The Cutter.' Before he had finished the sentence, Darlene had sped around the car and jumped into the passenger seat.

'How about The Prince Albert? Know that one?' William shook his head to Darlene's query. 'Cute place with nice staff, round the corner from the Cathedral. Been there a few times with Betty and my other friends.'

*

'Well, good evening, Dee. In on a Sunday? The gang coming in?' asked Bob.

'No, only us. Bob, this is my good friend, William Robertson,' replied Darlene.

William shot his hand out and had it swallowed up by the landlord's meaty mitt. 'Pleasure to meet you. Nice to know Darlene has regular haunt.'

'Aussie or New Zealander?' asked Bob.

'New Zealand. I'm with 75 Squadron.'

'Over at Feltwell? Good to have you lot here. Appreciate it. Usual for you, Dee? William, yourself?' Bob started making a gin and tonic while he waited for William to answer.

'Pint of Newcastle, ta.'

'It's quiet tonight. Why don't you take a booth in the snug round the corner? Give you a bit more privacy,' Bob gave them both a wink and a smile as he handed over the drinks. 'Put your money away. Dee knows it's my custom to give our colonial friends their first drink free.' William slowly put the coins back into his pocket.

'Thank you, Bob. You're such a darling. We'll take snug. If any of the mob come in, don't say we're here.' Darlene cocked her head as she spoke. Bob nodded and tapped his nose a couple of times with his index finger.

William opened the door to the snug for Darlene and they walked to the booth on the far corner of the room.

'Why don't we sit on the same side, we can snuggle and no one can see us from the doorway,' she said with a cheeky smile. 'You go in first. I'll probably need to powder my nose soon.'

'Here's cheers. So happy to see you again,' said William as they raised their glasses; the tinkle of glass echoed around the empty room.

'I was so scared for you last night. Betty said it was a thousand plane operation, which explained why we're on higher staffing levels now. Anytime there's a raid, I think I'll never see you again. It gnaws away at me,' she spun her glass for a couple of turns.

William took her hand, as she turned to look at him, 'You were on my mind for the whole run. You were the first person I thought of as soon as we landed. Odd thing about it, with the bigger ops, if we're right in the middle of the stream, it's a bit safer,' he said reassuringly. 'I'm two-thirds the way through now. A couple more runs and I'll be down to single figures left, so the finish line is coming into view.'

'Don't know if my nerves can take much more,' Darlene said. 'I can't imagine what it's like for you and the lads. You don't have to talk about it if you don't want to, but happy to listen if you do.' She squeezed William's hand. The heat of contact and sensation of skin on skin sent a warm wave through her body.

'It's tough to put it into any coherent words. What we see. What we have do. The chaos in your head and conflicted feelings. Knowing the line between life and death is absolute blind luck. The fires. Oh, God. The flames scorch your soul,' William cupped her hand in his as he spoke.

The high-pitched screech of the door's hinges pulled their gaze away from each other towards the entrance. Darlene let out a small sigh and her shoulders dropped. 'There goes our quiet night,' she said softly.

Her posture straightened quickly as she recognised Milena's voice. She started to slide out of the booth to say hello, but stopped short as Milena changed mid-sentence, from English to another language. Darlene turned to William and placed her index finger on her lips, then did the same on his lips. She leaned close to the booth's partition, so the neighbouring discussion wasn't so muffled. A heavy worry line formed across her forehead as she concentrated; beads of sweat burst onto her upper lip. She could feel William inching closer to her; she shot out her arm with her hand up and palm open, which froze him to the spot. She couldn't understand what the two next to them were saying; some sort of Slavic-based language, she assumed Czechoslovakian. Must be an old Czech friend of Milena's. She was about to give up on evesdropping when they changed back to English. A cold flush raced down her back, and her vision narrowed. Time took on a fluid form, changing from between double time to slow motion.

She didn't know how long she'd been listening, when Milena finally said, 'That's enough for now. We should go.' Darlene turned back to William, her eyes darting around the booth. The sound of their neighbours getting up to leave called for immediate action. Nothing for it; she jumped on William and kissed him heavily, ensuring her mouth completely covered his. She held him tightly as his shocked body started to relax. She heard the door to the snug open and a male voice with a central European accent say, 'Next week, Miss Dvořáček,' then the door slammed closed. Slowly, Darlene pulled away from William, his mouth still open.

'Sorry about that. Not sure it was wise in a pub,' said Darlene and she started fanning herself with her palms.

'No need to apologise. Was a surprise, but extremely pleasant. I've been wanting to kiss you all evening,' William touched her shoulder.

'I did want to kiss you, but I was in a bit of a panic. I didn't want those people to see me, I mean us.'

'What was that all about? Who are they?' asked William.

'The woman is another Nurse. She's Czechoslovakian,' replied Darlene.

'Do you mean the woman you pointed out acting strangely on the towpath a couple of weeks ago?' William interjected, 'Marlene, Melanie or something?

'Oh, yes. Good memory,' Darlene nodded at William as she spoke. 'Milena is her name. I was about to speak to her, but what they were saying made me stop. Don't want to be paranoid, but it didn't sound right.'

'You want to talk about it here, or find somewhere more private? Maybe in the car?' asked William

Darlene looked around the room, poking her head into the other booth, 'We're fine here. They started in English. Exchanged pleasantries, nothing odd. I was about to say hello, but then they switched to what I think was Czechoslovakian. I didn't understand, but it didn't last long, and they switched back to English. That's when it got interesting. They were speaking softly, so I missed the odd word here and there. Heard them talk about the thousand bomber raids and the Americans arriving this month. They finished up talking about meeting at the local Catholic Church next Sunday.'

'St Etheldreda's? Reggie and I go to Mass there. They sound a bit suspicious to me,' said William.

'Let's see what Bob has to say. Come on,' said Darlene, as she got out of the booth, grabbed William's hand and hurried back into the main bar area.

'Dee, so sorry about Milena, she took off straight for the snug before I could say anything,' Bob said, opening his arms in apology.

'Don't worry, Bob. She didn't see us. You know the man she was with? asked Darlene.

'Never seen him before. She said he was a Czech friend from London. Didn't introduce him, so didn't get a name.'

'But you got a good look at him, yes?' Darlene was clipped and breathless in her questioning.

'Oh, aye. Definitely distinctive. You want me to describe him? What's this all about?' asked Bob.

'No, no. It's fine, but if you could take some time to write it down. Be as detailed as you can. I'll come and pick it up tomorrow.

Nothing to worry about. I've got an odd feeling about him. Maybe nothing,' added Darlene.

Bob nodded to them both, flipped the tea towel he had in his hands over his shoulder and grabbed a small note pad and a pencil, 'Will get right onto it, Dee. See you tomorrow.'

Darlene and William thanked Bob and made their way to the car. William spoke softly to Darlene, 'So she introduced him as a Czech. Seems a bit fishy if they didn't speak in Czech the whole time.'

'Absolutely,' replied Darlene.

'The Sudetenland is part of Czechoslovakia which made up of ethnic Germans.' said William.

'Exactly. The Nazi takeover of the area was one of the last pieces of the puzzle which led to the war, wasn't it? I don't like the smell of it all,' Darlene shook her head as she spoke.

'You want me to go Mass next Sunday?' asked William. 'I can keep an eye out for them if you let me know what they look like.'

'I can come with you,' Darlene's voice went up an octave.

'But you're not Catholic. You'll be OK with that?'

'Hopefully I won't burst into flames crossing the threshold? It's fine with me but I won't take Communion. It won't bother you?' asked Darlene.

Suddenly William was pulled back to his childhood; visions of going to Mass with the family, Albert's Final Profession ceremony, Gary's wedding with Albert as the Priest, his mother's staunch, sometimes sectarian, position on Protestants. The memory which stuck was Albert in his full celebratory robes, doing the full wedding Mass for Gary and Sarah. He seemed so comfortable with being a Priest and appeared good at it too. The pride of the family; the apple of their mother's eye. Only a few years after later, he was gone, excommunicated and blacklisted from the family, all for the love of a woman. Now for himself, William has a small test between Catholic dogma and tradition, and his own love.

'William. You won't mind me coming to Mass?' Darlene prodded him for a response.

'Oh, yes. I mean, no. Not a problem for me. You know Milena, so you'll be able to spot her quickly. Hopefully, there'll be no op planned for next Sunday. Should be fine. We haven't had a Sunday op in six weeks. We'll keep our fingers crossed, eh?'

'Terrific. I'll come back to see Bob tomorrow and pick up his description of the man. My word. Exciting isn't it? I don't want to jump the gun, but we might be on the trail of some spies.' There was excitement in Darlene's voice.

'Probably a bit of a stretch, but have to admit, it seems a bit odd,' replied William.

# Chapter Seven

*7 June 1942*

William found Darlene standing on the street, a few yards past St Etheldreda's. Their deep hug lingered. Darlene regarded William and noted the dark rings encircling his eyes. 'You feeling alright?' she asked. 'You didn't need to come in after the operation last night. I could have handled this myself.'

'Don't worry, I'm fine. I got nearly four hours sleep. I'll take a nap this afternoon,' replied William.

'Sure? You've had so many raids in the last couple of weeks.' William nodded to Darlene's concern. 'I thought we could hang back and go in late, so we can scan the pews and see where they are. Then we can get a spot close to them, but on their blindside. We'll be able to keep an eye on them without them seeing us. We can also slip out before the end of Mass,' she said.

'Crikey, you've been thinking this through,' replied William.

'I've re-read a couple of Agatha Christie books to get some tips. Here's a copy of the description of Milena's friend. You look for him while I keep an eye out for her.' Darlene handed William a small piece of paper with Bob's recollections from last weekend.

William frowned as he read it, 'Bloody hell. A bit generic; six-foot-one, black hair, thin, angular face, sharp nose, chin dimple, black fedora. Oh, here we go; two-inch scar on right cheek, gold tie bar, gold cufflinks and silk scarf. If he wears those accessories, that'll make him stand out like dog's bollocks. Even on a Sunday.'

'Language, William Robertson. Technically, you are on holy ground,' Darlene scolded him.

They turned back towards the main door of the church and surveyed the parishioners as they mingled outside and trickled into the church. Darlene took in the exterior of St Etheldreda's; it was hard to tell how old it was, as its plain Gothic style in grey stone and brick, didn't give away too many clues. Given it was wedged into a relatively small plot of land on what would have been the edge of town in the 1700 and 1800s, she guessed mid-late 1800s. The small row of terraced houses next door to the church looked no more than fifty years old.

William looked at his watch, 'Ten minutes till the start of Mass. Best we go in.' He gave Darlene his arm.

'See. I didn't spontaneously combust,' Darlene poked William in his ribs when they went over the flagstone front step. She looked down and noticed a dip in the middle of it, well worn by thousands of the faithful.

William smiled broadly as he dabbed his fingers into the Holy Water vessel and crossed himself. They turned right and took up a position up against the wall, giving them a full view of the congregation. William grabbed a couple of hymn books and Parish newsletters. 'Here, we'll need these, be good to pretend we're reading something. Standing around looking like a couple of stunned mullets will raise alarm.'

'Now who's thinking like a detective? You see them?' asked Darlene.

'Not yet. Oh, wait a second. Far side on the aisle, about a third of the way down from the back. Adjacent to the Fifth Station of The Cross.'

'Remember I'm not Catholic. You may as well be speaking Gaelic. Hmm, third of way down … no, not them. The man has jet black hair and a nice suit alright, but the woman is blonde. Milena is brown-haired.' Darlene took in the interior of the church; smaller even than the outside would indicate. There were only ten rows of pews, with two banks of pews and a middle aisle in the main, central section and a few extra pews on the side. She calculated a capacity of no more than one hundred and twenty. Shouldn't be too hard to spot Milena. The central section was flanked by wings, separated by three arches, mirrored on both sides. The front of the church was flooded with coloured and diffused light streaming in through the stained-glass window. The sun illuminated the large crucifix suspended over the altar. Overall, she thought it a nice, warm and welcoming church, significantly different from the Cathedral. She actually preferred it; understated, not overly ornate, almost cosy.

Minutes ticked by, getting close to the ten o'clock start of Mass. They were both fidgety, nervy as they scanned the church.

'Wait. Got them. Far side, by the pillar. Fourth row from the back. No idea what Station of The Cross they are next to,' said Darlene. She turned to William, gave him a nod and inclined her head towards the pews. They found two empty seats on the aisle, two rows back from their targets. They both had good views of the pair, allowing them to see if they did anything untoward.

The Mass started and between hymns, prayers and the constant up, down, up, down movements, Darlene and William kept watch over their targets as much as they could, while trying to retain some discretion. During the sermon, Milena opened her handbag, took out a piece of paper, placed it into a Hymn Book then passed it to the man. He flipped through the book, and it fell open with the note sticking up. He placed it in his left breast pocket. Darlene turned to William and winked.

The Priest called the congregation up for Communion. As the pews emptied and the worshippers made their way to the front, Milena and the man stood to the side, then turned and walked to the back of the church.

'They're leaving. Should we follow them?' asked William.

Darlene turned away from them, so Milena wouldn't see her face, and whispered to William, 'No. Let them go. We know they kept their appointment, passed something between them, and they skulked out early. Adds to the overall picture. Going after them would alert them that we're onto them.' She looked over her shoulder as the couple scuttled out of the church.

*

*Date – 8 June 1942*
*Tour of Operations Count – Operation 29*
*Target Location – Essen, Germany*
*Assigned Aircraft – Wellington Mk.III X.3538 AA-N*
*Take-off – 23:30*

'Jesus, lads. Sixth op in ten days. Like that run of eight in thirteen days in April. I'm shattered,' said Tas, rubbing his face with his hands. 'Might need to pay a visit to the doc for some "go-juice" to keep me sharp.'

'And the fourth into the heart of Happy Valley since the start of the month. Robbie, is there anything left to hit in Essen?' asked Gordo.

'Bugger all, to be honest,' replied William as he looked at the operation briefing papers. 'Target list is the rail yard, the Krupps' factories and the industrial areas in the east and northeast. Which we've hit loads of times before. It'll be another blanket bombing run.'

The crew were gathered around a table, looking at the map. 'Shall we hold off until Pruno is back?' asked Boss.

'Yeah, good call. He went to chat to Ossie straight after the briefing. Tas, I'd be careful about those pills. They knocked Reggie for six when he took them during those back-to-back ops earlier this month. Took him nearly two days to come off them,' said William.

'Bloody hell, really? He's a big and hard unit. Thanks, Robbie. I'll try to get in a decent nap this afternoon,' replied Tas.

The door latch clunked and all four men looked up from the map, turning their heads to the entrance. En masse, their faces lit up as they exclaimed 'Ossie!' They turned back to Pruno with quizzical looks.

'Grab a seat, gents. I've got some good news for us,' said Pruno. Chair legs screeched as the men sat down. 'We need to talk about the taboo topic of the end of a tour.' All the crew immediately shifted uncomfortably in their seats. A couple of them gazed around the room. 'Although unspoken, we not only keep track of our own op numbers, but also those of our mates, so it won't come as any surprise to you I'm three shy of finishing my tour.' Pruno looked at each man as he spoke; they nodded slowly at his last sentence. 'I've been thinking about this for a week or two, and what's important to me is keeping this great crew together. I'm delighted to let you know the top brass has agreed to assign our mate, Arthur Osborne, as my replacement and Ossie will join us tonight as second pilot to reacquaint himself with us. As if it's actually needed.'

A crescendo of cheers erupted. Handshakes, backslaps and words of congratulation came from them all; in part from relief as much as excitement. Their old mate and trusted colleague would soon lead them into the fight.

'Right, lads. Let's go through tonight's run,' Pruno interrupted the celebrations.

*

'This is brilliant. How did you and Pruno swing it?' William asked Ossie as they walked back to the barracks.

'Took a bit of cajoling the bosses, but we played the consistency card. I've had only three active runs as Skip since I left you guys. There were a few changes on each op, so really didn't have a settled crew. We had fourteen runs as a consistent unit before they broke us up, so we were able to persuade them to reunite us.' Ossie put his hand on William's shoulder as they walked. 'I'm bloody rapt to be back with the lads.'

'Without jinxing it, if it all stays on track, you'll take Gordo, Tas, Boss and me through to the end of our tours. Can't tell you what that means to us. You and Pruno are the only ones I'd want as our Skip for the run to the end.' William smiled broadly as he spoke.

'Don't know why, Robbie, but I have a feeling we'll get through OK. Let's get some shut-eye and be razor sharp tonight.' Ossie gave William a wink as they parted towards their rooms.

As he approached his room, he heard a couple of voices, including Reggie's, through the open door.

'Hey, Billy-Bob. This is Joe Quin, the Navigator in my crew. Joe, meet Billy Robertson.' Reggie nodded as they shook hands.

'Absolute pleasure to meet you, Billy. Reggie raves about you,' said Quin.

'Call me Robbie. The big man here is the only person who calls me Billy. You're a Navigator too? Big job, along with the bomb aiming. How you tracking?' asked William.

'Well, see now, Billy-Bob, that's why I told Quiney to stop by. Young fella's hit a wall. Needs some advice,' Reggie spoke up for Quin.

'Right. Reggie, could you give us few minutes?' asked William.

'Y'all take as much time as y'all need. I'll go check on our bird. Make sure dem Erks have got me guns ready to kill some Nazis.' Reggie turned and closed the door on his way out.

'It's gotten too tough for you, Joe?' William gave Quin a chair and he sat on his bed.

Quin dropped his head, 'We've had some bloody dodgy dos. A couple of times I swear we were goners. I've had a guts full of this. I'm gonna give it away. I've been taking the doc's happy pills to get me through the last couple of runs. I've got six days leave due after tonight's op. I'm going to go home and get married to my girl. Once I'm hitched, I'm done.'

'First off, congratulations. Wonderful news. Focus on her, keep her in your thoughts throughout tonight's raid. Make her the reason you go up and do what we do. Calling it a day is a big decision, Joe. You're not thinking of deserting? Have you spoken to the brass?' asked William.

'Yeah, I met with Squadron Leader Olsen. Wasn't much help. He told me to take my leave, sort my head out and come back fresh. Bloody easy for him to say. He doesn't go up three or four days a week. I've made up my mind. I'm cashing in. Not sure how to do it. I know they won't let me walk away,' said Quin.

'I can't tell you one way or the other, but be bloody careful. A bad decision could ruin the rest of your life. It's up to you, but try to hold on to what's precious to you. Sounds like it's your girl. Make her your North Star. I found my mind became clearer once I sorted those things out,' said William.

'Thanks, Robbie. Appreciate the advice. You know you Leggett boys are legends, right.' A look of surprise broke across William's face. 'Well over twenty runs and ne'er' a scratch on ye, and the lads still talk about the fire you put out on the Lübeck do. We all want to be like you lot.' Quin left William in stunned silence. He turned back to his chest of drawers and grabbed the two photographs that now went with him on every operation; the picture of all four Robertson brothers, at Gary's wedding, with Albert in full ceremonial priests' robes, and the shot of Darlene and him at The Cutter Inn the young girl had taken. His North Stars.

*

'Looky, looky, there goes the cookie. Bombs gone,' William announced as he pressed the bomb release trigger to drop the last of the bomb bay's load. He checked for bomb detonation and took a handful of target area photographs; it wasn't another thousand bomber operation, so the devastation at ground level and subsequent fires wasn't as heavy as the last couple of runs to Essen, so he was able to see their payload hit. 'Target hit confirmed. Let's go, lads.'

Pruno immediately pulled the nose up to take them into the comparative safe zone between the low altitude flak of ten thousand feet and the high-altitude flak of fifteen thousand feet, which would help them save fuel on the journey home, 'Hang on lads. We're about to go through some flak,' he told the crew.

Ossie came on the intercom, 'Loads of searchlights and flak ahead. Get ready for evasive action.' Gordo and Tas started firing at the searchlights and the flashes and thuds of exploding flak started up on cue. The plane continued weaving, dipping and climbing as Pruno tried to keep them from being pinned in the coned searchlights.

William hauled himself back from the plane's nose to his navigator's position, and gave Pruno the flight instructions. Suddenly a loud explosion drowned out the engine noise. The aircraft shuddered, glass exploded inwards, and a wave of frigid air flooded the plane. 'Bugger me. That one was close,' thought William.

Pruno came on the intercom and for the first time the crew could remember, there was panic in his voice, 'Ossie's been hit. Robbie, get up here.'

William reached the pilot seats to find Ossie slumped against Pruno, limp and lifeless. The brutal air blasted William's face as it poured into the cockpit from the hole in the glass. He fumbled to release Ossie's seat restraint, then pulled him back to the void behind the cockpit, laying him on the floor next to Boss at the wireless station. Inspecting Ossie's wounds, he found a deep cut in his leather flight helmet from which blood was bubbling out, flowing down his face.

'Jesus Christ. Is he dead?' shouted Boss.

William didn't respond out loud, as the words 'Don't die on me Arthur Osborne, don't you dare, not today,' were going around and around in his head. He grabbed a couple of first aid packs, tore one open and took off Ossie's helmet to look at the wound. Blood poured freely. He grabbed a couple of wedges of cotton wool and pressed them down on the wound, licking the back of his free hand and placing it under Ossie's nose; yes, still breathing. Then he grabbed Ossie's wrist to check his pulse; weak, but still there. Turning to Boss, he said 'He's still alive, but the blood's pissing out of him. Gotta stop it, otherwise he might not make it home. When we're in range, make sure you tell base to have an ambulance standing by for us.' Boss nodded and said he'd try as soon as he could.

William rummaged around the contents of the first aid packs, finding a couple of wound dressings and bandages, more cotton wool, morphine and some anti-burn jelly. Not much bloody use, he said to himself. Looks like it'll be all the cotton wool, a wound dressing, then bandage him up as tight as we can. A prayer for a fast flight home might also help. He checked his watch; at least two hours, but more likely two and a half, till landing. 'Hang in there, Ossie,' he whispered.

As he pulled the first wedge of blood-soaked cotton wool off Ossie's head, the flow seemed to have slowed; he hoped the wound was clotting. He pressed a fresh batch onto the cut and placed a dressing on top, tying it off underneath Ossie's chin. Before he could start wrapping the bandage around his head, blood had already begun seeping through the dressing. This'll need redoing a couple more times, William said to himself. After he had finished the first aid, William used his own handkerchief to clean Ossie's face. Knowing they must now be between twelve and fourteen thousand feet, he grabbed Ossie's mask, checked oxygen was still flowing and cradled Ossie in his arms. He then put the mask over his mate's nose and mouth and started gently rocking back and forth, whispering 'Stay with me Ossie. We're not losing you today. Not if I can help it.'

A further check on Ossie's breathing and William tried to prop him up, using his and Boss's parachutes. He then wedged him against the fuselage in an attempt to keep his head upright and stable. Happy this would do for a couple of minutes, William returned to his instruments and charts. Despite the bitter cold, William felt hot and flushed, with beads of sweat running down his back. He blinked a dozen times in quick succession as he focussed on the map. He wiped his hands on his jacket, but traces of Ossie's blood still rubbed off onto his charts. After a couple of calculations and a check of the GEE, he got on the intercom, 'Skip, we've passed Deventer and we're on track for Schiphol. Keep on this heading. Looking good.'

'Roger, Navigator. How's Ossie?' replied Pruno.

William looked back to his mate, whose chest was still rising and falling, 'Hanging in there, Skip. Lost a lot of blood, though. Will do another dressing change soon.'

Half an hour later, Pruno announced they were about to cross the Dutch coast. Time for a new dressing, thought William, looking down on the sodden bandage. He took off his flight gloves again, exposing his silk under-gloves, now soaked with Ossie's blood. Gingerly, he lifted the dressing and cotton wool, wrapping it up to throw it away; Ossie's blood streamed down William's hand, pooling around his wrist, then disappeared down the sleeve of his flight jacket. The flow from the wound was now down to a trickle. He let out a huge sigh.

He was tying off the new dressing when Tas come on the intercom. 'Buckle up, lads. Two fighters coming in at four o'clock. Your eight, Gordo. Got 'em?'

'Yep. They're firing at us now. Time for a dust up,' replied Gordo from the back.

Both men opened up on the enemy aircraft immediately; the sound and recoil of their machine guns reverberated throughout the plane. Sitting on the floor, William could feel the vibration when all the Browning 303 calibre guns were going full bore.

'They've gone underneath. They'll be coming back from above. See them Gordo?' asked Tas.

'Two o'clock. Your ten, Tas. Light 'em up,' replied Gordo. The guns blazed away for five seconds, Gordo came back on, 'Got one of the fuckers. Stick that in your pipe, Hermann.'

'Good shooting, Rear Gunner. Let's get the last one, lads,' Pruno added.

They opened up as the remaining fighter made another attack. Rounds from the fighter started to rip into the Wellington's fuselage, William instinctively lay on top of Ossie. Sparks lit up the inside of the plane; the zing, zing, zing of the bullets almost drowned out the noise of the bomber's engines. William felt something tug at his flight jacket but didn't move for fear of exposing Ossie.

'Bugger it. Missed him,' said Gordo.

'He's coming back, my eleven o'clock. This time, mate,' Tas replied.

Another barrage of fire from the gunners added an erratic vibration through the plane's fuselage which shook Ossie and William as they lay together.

'I think I hit 'em,' yelled Tas. 'Yep, he's smoking. He's going down. He's a goner,' said Tas

'Good show, lads. Full throttle home. I've had enough of this,' replied Pruno.

Never had time seemed to slowdown so much to William, as the last hour from the Dutch coast to when the landing gear came down. He allowed himself a modicum of relief, but landing with a shot-up aircraft was always fraught with danger; had the flak or fighter bullets damaged the landing gear, or severed important hydraulics and wiring? He'd seen too many planes crash on landing to think Ossie, and all of them, were safe home yet. As the plane's vibrations and change in engine noise indicated touchdown was near, William prepared by supporting Ossie's head. Any sudden jolt would make his head bounce on the fuselage. The first thud of the landing gear hitting the ground threw the two of them six inches into the air. William held Ossie tight. Second contact was softer than William expected, then the third and final touch of the wheels on the ground was greeted with a chorus of cheers from the crew.

Almost immediately, as Pruno brought the aircraft to a halt, the main hatch was opened and a medic stuck his head inside, 'You lads got a man down?' he asked.

As the ambulance drove away with Ossie, William felt something warm and wet on his lower back. He put his hand underneath his jacket, pulled it out to find it covered in fresh blood. 'Shit. When did that happen?' he asked. He took two more steps then fell to the ground.

*

William woke disorientated; the unfamiliar surroundings confusing for a minute. He looked around the hospital ward; he was in the end bed of ten on his side, with the same on the other side. The summer sun was pouring through the window behind him, making the white bed sheets glow. He squinted to ease the brightness on his sleepy eyes. As he looked down the row of beds, he saw a figure he thought he recognised. William concentrated on the person to get a clearer image. As they moved closer, his eyes grew wider, his heart rate picked up and he felt a rush of blood to his face.

'Well, hello Flight Sergeant Robertson. Finally awake?' asked the Nurse.

'Darlene. I mean Nurse du Toit. What the hell happened?' asked William.

'You were brought in last night. Almost gave me a heart attack when I saw your name on the patient list.' Her eyes started to glaze over as she tried to compose herself. 'How are you feeling?' She placed her hand on his shoulder; the lightest of touches, yet it electrified William's body from head to toe.

'Not bad, a bit groggy, and bloody thirsty.' He looked around for a water jug and a glass.

'Good to hear. Let me get you a drink.' She passed William a glass. A warm flush shot up both their arms when their fingers touched.

'Thanks. We should try to stop meeting in hospitals,' he quipped.

'For the sake of your long-term health, I completely agree,' Darlene replied, giving him a broad smile.

'I'm surprised to be here. Last thing I remember was the ambulance taking Ossie away. Is he here?' Darlene tilted her head quizzically. 'Sorry. Sergeant Arthur Osborne. He had a nasty head injury,' added William.

'Oh, Arthur. Yes, he came in about an hour before you. He's in bed three on the other side.' William pulled himself up to look down the row of beds and winced as a bolt of pain shot up his side. 'Don't worry. He's fine. Looked worse than it was. The impact knocked him out, but the wound itself wasn't too deep. Like a lot of head injuries, the amount of blood makes them look worse than they actually are. You can go to see him,' replied Darlene, as she eased him back onto his bed. 'As for you, we took a piece of shrapnel out of your back. It was a decent size but it missed your kidneys. Lucky boy.'

'Each time we land safely, we're lucky. Don't want to use up too much of my allocation. When can I return to operations?' asked William. He was studying the curves, angles and features of her face.

'Why so eager to get back into the fray?' she asked.

'I'm getting near the end of my tour. Only seven ops to go. Want to try to get them under my belt as quick as I can,' he replied.

Darlene's face dropped as disappointment etched itself on her, 'So you won't be here much longer?' she asked.

'Can't really say. I haven't given the next step much thought. In Bomber Command, you only take one day and one raid at a time. You'd go batty if you looked too far into the future. Might stick around and train the newbies,' replied William.

'That'd be nice. I mean good for the squadron. Look at me, spending too much time with you and neglecting my other patients. Best I get on with rounds. I'll be back later in the day. Lunch will be served soon. Rest up, William.' She touched his hand as she walked away. The now familiar feeling of exhilaration flowed through his body.

William pulled himself up, gritted his teeth and swung his legs over the side of his bed. The pain was more uncomfortable than excruciating, but it didn't stop him moving about. He lifted up his hospital smock and inspected the bandage around his torso. He placed his hands on the wound; through the dressing, it felt warm to the touch. 'Just missed the kidneys? A lucky break,' he said softly. He shuffled over to Ossie's bed; each step half the distance of his usual gait. He'd almost made it when his friend recognised him.

Ossie's face beamed a wide, bright smile, as he boomed William's nickname, then changed to worry and confusion. He lowered his eyebrows and narrowed his gaze, 'What on earth are you doing here, mate?' He offered his hand to William.

'Took a bit of shrapnel last night. Had a dust up with a couple of night fighters off the Dutch coast. It's good as gold. Expect to be out of here soon. Much more important, how are you?' William replied and rubbed Ossie's shoulder after the handshake.

'Apart from a ripper of a headache, bloody good. They reckon because of where it hit me, it looked more gruesome than it was,' said Ossie.

'Mate, you had us scared to death we'd lost you,' replied William.

'Doc reckons a half inch lower, and I would have bought the farm. We'll chalk this one up to lady luck. I should go to the gee-gees and back a few winners,' Ossie said with a wide smile.

'God, it's great to see you're OK. There was so much blood, I didn't think you'd make it,' William clenched his fists so hard, his knuckles turned white, and he dropped his head.

'Must have been a bit of a scare. Amazing to think after all our runs, we're the first injuries. Say, did you save my helmet? Nice memento to go along with my gloves from the flare shenanigans. Arthur Osborne, cheater of death, with souvenirs to prove it,' Ossie beamed.

'Bloody hell, Ossie. Some great gallows' humour. Yes, I did keep your helmet. Well, I'm pretty sure I had it in my jacket when I passed out,' replied William, smiling as well. Ossie winked at him. 'When do they think you'll be able to get out?'

'They said they'll check the stiches and do a concussion test tomorrow. If I pass, I can go straight away. You?' questioned Ossie.

'Not sure. Need to talk to the doctors. Hopefully I can go with you. Don't much care to be hanging round here. Rather be back with the lads.' William knew he wasn't fully committed to the statement. The presence of Darlene meant a day or two's extra stay would be pleasurable.

*

After breakfast the next day, the doctor gave him the news which left him both happy and disappointed in equal measure; he could leave later in the day, he'd have a further four days of medical leave, then return to operations after his stitches were removed. Half of him wanted to get back to the gang and operations as quickly as possible, so he could complete his last few operations. The other half wanted to stay close to Darlene.

William could sense when she entered the ward; the lightness of her step, the waft of her English Rose fragrance, the change in atmosphere as soon as she appeared. This morning she was laden with clothes, including a leather flight jacket.

'Flight Sergeant Robertson, you are a free man. I took the liberty of collecting your discharge papers and medical clearance. Make sure you see the base doctor early next week.'

'Thank you, Darlene. You didn't need to. Am I getting special treatment?' asked William.

'Not at all. Don't be getting any ideas. I was passing the office.' She placed his uniform on the chair beside his bed, 'You'll find a new shirt and undershirt there. The ones you came in with were bloodied, so I picked up some replacements.'

'No special treatment? Right.' William raised his eyebrows and gave her a grin.

'I also had your flight jacket cleaned. The wool liner soaked up some blood. It was a bit smelly too. Nasty,' she added.

'Easy. That jacket probably saved my life. Is there still a flight cap in the pocket? It's Ossie's. He wants it as a souvenir,' replied William

'Yes. It's there. You airmen love your ghoulish mementos.' She shook her head at him. 'I also saved the pictures you had in one of your breast pockets. It means a lot that you keep the one of us close to you. Need to ask you about the other one sometime. Must go. Be careful out there. Let's organise another river walk soon,' Darlene squeezed William's hand as she walked away.

# CHAPTER EIGHT

*11 June 1942*

Taking advantage of being on a night shift, Darlene walked into the Ely Library for an afternoon's research. First stop was the Reference Section to get the volumes of the latest edition of the Encyclopedia Britannica which covered Czechoslovakia, Sudetenland, and the 1926 and 1938 Year Books. The muscles in her forearms strained as she carried the weighty tomes to the closest desk. A loud thump echoed through the library as she placed them down.

'Where do I start?' she whispered. She took out her notebook and pencil, opening the book to a fresh double page. She picked up the volume for Czechoslovakia and flipped through to find the first entry on the country. Her finger ran down the text looking for words to jumped out at her; Origins, Austro-Hungarian Empire, The Great War, First Czechoslovak Republic, Ethnicity, Munich Agreement, Sudetenland. Nothing piqued her interest until the Sudetenland section, when Milena's surname, Dvořáček, popped up. Darlene's straightened her posture and focussed her gaze on the text which referred to Konrad Henlein, the leader of the Nazi Party in Sudetenland. It listed his father as Konrad Henlein Senior, and his mother as Hedvika Anna Augusta Dvořáček.

'What's the connection? Is there a connection?' she whispered.

She opened the volume which covered Sudetenland and quickly found the text referring to the Nazi annexation and Henlein being installed as Gauleiter of the Sudetenland. She then got the 1938 Year Book and cross-referenced with the Sudetenland entry. She found a throwaway line at the end of the section, "There is a British connection with Henlein, with him being the nephew of the Henrich Dvořáček, Czechoslovakian Deputy Ambassador to the United Kingdom between 1926 and 1930."

'Bloody hell. This means...' She chewed on the end of her pencil, then drew up a mini-family tree in her notebook.

Her next port of call was the newspaper section. 'Good afternoon,' she smiled warmly at the clerk, 'I'd like to review all the editions of The Times from June to August 1926. Do you have them?'

The clerk's shoulders shot back, and her eyes grew wide, 'That's nearly a hundred editions. It'll take some time. You could go down to the Cambridge County Library. They have newspapers on that new microfilm system thingy,' she told Darlene.

'Thanks for the option, but I don't have much time. I'd rather flip through them here,' replied Darlene.

'Alright. Your choice. It will take a few minutes, though,' the clerk's shoulders slumped as she turned back towards the storage area. A few minutes later, she came back with a large pile of newspapers. She flopped them down on the desk, 'There's the first week of June. Good luck.'

Darlene started speed reading through the editions, hoping the unusual name of Dvořáček would stand out. Page after page, edition after edition, there was nothing. The second and third week's editions came out before she'd finished week one.

'I'll wait until you finish the first lot before I bring any more out. OK?' asked the clerk.

Darlene nodded, not looking up. First week done and nothing to be found. Second week, the same. She stood back, straightened her back, and rolled her shoulders. She wanted to rub her neck, but knew she'd get covered in ink smudges.

The clerk took away the first two piles of papers and brought back the fourth week of June. In the third edition of the fourth week, Darlene's finger stopped quickly. An announcement of the arrival in London of the new Czechoslovakian Deputy Ambassador, Henrich Dvořáček, his wife, Priska, daughter, Milena, and his sister Hedvika Henlein. There was to be a welcome ceremony and ball at the Embassy the next weekend. Darlene grabbed her notebook and scribbled down all the details.

'Thank you. Found what I was looking for. All done,' she said to the clerk who was returning with another handful of newspapers. She shot Darlene a sharp look. 'Sorry. Is there a public convenience for my hands?' Darlene held up her blackened palms. The clerk nodded towards the main entrance, turned sharply and disappeared into the storage area.

*

*12 June 1942*

Darlene handed out the round of drinks to mumbles of thanks and the tinkle of glasses touching. She slumped down into her seat and sighed, 'Not sure how to start this, so I'll be straight. I'm suspicious of Milena. She might be an informant for a German spy.'

'What? No. That can't be right,' said Stan, sitting bolt upright in a flash.

'Argh, rubbish,' added Harold, not bothering to look up from his pint.

'Actually, I'm not surprised. What's the story, Dee?' asked Betty, staring intently at Darlene.

'I know it sounds crazy. I've been going over what's happened, rehashing it again and again, and I keep coming back to the only logical answer; she's up to no good.' Darlene took another mouthful from her drink and started to reveal her information about the river and pub interactions.

'How do you know what they said? In two languages?' asked Stan in response to the Sunday night at the pub.

'I'm fluent in English, Afrikaans and Dutch. Good at German and can hold my own in French too,' added Darlene.

'Touché. Lads, never underestimate a quietly spoken woman,' Betty shot both Stan and Harold a sharp look.

'Plus, their odd behaviour at St Etheldreda's last Sunday. William and I went to Mass to keep an eye on them. Lastly, I was on night shift yesterday, so I went to the library and found out Milena's father and the mother of Konrad Henlein, the leader of the Nazis in the Sudetenland in Czechoslovakia, are brother and sister. Milena is the first cousin of Henlein. They're close family with the top Nazi in Czechoslovakia. So, all these things put together have got me worried.'

'A major stretch, if you ask me. Loads of coincidences, and reading something into innocent meetings,' said Harold, as he leaned back and drank nearly a quarter of his pint.

'She seems so nice and aren't the Czechs on our side?' asked Stan.

'I knew it. Something isn't right about her,' said Betty. 'You blokes are blinded 'cause she's a looker and is a bit of a toff. Why are working class lads fixated with posh tarts? I'm with you, Dee. You don't go into a quiet corner of an empty pub and share military news, unless you're up to no good. As for coincidences, there's no such thing. Especially in wartime. So, we've been feeding her intel. Makes me sick,' Betty cupped her face in her hands for a few seconds.

'What about Miriam? If this is true, should we have her here for this,' asked Stan.

'I've been thinking about Miriam all week. I can see her any day at the hospital and fill her in. She'll be here soon after picking up Milena. They seem to be getting pretty close. If Milena is a spy, or informant, I hope she's not trying to isolate Miriam.'

'So, little Miss Spy-Catcher, what's your plan?' Harold folded his arms as he spoke.

'You're being a prat,' Betty snapped back, 'You may not remember the spies who were captured in Kent in late 1940. You were probably still recuperating from your Dunkirk wounds. Four spies who came across from Holland were picked in Romney Marsh. Apparently, one of them was arrested in a pub in Lydd. These bastards are around, no doubt about it. Dee, don't mind Harold. Go on.'

'I want to plant some false gossip with her tonight and see if it pops up with her contact. I'm going to give her a couple of false tips about 75 Squadron. Betty, could you put a spin on something about the Yanks? Lads, are you in on this?' asked Darlene.

'Absolutely. Easy. I was going to give you an update on the arrival of the first wave of American aircraft. I'll flip it around a bit. Stan? Harold?'

'Don't know. Sounds a bit like a cheap spy novel to me,' said Harold. 'You know I usually don't have much to say. Probably best I keep my trap shut.'

'Don't act too different. Don't want to alert her. Say things are pretty quiet on the Home Guard front. OK? Stan?' added Betty.

'Fine by me. I'll say the number of Yanks coming through the station has slowed this week. It's not true. Here look, I made four bob and six in tips from them since Monday,' Stan showed them the handful of coins he had in his pocket.

'Great, thanks. I think to be safe, whenever she's around, we should pull back on details in our gossip sessions. OK?' asked Darlene.

Harold shrugged his shoulders, 'Going to make for boring Friday nights,' he said. Stan nodded.

'What'll you do if you spring her with the dodgy news,' asked Betty.

'No idea. Haven't thought too far ahead, to be honest. Suppose I'll need to take it to the MPs,' said Darlene.

'If things go the way you expect, come and see me at mine right away. Day or night, I can take you to see our base Intelligence Officer. He'll know what to do,' said Betty.

'Thanks. If anything pops up, I'll be straight round,' replied Darlene.

Betty looked up and past Darlene and her eyes grew wide, 'They're here.'

*

Darlene took up a strategic position on the deck outside The Cutter Inn. She had to wait a few minutes until a couple vacated the corner table which gave her an unobstructed view; less than one hundred yards straight down the towpath to the spot where she and William had seen Milena leaning against the bridge. She set up her gin and tonic and a packet of pork scratchings on the table. Not as nice as the biltong her dad made, but tasty all the same. She opened the bag and popped a piece in her mouth; the crisp, salty skin tickled her tongue. She bit down; the loud crunch surprised her. She looked around in mild embarrassment, then took a quick sip of her drink.

Although it was a mild evening, warm for the English, but not for a South African, so it was easy to wear a jacket, a scarf and a hat, to give her face and hair some cover from being easily recognised. She had picked through her wardrobe to make sure she put together a complete outfit she'd never worn before around Milena. Thankfully, most of their interactions were in their Nurse's uniforms, but Darlene still had to mix and match.

Looking down the path, she could easily see the flowerpot nestled up against the base of the stone bridge. She'd walked past it on the way to the pub and it was sitting upside down. The loose rock was in its usual spot, devoid of mortar, thus allowing it to be easily lifted out. Thinking back to last month, she remembered

Milena had used a side street on the far side of the pub to get to the bridge, and exited the same way. Hopefully, she'd take the same route today, but she wore the hat and scarf in case Milena walked close the pub. Darlene shifted her chair so her back was to the path, for some added protection. She took another pork scratching, then sipped her drink. Now the wait.

Minutes ticked away and the light changed as the early evening took hold. The summer solstice was only nine days away, so she knew sunset would be late, after ten o'clock due to double summertime the country was on for the war. There'd be plenty of light for her surveillance. Good Lord, who did she think she was? Play acting as a private detective; she couldn't pretend to classify herself as a spy or an intelligence officer. Maybe she had read too many Hercule Poirot novels. Was Harold right? Had she become paranoid, and jumped to ridiculous conclusions based on what? Milena taking an evening walk along the riverbank, an overheard conversation in a language she didn't know and a visit to a church service? Did she hear what she thought she had heard at the pub that night? She was positive she had. She took out her notebook and flipped through to her research from her visit to the library; more dots connecting Milena to being an informant, or merely coincidences, resulting in her clutching at straws?

She was about to nibble on another snack when she caught sight of movement. Slowly, she turned her head to take in the whole path, narrowing her gaze to focus on the person in the evening light; tall, slim build, dark hair below her hat brim, immaculately dressed, but with her back to Darlene. It has to be Milena, she thought. 'Turn around,' she whispered. Seconds dragged out and the space around her slowed down. Her temples began to throb, her heartbeats boomed within her. 'Damn it, woman, turn around, let me see you', Darlene whispered.

Almost on cue, the woman gave four quick glimpses; two left and two right. Yes, target confirmed, thought Darlene. She let out a deep sigh, and took in her first normal breath in a couple of minutes. Milena slipped her right hand from her jacket pocket, lifted the loose rock with her left hand, moved her right hand towards the bridge, then replaced the rock. She gave two more quick looks up and down the path, scratched the back of her neck, then crouched down and turned the flowerpot the right-way-up.

Darlene held the glass to her mouth and pulled the brim of her hat down. Milena looked back towards the pub and held her gaze for a few seconds longer than Darlene thought was necessary. 'Christ, has she recognised me? Look away, look away,' she whispered. Just when Darlene thought her cover was blown, Milena's gaze turned downstream, she plunged her hands deep into her pockets and started to walk down the path towards the pub. 'Shit, shit, shit.' She tried to look normal, whatever that was when you were watching a potential spy. She grabbed a pork scratching and munched down hard on it, then another. 'She's definitely got me.' As Darlene contemplated making a break, Milena turned a sharp left onto the street which took her back towards town. Darlene thought she was about to hyperventilate, so she took in a half dozen quick, deep breaths, grabbed her drink, which was still about a third full, and drained it. She used the ends of her scarf to mop her forehead. Beads of sweat also ran down her back and between her breasts.

'Pull yourself together, woman. The operation is only half over.' She held on for a couple more minutes to make sure Milena was on Board Street or into Cherry Hill Park; well past a position where she could look back at the river path. Two more deep breaths and Darlene stood up but felt light-headed and grabbed the seat to steady herself. Another couple of deep gulps of air settled her, then she walked towards the bridge. She felt her head was on a swivel, as she flicked left to right. Where the path met the side street, she stopped, scanned the area, and focussed on each tree and building. She decided to go past the bridge and look back from another angle. There was no sign of Milena, so she double-backed to the bridge.

Stopping at the flowerpot, she picked up the loose rock to find a double folded piece of paper. Her heartbeat started to increase again and beads of sweat reformed on her forehead. She picked the paper up and unfolded it, but had to take a couple of seconds to focus on the writing – it was in German. 'Concentrate, woman,' she whispered. She read it twice, to be sure. A small smile broke across her face; amongst the information on the note were the three false leads they spoke about last night at the Prince Albert. The last line of the note sent a flash of excitement through her body, "Nächstes treffen: Sonntag, 28 Juni, Prinz Albert". She refolded the note, put it back in the cavity and replaced the stone. One last look around and she strode back towards the pub and onto Station Road to catch a bus back to the Nurses' Home. She allowed herself a smile.

Back down the towpath, underneath the rail bridge, about the same distance upstream as Darlene had been downstream, a well-dressed man, with jet black hair underneath a black fedora, folded up a newspaper, pushed himself off the bridge abutment where he'd been standing for the last few minutes and adjusted his tie and gold tie bar. His thin, angular face was tense as he flicked the paper under an arm and walked to the stone bridge, where he stopped at the flowerpot.

*

On the bus, Betty's words came back to Darlene: "Day or night, I can take you to see our base Intelligence Officer". Soon after the Oliver Cromwell House Museum, she got off the bus and walked down West Fen Road to Betty's house. She checked her watch; nearly eight o'clock. A wave of guilt hit her; was this too late to knock on Betty's door, although she did say anytime. She grabbed the door knocker and tapped.

'Dee. Bloody hell, you look like you've seen a ghost. Come in, Pet,' said Betty.

'Who is it, Betty?' a booming voice came from the front living room.

'My Nurse friend Darlene, Pop. We'll have a cuppa in the kitchen. You want one?' asked Betty.

'Oh, Love, that'd be grand. One for Mother too,' said her father.

'Come on down the back. I'll put the kettle on. You've got something, don't you?' she asked.

'Thanks, Betty, and so sorry for coming round this late, disturbing your family's evening. Yes, it's about Milena,' replied Darlene.

'Thought so. Here, grab a seat,' said Betty as they entered the kitchen. 'What's the latest news?'

'I took a punt Milena would have the note drop on the river path, and she did. Same place, roughly the same time as a month ago. After she did the drop, I checked it and there was a note there and it had all the erroneous information we gave her last night,' said Darlene.

'What? You took the note? Did you check you weren't being watched? Dee, definitely a bit risky,' said Betty.

'No, no. I didn't take it. I read it and put it back. Don't worry, I was careful. I made sure she wasn't around, and I couldn't see anyone who looked like her man. This is the piece of the puzzle we were missing. Any chance we can meet the Intelligence Officer?' asked Darlene.

The kettle had started to squeak and squeal, so Betty had to raise her voice, 'You think tonight? I do. This is bloody big.'

'Language, Betty,' a woman's voice came through from the living room.

'Sorry, Mum,' Betty rolled her eyes, took the kettle off the range, and poured hot water into the teapot. A cloud of steam engulfed her. 'I can borrow Pop's car and we can go now. He lives on base. You got your RAF Nurses card? If so, shouldn't be a problem getting you on base.'

Darlene nodded. 'It won't be too late to see him? He won't be out and about?'

'Highly unlikely. I know him, stepped out with him a couple of times.' Darlene raised her eyebrows to Betty's revelation. 'Didn't last 'cause he is a bit boring, a wet fish. I'd put two bob on him being in the barracks, reading a book and smoking his pipe. This is too important to wait a couple of days. We need to talk to him while it's fresh in your mind. Let me set the oldies up with their tea and grab the car keys from Pop.'

Betty picked up the tray with the teapot, cups, saucers, milk jug and plate of biscuits and walked through to the living room. 'Come on Dee, meet Mum and Pop.'

*

They were still navigating their way out of Ely, when Darlene brought up a sensitive topic. 'We need to talk about Miriam,' she said quietly.

'I've been worried about how much time she's been spending with Milena,' replied Betty.

'It's more problematic than you might know.' Darlene took in a deep breath before she continued. She noticed Betty's grip on the steering wheel had turned her knuckles white. 'I saw her in a rather compromising position with Milena at the dance a couple of weeks ago.'

'Bugger. You don't need to go into details. I can guess. I bet Milena has been targeting her since Mer picked her up from the station on day one. Cunning bitch,' hissed Betty.

'So, it's true about Miriam?' asked Darlene.

'Oh, yes. I've known for years. She's always tried to keep it quiet, but I've known her for too long and this place is too small. She ever tried it with you?' asked Betty.

'Not really. A bit of flirting, but I told her about William pretty soon after I arrived. I'm worried she's being manipulated,' said Darlene.

'Absolutely. If Milena is who we think she is, she'll be trying to entrap Mer. Bigger worry is what Military Intelligence will do to Mer if they find out. Christ, being that way inclined must be tough enough in normal times, but in combination with being compromised; they'll crucify her. The only people who get away with it are establishment toffs. The rest of us get buried.'

The inside of the car grew darker, as they left town and entered the countryside; the only light came from the dim glow of the speedometer, which barely illuminated Betty's face as she continued, 'We've got to find a way to protect her. Give me some time to think about it. In the meantime, if you see her at the hospital, get her to start pulling back from Milena. Nothing too abrupt. Can't alert her that we're onto to her. Get Mer to make up some excuse she's got loads more jobs on.'

'I'll track her down on Monday morning. So, we won't tell your Intelligence man about how much time they spend together?' asked Darlene.

'Good Lord, no. Given we were a bit blabby during our first few Friday drinks sessions with Milena, all of us are potentially on the hook, so we have to look out for ourselves. Makes me sick to think some of the stuff we talked about might have got back to Berlin,' Betty banged the steering wheel with the heel of her palm.

'We can't beat ourselves up. We weren't to know,' Darlene reassured Betty.

'But we had our suspicions, didn't we? After the first night, the red flag went up for both of us. Always believe your first impressions. Right, we're almost here. Get your Nurses card out and let me do the talking.' Betty started to slowdown as the lights of the base entrance guard post came into view.

*

The staff dining room was abuzz with the hum of conversation. Darlene scanned the room and estimated more than half of the tables were taken for afternoon tea. She narrowed her gaze to see if Miriam was in. She had checked the staff roster, to see if Milena was working. Thankfully, she was scheduled for a night shift, so hopefully Miriam would be alone, or at least not with Milena. After a couple of sweeps, she found Miriam near one of the back corners of the room. She grabbed a cup of tea and a couple of biscuits and made her way to Miriam.

'Hey, stranger. Can I join you?' Darlene's voice was bright.

'Oh, Dee. Um, sure. Yeah, sorry, I've been a bit absent recently,' replied Miriam, she barely held Darlene's gaze for a second.

'No need to apologise, Mer. We've all been a bit crazy in the last few weeks. Crikey, we've had two of those thousand bomber raids since the thirtieth. How've you been?' Darlene tried to raise a supportive tone to her voice.

'Pretty good. Yeah, bloody busy. The Yanks ramping up has had us on the run. Bloody hell, they are a demanding lot. Still, great they are here,' said Miriam.

'Yes, we've seen our first few Americans in here. Extremely polite. You know my William got hit by some shrapnel? Nothing too serious; he was out in two days, but gave me a heck of a fright.'

'I was shocked. Great to know he's alright,' added Miriam.

'We haven't caught up since the dance at Mildenhall.' Darlene noticed Miriam's go pale at her comment. 'No need to look so worried. I'm not here to comment on what happened or who you're attracted to. Miriam, you've become a good friend, and helped me adjust here. I am so grateful. I need to warn you though, about Milena.' Miriam's eyes grew wide, and her mouth opened. 'We think you need to cut down the amount of time you spend with her.'

'What do you mean? Who's we?' snapped Miriam.

'Betty and I,' replied Darlene.

'Oh, Betty. The nosy cow. She can get stuffed,' Miriam snapped back.

'We have some pretty serious concerns about her. You really do need to wean yourself off her. Best to let her know your workload has gone crazy, and you can't catch up with her as much as usual,' said Darlene.

'You're not making any sense, Dee. What serious concerns?' demanded Miriam.

Darlene, exhaled and looked around her, then leaned into Miriam, 'What I'm about to tell you is going to be a shock, but is also top secret.' Miriam raised her eyebrows: 'RAF Intelligence Branch has been informed we believe Milena is either a spy or a German informant.'

Miriam leant back, 'What tosh. You two are jealous of her. Just because she's smart and good looking,' Miriam hissed.

'Mer, I know this isn't easy to hear, but I've seen her meet twice with a man I think is German, and caught her leaving a note with information about the bases and squadrons for the same man. We think she's been trying to wheedle her way into your affections from the first day she met you.'

'This is absolute rubbish. I don't need to listen to any more of this,' Miriam jumped to her feet.

'Mer, the Intelligence Branch know about her, so they'll be watching her closely. It means if you don't pull back, they'll identify you and you'll be swept up in this. We don't want that to happen to you. You mean too much to us. You understand what the implications would be for you?' Darlene held Miriam in a hard stare.

Miriam glared at her but eased back into her seat.

'Yes, Mer, think about what they'd do to you. We want to protect you. The military don't need to know anything about your private life. If you continue to see Milena, you'll be stepping into a spider's web. Once in, there's no way Betty and I would be able to help you.' Miriam vigorously rubbed her hands as Darlene spoke. 'We're not saying change your feelings, but do what you need to do to protect yourself. No idea how long we're talking about, but now Intelligence know and are watching her, they'll probably want to act pretty quickly.'

'I'll think about it,' said Miriam abruptly, then with a screech from her chair which turned heads around, Miriam got up and left the room.

Darlene exhaled and shook her head. Picking up her cup, she sipped a mouthful of tea, while drumming the table with her spare hand. Thoughts raced through her head; would Miriam take her advice, had she told her too much, would Miriam confide in Milena, and if she did, would Milena slip away? 'Bugger,' she whispered.

*

*Date – 17 June 1942*
*Tour of Operations Count – Operation 31*
*Target Location – Frisian Islands, Wadden Sea, Germany & Netherlands*
*Assigned Aircraft – Wellington Mk.III X.3646 AA-M*
*Take-off – 23:30*

The Leggett crew sat in a small semicircle in the Briefing Hall, waiting for the night's operation details to be unveiled. Pruno was in the middle of the men, arms folded and legs crossed; but his usual smile was nowhere to be seen. The rest of the crew reflected his mood. Tas was already smoking his second cigarette by the time the Squadron Officers came in.

One of the junior officers pulled back the curtain in front of the operations board, with the target, take-off time, and the listing of aircraft and pilots revealed. A wave of sighs and heavy exhaling came from the crews, as they saw a mine-laying op to the Frisian Islands.

'You fucking little beauty,' said Boss, as he grabbed Pruno's shoulder.

Pruno leaned forward, dropped his head, unfolded his arms, clenched his fists and gave them a celebratory shake. The rest of the crew offered handshakes and backslaps.

'Settle down lads,' said the briefing officer. 'Yes, good to get a gardening run after three weeks of raids on Happy Valley.' He continued with the details of the operation to a more upbeat audience.

*

William sensed a different atmosphere in the plane. The tense nature of pre-flight preparations could never be completely dissipated, but there was always a lighter air within the crew when they had a gardening run, but to have one at the end of Pruno's tour ops, gave the crew added levity. The sadness of losing their long-serving, trusted and much-loved pilot was tempered by the relief he'd have a higher probability of coming through his last raid unscathed. Having a crew member finish their tour was close to a forgotten memory for William. It took him a minute or two to remember it was exactly two months ago since Slim Mayall finished his tour. So many ops, so many bombs dropped, so many close calls and lost crews between then and now, he wasn't surprised the few good news days got swamped by the tidal wave of grim memories.

'We set to go, lads? Stay sharp. Let's do everything bang-on, as normal,' Pruno's voice was steady and assured, as usual.

'Skip, you get us up there and we'll look after you,' replied Tas.

As ever, tension swept over William as the engines wound up, ready for take-off. Always one of the danger points of a raid, it was exacerbated tonight as they were flying in X3646 M-Mike for the first time. They didn't know the aircraft, its idiosyncrasies and foibles. They had huge confidence in the ground crew, but these feelings always arose whenever they flew an unfamiliar plane. 'What a night to get a different plane,' he whispered. The plane shuddered as Pruno released the brakes and they charged down the runway.

William flinched at each noise and vibration. Was this normal? Does their old faithful X3538 N-NUTS make the same sound? Should that piece of equipment be shaking so violently? 'Jesus, man. Will you relax,' he scolded himself. His chair suddenly stabilised as Pruno pulled the nose up and the plane rose into the night sky. Then it felt and sounded as smooth as N-NUTS. He let out a deep breath, crossed himself and turned to work on his charts and the GEE navigation system.

*

'Five minutes to target area, Navigator. There's a bit of sea fog around. Visibility is moderate to poor. Might be an instrument drop.' William sprang up from his desk on Pruno's update.

'Robbie-boy, light flak and few searchlights. Haven't seen a single fighter yet. You should have a smooth run in,' added Tas.

William lay down in the bomb aimer's bay and got settled. 'Thanks, lads. Yeah, it's a bit soupy down there. We're on the right line, so should be fine.' William checked his instruments and his watch and both confirmed they were on track.

'Over target area now,' said Pruno.

'Lead aircraft have dropped. Look for some flares, Robbie,' added Boss.

William reached over to the bomb bay control panel, flicked the appropriate switches, and pressed the release button, 'Mines gone. Let's get you home, Skip,' William told the crew. Cheers and muffled claps of gloved hands echoed around the plane.

*

'As our Pommy mates would say, this op was a wizard prang. Time for tea,' said Boss. 'Refreshments coming right up.' Boss poured the tea and he and William handed out the cups to the crew.

'Christ-almighty. It's got some kick tonight,' said Gordo from the rear.

'Bloody hell, Boss. What'd ya put in it?' asked Tas.

'Some celebratory brandy. Scammed a hip flask full from the Sergeant at the Mess. Congrats, Pruno. Captain extraordinaire,' added Boss.

'Thanks, Wireless. Tastes great. Let's hold the cheers until were parked up, eh?' said Pruno

*

William looked up from his charts when he heard the engines ease up and felt the landing gear go down.

'Prepare for landing in five. Almost there, lads,' said Pruno.

They'd been descending for the last ten minutes, but now the last high-risk aspect of the flight was a few minutes away. Visions of aircraft going up in balls of flames and landing gear crumpling underneath planes shot through William's mind. 'Trust Pruno and trust the plane,' he said to himself. As was almost standard procedure, time seemed to be suspended; seconds and minutes dragged on. His fingers grew numb and seemed to expand into useless, chubby sausages. 'Get down, get down,' he whispered. One last throttle down on the engines was followed by the hard thump of the initial touchdown, the bounce, then the second touch of the wheels. All fine, landing gear holding. The final touch and the engines drowned out by the cheers and shouts of the crew.

'Pruno, you bloody legend,' said Gordo.

'Great run, Skip. Smooth as silk,' said Boss.

'Top drawer,' added Tas.

'Brilliant op, Skip. Magnificent as ever,' said William.

'Thanks lads. Always a team effort,' replied Pruno. 'Let's get her parked and have a drink. Boss, got some left in your hip flask?'

'You bet, Skip. Plenty to go round,' said Boss.

*

As the crew pulled some seats together in the Debriefing Room, each man pulled out a hip flask from his tunic. Boss had a spare for Pruno.

'Argh, lads. You've come prepared. Bloody brilliant,' said Pruno.

William stood up, 'Pilot Officer Rufus Leggett. Our Captain, our rock. This, and all the Leggett crews, thank you for guiding us safely in all the ops. Through those flak fields, walls of searchlights and waves of fighters, you've always been a beacon of calmness and stability. We know there probably were many times when you wondered whether we'd get back here. The flare fire over Lübeck and Ossie's shrapnel come to mind.'

'Christ, that was some flying on the Lübeck run. Thought we were gone for all money,' added Gordo.

'As your longest serving crew members, Gordo and I thank and salute you on behalf of every airman who's had the privilege and good fortune to call you "Skip". Till we take our last breaths, we all owe you a debt we cannot begin to pay back. To our Pruno,' William put his arm around Gordo and they raised their hip flasks.

'To Pruno,' shouted the men, followed by long pulls on the drinks.

'Thanks Robbie, Gordo, lads. Was half expecting something tonight but thought Tas might be organising one of his legendary nights at the pub,' said Pruno.

'Never fear, Skip. It's on the cards as soon as we have a free night,' shouted Tas.

'That's what I'm afraid of,' Pruno's luminous smile broke across his face, puffing up his reddened cheeks, as a wave of laughter swept through the room. 'You know I'm not one for big speeches, more a quiet word, an understanding ear when someone needs to talk, and I suppose a bit of British stiff upper lip to get on with the job. I look around so many faces of blokes who've flown with me, or been here since I joined you crazy Kiwis, and I have to thank God I was assigned here. You're right, Robbie, there's been more than a few times I thought we might not make it back.'

Pruno stopped mid-sentence, took a deep breath and chewed on his lower lip for a couple of seconds, 'but as I've always said, it takes a full crew to get a plane back. Tas, Boss, Gordo and Robbie, but also Ossie, Slim, Cyril and Clem at the start of my tour, without you, there'd have been many times when I wouldn't have been able to get us home. It's me who owes you the debt. To the Leggett crews and all of 75 New Zealand Squadron, cheers.'

'75 New Zealand Squadron. Ake Ake Kia Kaha,' shouted the men. Gulping their drinks, they gathered around Pruno, quietly exchanging words, handshakes, shoulder taps and backslaps. After the men drifted away, William pulled Pruno aside.

'We never talk about the end of a tour, so I have no clue what your plan is,' said William.

'Robbie boy, I want to get home to Catherine for my end of tour leave. Take strolls with her around Thetford Park. I've signed up for the transport wing. Nice and quiet and no more bloody flak. Once the war is over, go I'll be down to Carrow Road as quick as I can to watch my Canaries play Ipswich. Get back to regular life, whatever that means now. How is life going to be normal after what we've seen, what we've been through?'

'No idea, Pruno. Park it all deep in the memory. Do our best to keep it there. The demons will come back when we least expect them. You've got to be ready for it,' replied William.

'How many runs did we do together. Twenty-five, twenty-six?' asked Pruno.

'Exactly thirty. Some accomplishment,' said William.

'Christ, Robbie. Thirty? We've seen a lot, haven't we?' Pruno rubbed William's shoulder warmly. 'That run to Stuttgart when we iced up. Felt like I was flying a brick and chunks breaking off, hitting the fuselage. The first thousand bomber run over Cologne. That's seared in my mind. The fires. It often comes back to me at night. Lord God Almighty.'

'All we can hope is they'll fade over time. You've got to build up better memories to swamp them. Push them right back. Have some young ones with Catherine. See Norwich City win the Cup. Good things. They'll crowd out the bad ones,' said William.

'You're a good man, William Robertson. Thirty runs. Can't count how many would have ended badly if you weren't guiding me. I'm knackered. Got to get some sleep, especially if we don't have a run tonight, it means I'll need to be ready for Tas's pub night. See you a bit later.' They shared a long handshake and knowing nods.

*

*Date – 19 June 1942*
*Tour of Operations Count – Operation 32*
*Target Location – Emden, Germany*
*Assigned Aircraft – Wellington Mk.III X.3538 AA-N*
*Take-off – 23:35*

William sensed the atmosphere inside the plane was different, more tense than their last run; one was as celebratory as a combat operation could ever get. The random chatter and usual banter from Tas and Gordo was missing; it reminded him of the feeling one used to get when facing a new teacher for the first time. The whole class was eager to see what they were like and slightly nervous about how they'd treat them. They all knew Ossie was an extremely good pilot; he'd taken over from Pruno many times during raids, acquitting himself with distinction, and the training last night couldn't have gone smoother. This was different though; the first full operation from go to whoa with Ossie as their Skip. He told himself if the crew did their jobs as normal, all would be fine, and thankfully they were back in X3538 N-NUTS.

They eased off the ground and climbed smoothly into the evening sky, light fading fast with the sun now set below the northwest horizon. Nice work, thought William, keep it up, Ossie boy.

There was solid cloud cover over Emden, when Ossie addressed the crew, 'No searchlights, lads. The front has made it soupy. Should keep the fighters away too.'

'Haven't seen one fucker yet,' said Tas.

'Looks like there's plenty of flak though. Could get rough. We'll descend to bombing altitude in two minutes,' Ossie continued.

*

Ossie taxied the plane to its parking spot amongst a din of jokes and banter over the intercom. The usual chat which came with the relief of yet another safe and successful raid, was there in abundance. A smooth landing was met with a round of congratulations from all the crew.

'Not bad for a first timer,' quipped Tas.

'Never in doubt,' added Boss.

*

*Date – 20 June 1942*
*Tour of Operations Count – Operation 33*
*Target Location – Emden, Germany*
*Assigned Aircraft – Wellington Mk.III X.3538 AA-N*
*Take-off – 23:40*

The smiles and levity dissipated as they de-suited in the kit room; a quick count of aircraft and crews found Gordo's roommate, Ray Trengrove and his crew weren't back yet. William noticed Gordo wasn't at his locker. He motioned to Tas to come with him. The two men didn't say a word as they walked to the Flight Operation hut.

'Come on Gordo. They'll be back soon enough. You saw how heavy the flak was. They probably took a longer route back. Time for some kip,' said Tas.

Gordo stood by the door, staring out at the airfield, not moving a muscle.

'Ray will be alright, mate. He's an experienced campaigner and old Fraser is a top pilot.' William reached up and put a hand on Gordo's shoulder.

'You're right, Robbie. Fraser's one of the best in the business. If anyone can bring 'em home, it's him,' Gordo exhaled heavily. All three men walked slowly back to barracks, constantly searching the morning sky.

*

William knocked on Gordo and Ray's door, 'Gordo, you there, mate?' No reply. Another knock and he opened the door to find the room empty. William jogged over to the Briefing Hall to find Gordo looking at the aircraft list for the previous evening's operation; he was still in his flight gear from earlier in the day. William's eyes ran down the aircraft numbers and pilot's names and found Wellington X3760, P/O Fraser, A.A. Next to the listing was FTR. 'Bugger, officially listed as Failed to Return,' whispered William. He turned to Gordo, who had tears flowing down his face.

'Four to go, Robbie. Same as you and me. He only had four bloody runs to go.' William held Gordo's upper arm; the big man fell into William's arms and started sobbing. 'I stayed up all day. He never came in.'

'Let it out, Gordo. Don't keep it in. There's too much we lock away. Not this time, mate. Let it go.' Gordo's shoulders heaved and sank with each breath. William gently patted him on the back, not saying another word.

Reggie appeared at the door; 'What's doing, y'all? We going to the Mess for a …' He didn't finish the sentence, as William shook his head and gave him a flick of his eyes. Reggie, put his hands up in apology and walked away.

Gordo pulled back from William, 'Sorry, Robbie. Didn't mean to lose it.'

'Shut up man. It's natural. I'd be more worried if you'd done nothing,' replied William.

'You're a good man William Robertson. Knew it the day we got our assignment together. Lord, seems like a lifetime ago. You get going. Don't want you to miss pints with the lads.'

'No worries, Gordo. I can stick around here. Make sure you're alright,' replied William.

'Not necessary, but thanks. I'll be right now. Anyway, Ray and I had a pact; if anything happened to either of us, the other would take care of personal things. He has a lady he's been stepping out with down in London, and he made a list of things to give to her. I want to sort those out. Got to see the Erks to grab Ray's special letters. Probably one for his lady. I'll request a leave pass to go to London to see her.'

'You sure. I'm happy to stay.' William held Gordo's upper arm as he spoke.

'On your bike, Robbie. Don't make me throw my weight around,' he smiled at his mate.

# CHAPTER NINE

*22 June 1942*

Darlene stopped in her tracks in the doorway of her room. Her upper body straightened up; a white envelope sat in the middle of the floor. She wasn't expecting a letter from William; he'd sent his last note only a week ago and they'd spent the day together less than two weeks ago. Who could this be from, she thought?

She picked it up, no closer to knowing the sender. Her address was typewritten and truncated:

Staff Nurse Darlene du Toit
Nurses' Home
RAF Hospital Ely

No return address, no stamp and no postmark. She flipped it over; no return address on the other side either. She stepped into her room, closed and locked the door. She sat on her bed and dropped her handbag beside her. She took the envelope in both hands and regarded it. 'Well, you won't know what it's about unless you open it,' she whispered. She flicked her thumb nail under the back flap and unfolded the letter. Finally, there was an indication of the sender: RAF Intelligence Branch, Air Ministry Intelligence Department, War Office, Whitehall, London. No insignia, badge or other identifier.

It was a short note and only a single page. She started reading:

*16th June 1942*
*To Staff Nurse Darlene du Toit,*

*This letter is a follow-up to your recent meeting with our RAF Intelligence Officer at RAF Mildenhall.*

*The information you provided is of significant interest to the RAF Intelligence Branch and as such, I would greatly appreciate the opportunity to meet with you in-person to discuss this further.*

*Please make arrangements to meet me at the University of Cambridge Library, West Road, Cambridge, at eleven o'clock in the morning, on Thursday 25th June. There will be seats reserved for us under your name, in the Main Reading Room. Ask for directions to the room at the main service desk in the lobby.*

*Apologies for the urgency of this request. I look forward to meeting you on Thursday.*

*Yours sincerely,*
*Flight Lieutenant Hector M.E. A'Court*
*Senior Human Intelligence Operator*

Darlene lifted her head and exhaled heavily. Well now, this was taking a serious turn, she thought. Someone from RAF Intelligence headquarters doesn't write to you direct, demanding an urgent meeting if there wasn't something of real interest about Milena. With no return address and no postage, she wondered if it had been hand-delivered. The thought of it added to the seriousness of letter; no trace of the letter in the system, no ability for it to be intercepted. Was she ready for this next stage? Up until now, it all had been happenstance, a bit detective work pulled from the pages of a cheap novel. Actually, a bit of fun, however, now the RAF Intelligence Branch was involved, it was very real. Her shoulders trembled as a wave of chills swept over her. What was the next step and what could it enable? Her mind pictured countless scenarios: the intelligence officer dismisses all the information as circumstantial and coincidence, leaving them to look like paranoid busy-bodies. What she'd found out was of interest, but unable to be actioned, leaving them with a potential spy in their midst. The officer sees this as a significant risk issue and needs to take action, so they could have to help entrap Milena and the man. She didn't know if she was up for being part of a spy catching operation.

She folded up the letter, put another fresh fold in it and put it inside a zipped pocket in her handbag. She made a mental note to talk to her Ward Nurse first thing tomorrow to move her onto a night shift on Thursday. She changed out of her uniform into civvies and headed off to the dining hall for dinner, her handbag clutched tightly against her body.

*

*25 June 1942*

The brown brick edifice of the Cambridge University Library and its one hundred and sixty foot tower was an easy landmark for her to follow from the town centre. The single-arched entrance enveloped her as she pushed on the revolving door. She tentatively walked up to the service desk, where a young woman greeted her with a warm smile; Darlene thought she couldn't have been older than herself.

'Good morning. How can I help you?' the woman asked.

'Oh, I hope you can. I have a couple of seats reserved in the Main Reading Room. My name is Darlene du Toit,' she gave the clerk a hesitant, half-smile.

'One moment, please.' The clerk picked up a clipboard, flipped over the top page then ran her index finger down a list of names, 'Yes, here you are. Row three, table one, seats one and two. I'm sensing you haven't been here before,' she added a head tilt to her smile.

'Thank you. Correct, never set foot in any Cambridge University building. All a bit daunting, to be honest,' replied Darlene, clutching her handbag straps so tightly her knuckles were turning white.

'I know how you feel. I was walking around with bulging eyes for my entire first year. It's easy to find; up those stairs, a quick left-right, down the Catalogue Hall, and through the double doors at the end of the hall. It's well signposted. Enjoy your visit.' The woman pointed to a staircase through a thirty-foot-tall archway.

'Thank you so much.' Darlene started off on her search for the meeting spot Hector A'Court had organised for them. She could hardly believe she was in the main library of one of the most prestigious universities in the world. Never had she ever believed she'd be in a place like this. Although it was a modern building, it reeked of higher learning and prestige. She wasn't sure why Hector had suggested here, but she was grateful for the opportunity to visit such a place.

At the top of the stairs, she took the left-right turns as instructed. As soon as she was in the Catalogue Hall, the musty smell of leather and wood hit her. It was over thirty yards long, maybe fifty, with oak bookshelves lining the walls, all with identical brown leather-bound volumes. A handful of well-dressed students, intermittently dispersed along the hall, were reading the tomes or flipping through their pages. At the end of the hall, she saw the double doors the clerk had mentioned. She stopped short upon entering the reading room, where her gaze was drawn to the exposed wood beams in the ceiling. A bank of twenty-five arched windows flooded the room with the strong summer sunlight. She made her way to the study tables to her left, where the first table had a brass badge inscribed with "Row 1 – Table 3". At the start of row three, she found a folded card with her name on it, not unlike what you might have on a table at a fancy dinner. Across the table was another card, which she turned around to see Hector's name.

She sat down, took out a small notebook from her handbag, patted down the front of her skirt, puffed up the shoulder pads in her jacket and flicked some stray hairs off her face. She had barely got herself settled, when a man walked past her from her blind spot and sat down opposite her, dumping a couple of books on the desk. She pushed back into her chair and her eyes widened.

'Darlene du Toit? Flight Lieutenant Hector A'Court. Pleasure to meet you. Please act normally, as if we're regular students, acquainted with each other, sharing a study space,' he said softly. At the low volume, the words of his refined English accent, were difficult for her to pick up.

She nodded, but too quickly and nervously than he would have wanted, she thought, 'Nice to meet you, Flight Lieutenant.' She offered her hand, but quickly pulled it back. 'You're nice and early,' she added.

He opened his bag and took out a pad, 'I was in the Catalogue Hall when you walked through. Needed to check you weren't being followed.'

'But you didn't know what I looked like,' her sentence tailed off as he cocked his head at her, raised his eyebrows, and gave her a knowing smile. 'Of course, you're in intelligence. You must have had me clocked the second I walked in the building. Probably getting off the train, too.' He gave her a small nod.

She noted his thick brown hair, a side-part on the left, with a liberal dose of hair cream, fine facial features and a slightly lopsided smile, turning up on the left, a grey herringbone suit, white shirt and a green, brown and white diagonally striped tie.

'Before we get started, I have to thank you for agreeing to meet. It can't be easy to talk to us about a friend and colleague,' he said.

'Wouldn't go so far as calling her a friend. I've met her half a dozen times at most, and had my suspicions about her from the get-go,' Darlene replied.

'Still, I appreciate what you're doing. As it happens, we've had our eye on her for a few years. Probably back to 1938, but I'll come back to that later. Now let's review a few facts.' Hector took out a fountain pen from one of his inside jacket pockets and opened his notebook. 'You are Staff Nurse Darlene du Toit from RAF Hospital Ely,' Darlene nodded. 'Originally from Capetown, South Africa, and been in service since March 1941. First assigned to RAF Hospital Exeter. We're here to discuss Staff Nurse Milena Dvořáček, also a Nurse at RAF Hospital Ely and originally from Czechoslovakia, and a currently unnamed male acquaintance of Miss Dvořáček. Correct?'

'Yes, all correct,' Darlene nodded.

'Thank you. Now take me through the last few months, from the time you first met Miss Dvořáček, to the time you contacted RAF Intelligence Branch at Mildenhall,' Hector fixed Darlene with an intense gaze.

She took a deep breath, opened her notebook and started retelling what she'd seen, heard and uncovered since the first Friday night when Miriam told them about collecting Milena from the train station. 'Then I went to see the Intelligence Officer at Mildenhall. They have their next rendezvous this coming Sunday, the twenty-eighth at the Prince Albert pub in Ely. It fits a rough routine I think they are keeping: the first Sunday of the month they meet at St Etheldreda's; the middle Saturday is the note-drop off on the river path; and the last Sunday is when they meet at the Prince Albert, the meet I saw on the note,' Darlene exhaled for what she thought was the first time in minutes.

Hector scribbled down some additional items, then looked up at Darlene, 'Outstanding, Miss du Toit. This is excellent information. I like your deduction on their routine. All fits a pattern of regularity of contact and all hidden in plain sight. Not trying to be too clandestine and so irregular that things stand out. Now this airman who keeps popping up, Flight Sergeant William

Robertson, and the WAAF, Betty Hardwick. Some background on them?' he asked.

Darlene wriggled around in her seat and felt her face redden, 'Well, William and I are close friends. Actually, we've been stepping out together. He's a New Zealander, a navigator in 75 Squadron. Almost finished his tour, but I'm sure you know most of this already. Betty works at RAF Mildenhall. She got me on base to meet the Intelligence Officer there. She was worried about Milena almost immediately too.'

'Thank you. Yes, I know the official details of them both. How much you trust them and how much they know.' he asked.

'I trust both of them with my life. William has almost died a few times already. Nothing unusual for Bomber Command aircrew, I suppose. Betty is so committed to the fight. She's a real tiger. She's been a great confidante,' said Darlene.

'And the other members of your Friday night social group?' he questioned.

Darlene eyes grew wide, and a surge of heat went through her body. How did he know about the Friday sessions? She couldn't remember telling him or the other Intelligence Officer. Maybe she did. Perhaps Betty told her contact. 'Um, well, there's Stan and Harold. Both in the Home Guard. Good lads, hard workers. Harold was in the Army. Wounded at Dunkirk. Stan is unable to serve. Wouldn't have any worries about them. Miriam is in the Women's Auxiliary, great person, so dedicated. Since we first had our concerns about Milena, we stopped talking about anything of significance and cut down how often we get together. Need to be safe.'

'Thanks. We have to be sure about them and any additional sources of leaks and information. Do you know what the gentleman looks like? Could you describe him to me?' asked Hector.

'Better than that. Here you go,' Darlene flipped through a few pages of her notebook and pulled out the notes Bob had written up, plus some additions she'd made after they saw him and Milena at Mass. She slid the paper across the table, Hector's hand lightly brushed hers as they exchanged the note. A jolt of electricity shot up her arm.

Hector unfolded the paper and read the note; he pursed his lips and a worry line formed between his eyebrows. 'Interesting,' he murmured.

'How so?' Darlene shot back.

'Overall, reasonable generic, but the combination of the black fedora, face scar, gold tie bar and gold cufflinks. It matches someone we were notified about earlier this year. A nasty piece of work, from what they say. Now, onto this possible meet on Sunday,' Hector capped his fountain pen as he spoke; the click echoed around the room.

'Probable, if not a certainty, they'll meet up. I've planned ahead and organised a room with the landlord, where we can listen in on them,' said Darlene.

'Excellent work, thank you. Not a lot of things are certain in my line of work, but I take your point. Why don't I pick you up about six o'clock?' he started making notes again as he spoke.

'Best make our own ways there,' Darlene said. 'Ely is small, so if I'm seen with a man other than William, tongues will start to wag. You should aim for five o'clock. They came in soon after six last time. It will give us some time to set ourselves up. Now, if you don't mind, can I flip things around and ask you some questions?'

'An unusual request, but your level of preparation and detailed information have earned you some tokens with me. Go ahead,' Hector replied.

'You said you've been watching Milena for a few years. Why so, and why haven't you picked her up yet?' she asked.

'As you've discovered, there's a family connection with Konrad Henlein. You are correct she is a first cousin of Henlein. She returned to Czechoslovakia infrequently up until spring 1938, then visits ramped up to every other month until the invasion of Poland. We haven't acted yet as her father was, and still is, well connected to many people within government, some at high levels. He did an exceptional job of networking when he was Deputy Ambassador, so we've had to tread delicately,' he said.

'And you think she's been planted in Ely, in the heart of Bomber Command bases, to secure intelligence and give it to a German spy?' added Darlene.

'Not sure if it's your interpretation looking for confirmation, but it does appear to fit the facts on the ground,' replied Hector.

'Why here and why no uniform for you?' she asked.

'Much like them. Why not hide in plain sight? Meeting in odd places in the dead of night is too hard to organise and stands out too much. This is where I went to university. I know it well and they know us. The woman on the front desk?' Darlene nodded to his question. 'She's one of ours. The uniform, well, again, why draw attention to oneself? I wear it when I'm at official RAF functions, but as a Human Intelligence Operator I need a high level of discretion; a uniform is like an air raid siren.'

'Thank you. Good to know. Lastly, personally, you have French ancestry, with A'Court as a last name?' asked Darlene.

'Yes and no. Huguenot, to be specific. My family escaped the Protestant persecution in France back in the late 1690s. We pronounce the T in our name. Have embraced the Anglicised version. Quite the interrogation. Impressed. Anything else?'

'No, that will do for now,' she said with a smile.

'Perfect. See you on Sunday. You pack up and leave before me. I'll check no one follows you and will be a minute or two behind you.' He closed his notebook, put his pen back in his jacket pocket and gave Darlene a warm smile.

# Chapter Ten

*27 June 1942*

Through the trees and hedgerows, thick with their luxuriant coats of summer growth, the Cambridgeshire countryside revealed itself to William in fleeting glimpses. Flat, without what a Kiwi would call a hill, as far as he could see. The fields of rapeseed and corn, broken up by the odd paddock with a herd of dairy cows idly grazing. It reminded him of the Manawatu, back home, and the train trips to Palmerston North to see Albert when he was at Highden Seminary.

His mind wandered back to 1931 when he and a mate bicycled all the way from Wanganui to Palmerston North to visit Albert. A couple of fourteen-year-olds biking forty miles with nothing but a couple of sandwiches and apples between them. A grand adventure. The look of surprise and delight on Albert's face when they rode into the Seminary made the hard slog of nearly eight hours on the bike worthwhile. After Albert organised some dinner for them, he presented them both with St Christopher medals, 'Here's something for our intrepid travellers. He'll watch over you for your trip back,' said Albert, as he blessed the medals.

William dug the medal out from under his shirt and tie and rubbed it between his thumb and index finger. Yes, back then he idolised his older brother. When Albert was the apple of their mother's eye, when he was the pride of the family. The smile on William's face faded. Less than six years later, all had changed; shame brought upon the family, Albert disowned, banished, his name never to be spoken again. All for love. This had always eaten away at William; why all the vitriol for Albert following his heart, for doing what made him truly happy. If he'd killed someone, robbed a bank, then yeah, brand him a black sheep, but for love?

Their mother's position always struck him as an overreaction. He had some empathy for her feelings of shame, but felt railroaded into the extreme measures meted out to Albert and Abigail, and he never felt strong enough to defy Mother.

As the train swept through the wide right-hand turn on the approach to Alexandra Palace station, a wide panorama of London came into view. William and Gordon's eyes widened, and their mouths dropped open. Plumes of smoke, too numerous to count, rose like writhing, black serpents into an otherwise clear summer sky. They'd noticed the extent of bomb damage had increased for the past half-hour, but as they got closer to central London, it grew exponentially.

'Jesus wept,' said Gordo, 'I thought Jerry had eased off the bombing.'

'They have. This is nothing.' Both men turned to regard the train's conductor, who was stooped over, peering out their window. 'We're only getting about a quarter of the raids we were last summer. There'd be some days this view would be completely black, thick with smoke from the fires. The sun blocked out.'

'Where are you from?' asked William.

'North London, Finsbury Park. Not far from here.'

'How's it there?'

'Not too bad. Well, it's all relative. A couple of hot spots around Brownswood Park and Manor House. Nothing compared to those poor buggers in the East End. Had the shit blown out of 'em. You lads RAF?' the conductor asked.

'Bomber Command. 75 New Zealand Squadron,' replied Gordo.

'Hmm, right. Thanks for coming to help us. We need all hands on deck for this fight. Don't spare them a single bomb. Give those bloody Nazis a taste of their own medicine, and then some. Either of you been to London recently?' William and Gordo shook their heads, 'You're in for a shock, lads.' He stood up and walked through to the next carriage. Silent and ashen-faced, both men turned back to look out the window.

Half an hour later the spires of St Pancras station came into view; their terminus at Kings Cross was only moments away. 'You got the hotel details handy?' asked Gordo.

'The Skinners Arms on Judd Street,' replied William, as he unfolded a piece of paper from his breast pocket. 'Says it's round the corner from the station.'

The train hissed as it came to a halt in a cloud of steam. The men grabbed their bags and stepped onto the platform where they were engulfed in a stream of other passengers, shuffling to the front of the station. They emerged from one of the station's arched doorways to a swirling mass of humanity; the majority of the crowd wearing military uniforms. They fought their way to an empty spot next to a tobacconist. 'Says walk out to Euston Road, turn right, go past St Pancras Station, then left on Judd Street,' said William. 'This way,' he added as he dove into the flow of people.

Dodging the other pedestrians, William was transfixed by the gothic revival grandeur of St Pancras Station hotel. The gold trim glistening in the summer sun, contrasting to the building's dark red brickwork. He turned back to get another look at the hotel's clock tower. Its four mini-spires guarding the clock faces and main spire rising atop the whole clock tower, reminded him of a cathedral bell tower.

As they approached the corner, a pile of rubble on the street drew their gaze away from the hotel. Crossing Euston Road towards Judd Street, they saw the remnants of a building which had taken a direct hit. The fresh wound in the fabric of this majestic city was raw and vicious. Either side of the relic were elegant Georgian buildings, with long arched windows, now missing their brethren, like a missing tooth in the smile of a boxer.

'Must have been trying to hit the station,' said Gordo, 'Didn't have a bomb aimer as good as you,' he added, patting William on the shoulder.

Two blocks down the street, The Skinner's Arms beckoned them in with vibrant hanging baskets of flowers framing the entrance. Blue, purple and orange petals cascaded over the baskets and down the white plaster of the outer doorway. A blackboard proudly announced in scrawling writing, "Hearty Homemade Meals and Great Ales". As they stepped through the door, William's eyes struggled to adjust to the dark environs of the pub. The décor, at last, came into focus: the etched glass and mirrors behind the bar; the stained-glass windows; the dark wood of the bar itself and the panelling throughout the pub.

'RAF boys?' asked the bartender, 'Always a pleasure to have you lot in. What can I get you?'

'Afternoon, Sir. We've got a booking for a room. Flight Sergeants Robertson and Newdick,' replied William, as he stepped towards the bar and handed the bartender the document he'd got from one of the WAAF's at the base.

'Aussie's? Let me get me book,' said the bartender.

'New Zealanders, actually. Bomber Command, 75 Squadron,' Gordo corrected the bartender.

'Top lads. Giving Jerry a right bashing, I hope. Thank God the bastards have eased up on us. Too busy with the Russkies. A decision I reckon they'll come to regret. We had a couple of bombs hit down the street. Too close for comfort. Anyway, got you in room five. Twin singles at the back of the building; away from the street. Stairs are next to the loo,' he finished, pointing down the corridor.

They took the key, said thank you and went to find their room.

'Want to go for a wander?' asked William, as they dropped their suitcases on their respective beds. Gordo nodded.

The late afternoon sun blinded them after the dark interior of the pub. They turned to each other and William gave a nod to go left, away from Euston Road. No more than eighty yards down the street they found the next bomb site. Carved out of a neat row of residential Georgian terraced townhouses was a hole wide enough for two of the dwellings. No debris littered either lot. The site was clear, save for a small white cross in the centre of the space. Two bouquets and a teddy bear formed a miniature shrine around the cross.

The flowers were withered, with bows so faded and dirty, William couldn't make out the original colour. He could tell they were roses and carnations; three of both in both bouquets. Most of the rose petals had fallen from the stem, and lay forlornly next to the cross, like tears shed for the dead, but long since dried.

The heads of the carnations looked so delicate like they'd disappear with the slightest breath of wind. The bear was blackened with dirt and soot, but its button eyes still glowed fire orange in the summer sun.

Who had lived in the houses, William mused; a young family, cut down long before their time; an elderly couple, trying to survive the war so they could live out their golden years; a civil servant at the War Office, killed by the war they were helping plan? 'Brings it home,' he said.

Gordo tilted his head and raised an eyebrow.

'The destruction we're inflicting on each other,' continued William, 'Got to keep telling ourselves we're on the side of righteousness.'

'I'm bloody well sure, Robbie,' replied Gordo. 'The Nazis didn't come to power by revolution or coup. The Germans voted them in. They're reaping what they sowed.' William gave a couple of slow, deep nods.

Coming back onto Euston Road, they saw a small trailer with a window in it. A sign on its roof read, "Free tea for Military". They joined to queue for a cuppa.

'What'll ya have, darlings?' asked the woman in the trailer.

'Two teas, thanks. Any biscuits?' replied Gordo.

'Oh yeah, Luv, but only them nasty ration pack ones. You'll need to dunk em. Break ya teeth otherwise. You lads Kiwis or Aussies?' she asked with a warm smile.

'New Zealanders. 75 Squadron, Bomber Command, up by Ely,' replied William.

'Not too much information now, lads. Never know who's eavesdropping. Kiwis huh? Keith Park is one of yours, right. Top lad.'

'Yes, he is. You know him?' asked Gordo.

'Not really. Stops by for a cuppa when he's taking the train from these stations. Lovely bloke. Don't think we would've beaten back the Luftwaffe without him. There ya go, darlings,' she handed over the mugs and biscuits.

'Thank you. And your name?' asked William.

'Patience Brand, but folks call me "Boo". You in London town for long?'

'Only tonight and tomorrow. Need to be back on base by lights out tomorrow,' said Gordo.

'Not much time for sightseeing,' replied Boo, as she leaned over the counter of the mobile canteen, lifting the front of her wide brimmed hat.

'It's all the leave we could get. On a humanitarian trip, really,' said William. Boo cocked her head and gave them a quizzical look. 'Gordo's roommate died last week, and we've come down to see the woman he was stepping out with. They aren't married, so we don't think she knows. Going to be a tough day,' said William, then took a long drink from his cup of tea.

'So sad. Lovely you've come to see her in person. Suppose it's the one side of war us women get a lot of practice at – the heartbreak and the consoling. Never get used to it, mind,' said Boo, her gaze drifted away from the men into the evening sky, as she spoke. 'Godspeed me lovely Kiwi lads. Come see me tomorrow, if you have time before ya train.' She gave them both a warm, genuine smile, as she turned her attention to a British Army officer, standing next to Gordo.

They both finished their tea and put the mugs down on the counter and simultaneously said "Beer".

*

They stepped onto Whitechapel Road from the Tube Station of the same name. For a Sunday morning, there was an unexpected bustle they didn't experience on Sunday visits to Ely or Cambridge. To their left, a line of market stalls hugged the footpath, spilling over onto the street. All the stalls were closed, but various forms of detritus from yesterday's market day was strewn around them. Across the street, to their right, was the moderately grand façade of the London Hospital. It was the standard tan brick and blockwork of so many London buildings, but two distinct features caught William's eye; the five-arch main entrance and the large clock face at the top of the building. A noble attempt to bring some of the magnificence of Central London and the West End to the downtrodden East End.

They turned right and walked down the street, back towards the City. Within thirty yards, a now familiar ten-yard gap in the terraced buildings heralded another bomb site. Two properties were demolished; the damage looked new, with much of the debris of the buildings still in place. Next to this was a bookstore with its front blown out; the footpath was strewn with books, many mangled, torn or burnt, and the wood, glass and bricks of the building's destroyed façade. William and Gordo had to step onto the street to get around the mess. To their surprise, sitting on some of the debris, reading a book, was a young man. Looked like mid-teens to William; dressed in a tweed jacket, a black vest, dirty white shirt and tie, and black trousers. Dust covered his lapels, trousers and shoes. He appeared completely oblivious to the mayhem around him, so engrossed was he in the book. William peered into the darkened core of the shop and saw an elderly man sweeping the floor, stopping after two or three strokes to pick up another book jettisoned from the shelves by the blast's force.

A couple of boys walked past the men, stopped outside the book shop for a couple of seconds, then in a rush of grabbling hands, they scooped up a few books and started to sprint away. The old man had seen them pilfering his stock, took chase, and shouted, 'Come back here, ya little fuckers.'

'So much for the spirit of pulling together, picking oneself up, dust off, help with the clean up and get back to normal. Whatever normal looks like,' said William.

'Mongrels pop up whenever misery does. Human nature, Robbie,' added Gordo.

William opened up his satchel and pulled out a "Geographers' A to Z Atlas to London" they'd borrowed from the Base's library. He'd pre-marked the pages for this part of town and their route to get to Anne's house.

'There we are, New Road,' he said to Gordo. 'One street down to Fieldgate, then Parfett Street should be third on the left,' he continued as they crossed the street.

Approaching Parfett Street, the lot at the top of the street was another bomb site, but this one had something they hadn't seen before; vegetables growing in neat lines. Most of the rubble had been cleared, except for some remnants up against the dividing walls of the adjoining terraced houses. Most of the land had been dug up and was well tilled. Two young boys, not yet teenagers, were tending a line of beans. William also recognised peas, potatoes and carrots. The boys looked up from their work, and recognising the men's uniforms, jumped up to attention and gave two perfect salutes. Gordo and William stopped, turned to the boys and returned the salute. Big grins broke across both boys' faces before they returned to their chores.

'It's number thirty-nine. Should be about halfway down this block. There's fifty-one,' said William, as they turned the corner and crossed the narrow lane. The entire street was made up of identical, neat three-storeyed terraced houses. All houses had a brightly-coloured front door; on the left of the house on the even-numbered side of the street and on the right of the house on the odd side, a big window at ground level, and two sash windows on levels one and two. Some had attics, with dormer windows that peeked out from their roof lines.

They reached a green door, with an arch and half-round leadlight window above the doorway. Gordo knocked, his large hands creating a deep thud. The two men simultaneously inhaled a deep breath. As Gordo raised his hand again, the lock turned with a dull clunk. The door opened about five inches, revealing half of a woman's face.

'Can I help you?' she asked.

'Anne Bennett? It's William Robertson and Gordon Newdick from 75 Squadron. Can we come in to talk about Ray? William tried to ensure his voice portrayed as much empathy as possible.

'Ray? What's happened?' The door flew open and the hallway was flooded with light. Anne shielded her eyes and blinked a couple of times. The sunlight flickered off a wedding band on her left-hand ring finger. Both men turned towards each other; "Married?" Gordo mouthed to William.

'There's some bad news, afraid to say. Is there somewhere more private than the footpath?' asked William.

'Oh, yes. Please forgive me. Come this way.' She led them down the hallway and turned left into the sitting room. On a side table near Anne, William noticed a framed photograph of Anne in a wedding dress, arm in arm with a man dressed in a British Army uniform. They took a seat, and William had a chance to regard Anne; the first thing he noticed was her eyes – ice blue, piercing, knowing and already tinged with sadness. Her bright red lipstick was set against pearl white skin, which was dotted with small freckles across her cheeks. Her brown hair, with a high fringe and curled ringlets at the back, suggested a likeness to Judy Garland.

As they had agreed, Gordo led the discussion; 'I know you and Ray have been stepping out for a few months. Don't know if he talked about me, but he's one of my best mates.'

'Yes, he has, Gordon. Many times. Sounds like you two have been through a lot together,' replied Anne. William noticed her hands were clenched tightly in front of her, veins popped out and knuckles turned white from the pressure.

Gordo twisted his cap, in discomfort. 'Anne, I don't want to beat around the bush, so I won't. Ray was lost on an operation over Germany about a week ago. There's still a chance he's alive, maybe he parachuted out, got captured, or is on the run, but at the moment he's listed as Missing – Presumed Dead.'

Anne straightened herself, unclasped her hands and patted down the front of her dress. Tears fell from her eyes. 'I thought as much. He normally sends two letters a week and calls once a week; but there's been nothing in nearly two weeks.' She pulled a small handkerchief out of her left sleeve and dabbed her eyes, which were now flowing with a steady stream of tears. 'What are the chances of him being alive?'

'There's always a chance, Anne, but not great, I'm afraid,' replied Gordo.

'The flak was particularly heavy on the run,' added William. 'If they took a direct hit, well, no,' he added, as he shrugged his shoulders and gave a small shake of his head. 'There's a couple of reports from crews in their group they did.'

'Damn this war,' Anne shot the words out through gritted teeth.

'It's taking everyone.' Her shoulders rose and fell, as she gulped air to keep her emotions in check. 'Did he tell you we had plans on getting married next month?'

Both men stared with eyes wide. 'No, but aren't you?' Gordo queried, tapping on his left-hand ring finger, as William glanced back and forth between Anne and the wedding photo.

'Oh, yes, I mean I was married. War widow.' Pointing to the photograph, 'That's Peter. He was killed at Dunkirk.' William and Gordo exhaled together. 'Ray, Peter and my brother Stewart, all gone. Stewart died in North Africa. I think it hit me the hardest; tough when you lose kin for the rest of your life. Apart from Dad, there's no more men close to me for those shithouse Nazis to take.' She buried her face in the handkerchief.

'I'm so sorry to hear, Anne. It's taking a lot of good people. Ray didn't tell us about the wedding. We all would have been there for you both, had we known. Right Robbie?' William gave a small nod to Gordo's question; his mind focussed on memories of Albert, Gary and himself playing cricket on the road outside their parent's home.

'It was going to be in the local registry office. Nothing big. He said he expected to be done with his tour of operations by the middle of next month, so we had planned a week or two after,' added Anne.

Now visions of Darlene flashed across William's mind, followed by a warm glow. He shook his head to bring himself back into the conversation.

'Yeah, we're all down to a handful of ops left to go. Can't deny the anxiety levels have risen in the last few weeks. I want to be done and get through in one piece,' said Gordo. 'We don't often talk about the what-ifs, the chances of not coming back, but most of us write letters to the special people in our lives, in case the worst happens. Ray wrote one to you. There are also personal things he put aside for you,' Gordo's voice lowered as he handed the letter and a small box to Anne.

'Oh, thank you so much. I'll read it a bit later, if you don't mind,' said Anne to nods from both men.

'Also, we had a bit of a whip round amongst the crews. There's nearly fifty quid and some extra ration coupons for butter, milk and eggs,' said William, as he handed over an envelope. 'If there's anything else we can do for you, don't be afraid to ask.'

'So, so generous. Thank you. There's really no need. I have a good job at the War Office, but the coupons will certainly come in handy.' Anne stood up, straightened her dress, walked over to a sideboard and placed the envelope in one of the drawers. 'How rude of me, I haven't offered you anything to eat or drink. A cup of tea? The kettle's boiled.'

Both men nodded. 'That'd be lovely. Thanks,' said Gordo.

A few minutes later, Anne returned carrying a tray with a teapot, three cups and saucers, and a plate of biscuits. 'Plain old digestives, I'm afraid. Not much else in the shops these days. Not even shortbread,' said Anne as she poured the tea. 'Got some milk though.' She added a splash into each cup and handed the men their drinks. 'You Kiwis are such nice people. There's a couple of girls from New Zealand at the War Office. Ruth Teasdale and Mavis Kupo-Norton. You know them?' Both men shook their heads. 'I was coming around to the idea of moving there after the war. Ray was doing his best to persuade me. A new house on a quarter-acre, fruit trees, no rationing, and lovely beaches only a short drive away; it would've been some change from Whitechapel.'

'Still hold on to some hope he's made it, Anne. We know a few of our blokes are POWs, and when this is all over, they'll come back to us,' said William.

'I've found holding on to too much hope destroys you. In war, it's always shattered. That's what happened with Peter and Stewart,' Anne replied, taking a big mouthful of tea.

'We'll make sure we keep you updated on any news we get,' added Gordo. He finished his tea, 'Anne, if you don't mind, we'd better get going. We're on the last train back to Ely. Have to be back on base tonight.' Anne gave a couple of quick nods. 'Been lovely to meet you. So sad it was under these circumstances.'

'Now we've made the connection, we'll make sure we come to visit whenever we're back in London. Would that be alright?' asked Gordo.

'Yes, very nice. I'd enjoy the company. Thank you both. Look after yourselves. Be safe,' Anne said as she led them to the front door.

*

Late afternoon sun drenched the carriage in a golden hue, warming the faces of both men. The train started to pick up speed as it cleared the northern outskirts of London, and headed to Cambridgeshire. They took the last mouthfuls of tea from carboard cups they'd got from Boo and her Women's Voluntary Service canteen on Euston Road, when Gordo started to talk, 'Bloody hell, I can't imagine the loss and anguish Anne's been through.'

'Tough. No two ways about it. Brother, husband and fiancé? I'm amazed she's still in one piece herself. One or two losses like those would break most people,' replied William.

'It'd devastate me if I lost my brother. Thankfully, he's in the public service back home. No chance of him being released to join up. Your brothers in the forces?' asked Gordo.

'Um, no, no. One's like yours, a government worker, and the other is in the clerg…' William cut himself off. 'Actually, not sure what the other one is doing. Living in Auckland somewhere. Kind of lost contact.'

'Oh, sad, especially in these times. Best to keep blood close to you. Never know if we'll ever have a chance to tell them what they mean to us. Think I'll knock out a letter to mine on the way back,' Gordo added, taking out his notebook and a pencil.

William turned to the window, his mind drifted to Albert, as the green fields of Hertfordshire became a blur. Was he in good health? Where in Auckland were they living if they were still there? What did he do for a job? Did he ever think about him? What would he think of him fighting in the war? Anne's words from earlier in the day repeatedly returned to, "Tough when you lose kin for the rest of your life."

When millions of people around the world had already lost family, and millions more would before the war ended, it hit William that he, and his family, had knowingly, wilfully, lost Albert. They had banished him and Abigail, from their lives, to the point of not speaking his name when Mother was within earshot. He dropped his head, cupped his hands around his temples, and whispered 'No more. I'll find you Albert. Don't worry.'

# CHAPTER ELEVEN

*28 June 1942*

'Evening Bob. Good to see you,' said Darlene as she took a seat on one of the bar stools.

'Hello Dee. Likewise. A new outfit? Haven't seen it before. Nice,' replied Bob.

She patted down the front of her gun-metal grey pant suit. It was one of her nicest outfits and she had worn it only a couple of times since coming to Ely. Once for one of the river walks with William. 'Oh, thank you for noticing. Had it for a while, but haven't trotted it out for Friday drinks yet. We all set for tonight?' asked Darlene.

'Hope so. I've given the storeroom a bit of a tidy-up. Didn't know how you wanted it set up, so you might need to move some things around. You want a drink?' asked Bob.

'No, thanks, Bob. Better stay sharp,' replied Darlene

'Lemonade or water? Bob raised his eyebrows.

'Go on, then. I'll have a lemonade, thanks,' she said.

'You sure Milena will be in tonight?' asked Bob, as he grabbed the jug of homemade lemonade and poured some into a tall, thin glass.

'Can't be certain, but if she is sticking to her routine, she should be. You haven't noticed anything else odd about town?'

'Been keeping my eyes peeled, but nothing I would call strange. Seen Milena around a bit. You know, on the streets and in a few shops. Kept an eye on her, but nothing out of the ordinary. Oh, I did see her and Miriam driving through town. Wednesday, I think.'

Darlene exhaled, pursed her lips and drummed her fingers on the bar, 'Thanks Bob. Good to have an extra set of eyes out there. Keep thinking I've overreacted, or I'm dreaming about all this,' she said, and took a long pull from her drink.

'Don't doubt yourself, Dee. My heckles went up the first night she came into for your Friday sessions. Then that Sunday night with the black hat man? It was like a bloody air raid siren going off for me. As far as I'm, concerned, you've done the right thing. Can't be too careful these days,' he held a powerful stance, with his arms spread wide and his hands gripped the edge of the bar top.

The door opened and Hector walked into the pub. He took off his hat, ran his fingers through his hair and scanned the room, his eyes lit up when he saw Darlene.

She stepped off the bar stool to greet him, offering her hand as they drew closer, 'Hector, you found it alright?' His skin warmed hers as they shook hands.

'Darlene. Pleasure. Early again. Yes, easy enough to find. Nice pub,' he replied.

'Here, let me introduce you to the owner, Bob. This is Flight Lieutenant Hector A'Court,' Darlene pointed to Hector as she introduced him.

'Bob. Pleasure to meet you. Nurse du Toit has told me about your support and vigilance. Thank you,' said Hector.

'Just doing what I can. Something didn't sit right about those two the moment I saw them come in together. I'll put them in the snug when they arrive. I told Dee about a storage room behind the snug and there's a serving window that opens up into it. If you leave the light off in the room, open the window a smidge and stay quiet, they won't know you're there. Come, let me show you,' said Bob.

He lifted the hinged bar-top and guided them behind the bar, and down a narrow corridor. Darlene squinted as her eyes struggled to adjust to the murky light and she turned sideways to get down the hallway. Half a dozen steps in, Bob opened the door to the room, and flipped the light switch, 'It used to be a food preparation and serving room when this was a coaching inn, back in the old days. Here's the serving window. Two doors open inwards and on the snug side, two carved lattice doors open the other way. I reckon leave the lattice doors closed and open one of the doors this side. Should give you all the listening ability you'll need. Remember though, keep the light off and the main door back to the bar closed.'

'Great, Bob. This should be fine. What do you think Flight Lieutenant A'Court?' replied Darlene.

Hector surveyed the room and serving window, 'If we clear away some of this stuff, it should be fine,' he said waving at the rubbish on the floor. 'Can you make sure no one comes in?' he asked Bob.

'It's only me working tonight, so there'll only be you two back here. Good luck. Hope you get what you need,' Bob nodded to both of them and went back to the bar.

'Let's move this lot to the back of the room,' Hector pointed to some boxes, 'We can use these two barrels as seats. Alright with you?' Darlene nodded. Coming back to the serving doors, he opened them both and looked into the snug. 'Two booths and one small table in the middle of the room. Where did they sit last time?' he asked.

'The booth closest to us. Flight Sergeant Robertson and I were in the far booth,' replied Darlene.

'Hmm, yes, I can see how they didn't see you when they came in. Lucky they didn't try for the secluded booth. And how close did you get to them when they were talking?' Hector asked.

'Right up to where the booths meet. Obviously behind the seat back, so they couldn't see my head. Heard them clear as a bell.' She stepped up to the small opening to point out where she was. She could feel the heat of Hector's body and a light breeze on her skin.

'Good work, Darlene. Nice surveillance skills. Exactly what I would have done,' he gave her a small, warm smile. 'Let's sit down and get ready for them.' Hector closed one of the doors completely, and half-closed the other, then went over to the main door, made sure it was firmly closed and flicked off the light. The room plunged into deep darkness, save for a narrow sliver of hazy, diffused light coming from the snug via the crack in the serving door. The light fell directly between the two barrels they'd set up as seats and the lattice work was clearly visible in the light cast on the floor.

'I say, it is dark. You alright with this, Darlene?' asked Hector as he sat down.

'Oh, yes, fine. Needs must,' she replied. She was sure he couldn't see her nervously rubbing her hands, as she couldn't see her own hands, 'How's your German?' she asked.

'Fluent. As is my French and can hold a reasonable conversation in Spanish and Italian,' replied Hector.

'Good. Last time they came in here, they used English and Czechoslovakian. Any good at the Slavic languages?' she asked.

'Not good enough to be dropped in Eastern Europe without getting into trouble, but can tell Czech from Polish, Ukrainian and Russian,' he answered.

'They only used it for a couple of sentences. Presume the man is German and isn't fluent in Czech,' Darlene concluded.

As the minutes passed, her vision become more accustomed to the room's environment. As long as she didn't stare directly at the open serving doors, she could make out the rough shape of the room and Hector himself, sitting less than two yards away from her. All her other senses exploded. Every squeak from the room, rustle of clothing, scratch of a shoe sole on the stone floor, reverberated in her ears. The musty aromas from the room's contents, her own perfume and Hector's aftershave and hair cream assailed her nostrils. The dust stung her tongue. Her clothes felt coarse and the barrel she sat on sent tingles up her spine. Time seemed suspended; she couldn't say how long they'd been sitting in the darkness – five minutes, twenty, an hour?

As the sensory overload began to worry her, the sharp sound of the main snug door handle being turned jolted her back into focus. Two sets of footsteps echoed around the snug and through the small window to their hiding place. Then came the dull thud of glasses placed on the booth's table, and the sound of bodies shifting along the seats.

'Prost! Frau Dvořáček. Good to see you again,' said the man, followed by the clunk of glasses being touched. 'Now, what have you been able to find out this week?'

'I've heard from multiple sources the lauded thousand bomber raids haven't achieved what they expected, and losses are high. I can confirm we get busy in the hospital straight after those raids. It's likely there won't be many more big raids,' said Milena.

'Yes, High Command tell me they are losing at least twenty percent on each raid. As the Americans say, it's a turkey shoot for our air defence and the Luftwaffe,' replied the man.

'Speaking of the Americans, apparently their morale is low. They are already homesick,' added Milena.

'They are soft. Don't have the backbone for the fight. Whining about a lack of Coca-Cola, cold beer and hamburgers, no doubt. They still planning daylight bombing raids?' he asked.

'As far as I'm aware,' replied Milena.

'Anything else?' asked the man.

'An unconfirmed report that 75 Squadron won't be growing. The New Zealand government is turning its attention to the Pacific. Lastly, we are supposed to have a VIP visitor at the hospital soon. No other details yet, but I'll find out more,' said Milena.

'I will pass on the New Zealand information to the Oberst for him to check. Does not surprise me. The Japanese have had their first defeats. We fear they have over-reached and are now vulnerable. Find out about this VIP. Could be a good target for information or assassination. Now, in terms of targets, at our last bridge drop off, a woman came from the public house and read the note you'd left. It appeared she knew where to look and what she would find.'

'What? Impossible. I did my normal surveillance before and after I left the note. There were a couple of people outside the pub, but they weren't watching me. What did she look like?' asked Milena.

'Hard to tell as she was wearing a coat and hat, both were brown, but she had a bright blue scarf on. We need to find and neutralise her quickly,' he added.

Darlene leaned closer to the opening and concentrated harder. In a matter of a seconds, her breathing became quicker and shallower. She felt the blood coursing from her hands and feet. The small shaft of light came in and out of focus.

Hector leaned next to her ear and whispered, 'It's alright, Darlene. Breathe. I'm right here.'

In spite of the room being cool and musty, she started sweating; droplets formed on her top lip. The clunk and thud of footsteps from the snug shocked her back to reality. The snug door opened then closed, and the room fell silent.

'Wait,' whispered Hector.

A minute later, lighter footsteps echoed from the snug and the door handle sounded once again. A few seconds later, there was a knock on the storage room door, 'All-clear,' said Bob.

'Hector, Hector. What did they mean? He saw me at the last river rendezvous. He wants to kill me,' Darlene was panting, eyes darting from side to side.

'Darlene, no one is going to kill you. He has no idea who you are. Milena didn't connect you with his mysterious woman who checked the bridge drop spot. You obviously did a great job of disguising yourself. He doesn't know how to find you. I guarantee nothing will happen to you. For an amateur, you are fantastic at this. You've done more, found out more than most of my colleagues ever have. You have my promise, I will protect you.'

They fell into a deep embrace. Darlene held onto Hector tightly. His arms felt strong and safe. She put her face into his neck and inhaled his aroma.

*

*29 June 1942*

Her tea was now lukewarm, which caused Darlene to purse her lips, crinkle her nose and push the cup to the side of her tray. She arranged the plates on her tray and prepared to stand up, when Milena sat down in front of her. A cold shiver ran down Darlene's back and she swallowed hard.

'Hello Dee. Not in a rush are you?' asked Milena

'Um, was about to leave. Was on an early lunch, but don't have to be back on the ward for another ten minutes,' replied Darlene, her eyes darting around the dining room as she spoke.

Milena looked down at her plate, 'Leftovers from yesterday's roast, I see. Yum.'

'Tastes better than it looks. The dozy Yorkshire Pud makes it look worse than it is,' said Darlene.

'Fun night on Friday. I like the Prince Albert. Nice place.' Milena started cutting up the meat on her plate as she spoke.

'Was a good night. The crew was in fine form. Betty and Harold were really sparking. They give each other some amount of grief,' replied Darlene.

'It makes me uncomfortable sometimes. I can't get the English sarcasm. That, and cricket, still baffle me. You go there much, other than the Friday sessions?' asked Milena.

Darlene felt her eyes pierce her soul. Relax, breathe, you knew this might happen, she told herself. 'Only once or twice. I took

William there back in March, when they weren't flying so many operations.' A mix of truth, half-truth and lie.

'I'd like to meet William. You seem to be an item,' replied Milena.

'He wants to come to a Friday session. He's only one operation away from finishing his tour. Weather is supposed to be settled for the next few days, so they are hopeful they can get it done soon,' replied Darlene.

'He might pop the question once he's finished. You better be ready. If it happened, would you use St Etheldreda's? It's your church, no?'

Darlene felt the blood rush from her face, her head swam, and some bile refluxed from her stomach. 'Argh, um, St Etheldreda's? That's the Catholic Church? No, no, no. William's Catholic and he goes once and a while. My mum is Anglican and my dad is Dutch Reform. I think I'd be struck down by lightning if I set foot in a Catholic Church.' She took a gulp of her now stone-cold tea.

'Strange. Could have sworn I saw you there a few weeks ago. Mustn't have been you. You seen much of Miriam lately? Apart from Friday, she's been a bit scarce,' said Milena.

'Yeah, I noticed too. She did say they've been piling on the work since the American's arrived. Probably rushed off her feet. Oh, crikey. Look at the time.' She flipped up the watch pinned to her left chest. 'I better fly. Lovely to chat, Milena. See you during the week.' Darlene almost broke into a jog taking her tray to the kitchen. She stopped by the toilets on the way back to her ward and had the vomit her body was aching for.

Before she went back to her ward, she ran over to her room at the Nurses' Home. She swung open the wardrobe door forcefully, and flicked through her coats and jackets. She grabbed the jacket, the hat, and the blue scarf she wore at the river and bundled them up into a tight ball. She reached underneath the bed for her small suitcase and stuffed the garments in.

'You lot won't be worn again,' she whispered.

*

The Cambridge train station tea room was full to capacity; a buzz of chatter filled the air as passengers waited for their trains to take them home from their day's work or study. Darlene scanned the room and found Hector sitting at a small table in the back corner.

He stood up as she approached the table, 'Darlene, thank you so much for coming in. It's hugely appreciated,' he offered his hand and pulled out the spare chair.

'Thank you, Hector. Must admit, I almost didn't jump on the train. I'd be lying if I said I wasn't scared,' she replied.

'After what happened last night, it takes a lot of bravery to stay involved. What he said at the end would have been a shock, but as I said, they don't know you're the woman he saw, and Dvořáček doesn't know you're involved.' Hector poured some tea into the empty cup, added some milk and slid it and the sugar bowl over to Darlene. 'I have to commend you. So far, all of your information and suppositions have been absolutely spot on.'

'Oh, I could kill for a cuppa. Oops, probably not the appropriate phrase. Yes, it's good to be proven right. At least it means I'm not going loopy and seeing things that aren't there,' replied Darlene.

'If they do keep to their timetable, they should meet at the Catholic Church in Ely this Sunday. Correct?' asked Hector.

'Should do. So far, they haven't deviated from their routine.' She took a long sip of tea and her shoulders dropped as she started to relax.

'We need to have someone there to see if they do meet up, and also positively identify them both. We're close to having enough to pick them up, but we need a confirmed identification for him. The last thing we want is to sweep up the wrong person, or let either of them slip through our fingers,' he said.

Darlene straightened up and her eyes widened. 'You want me to go to St Etheldreda's? I'm not sure it's wise,' she replied.

'Oh, no. I certainly don't expect you to go. I need to go, but I thought it would be helpful if Flight Sergeant Robertson could accompany me. I know what Milena looks like, we have file pictures of her, but I don't know the man, only the description you gave me. Flight Sergeant Robertson has seen him.'

Darlene exhaled and started to rub her legs, as a flash of heat shot up her back. 'I'm not sure but I will ask. I need to let you know, Milena might be onto me, or at least suspicious. She cornered me at lunch today, and said she thought she saw me at St Etheldreda's when I went there a few weeks ago. I think I deflected her well enough, but don't know for sure. It's scared me.' She told herself not to mention Milena asking her about Miriam. No need to bring any more attention to Miriam.

'Alright. That's a worrying development. You need to keep your head down on this now. It makes it more important I identify both of them as soon as possible. Once done, I can plan the interception and arrest them. My top brass is getting pressure from her family's contacts in government to drop my investigation, but I'm going to keep going. We're onto something,' he said. 'Can you let Flight Sergeant Robertson know I'll attend Mass at St Etheldreda's this Sunday. Best we meet before the service and sit together in a strategic position.'

Darlene's hands tightened around her cup of tea. 'Sure. We are due to meet as soon as he has completed his tour. He only has one more to go. I'll get him to meet you where we have been before. It's on Egremont Street, at the far end of the church. You know what he looks like?'

'Thanks, yes I do. We have access to profile photographs of all personnel in all squadrons. As for your situation, I'll get some minders to look out for you. I'll organise it tonight. Should be in place sometime tomorrow. If they do their job correctly, you won't notice them,' said Hector.

'Very reassuring. Much appreciated. Maybe I'm overreacting and I read too much into her questions. It rattled me,' she said.

'You've done more than enough on this. Far beyond the call of duty. If they meet at church, we'll make sure it's over soon,' he replied.

'Will you be going back to HQ when it's sorted?' asked Darlene.

'I'll head back this evening to organise the resources we'll need for the next couple of weeks. It won't surprise you this isn't my only active espionage investigation. I'll come back up on Saturday and stay at Mildenhall, then go to the Mass on Sunday. I'll plan the arrest operation with my colleague and the MPs at Mildenhall. Then it'll be back to Whitehall.'

'Thought that would be the case. Shocking you are so busy with spy cases. Such is the way of things in war-time.'

The station's announcer interrupted Darlene with the details of the next train, 'Platform Three for the 17:40 service to King's Lynn. Stopping at Waterbeach, Ely then all stations to King's Lynn.'

'That's me. I'd better go. So, this is goodbye, then. Thank you for taking me seriously,' said Darlene.

'Maybe not goodbye at this stage. When we move to intercept, I'll want to get details from you of their river path drop point. We might need to have a walkthrough at the location next week. I'll be in touch,' Hector smiled warmly as he stood up to see Darlene to the platform.

As she settled into her carriage seat, feelings of excitement, fear and worry flowed through her in equal measure. The train hissed and spat out a cloud of smoke and steam as it left the station, and Darlene started to think about how she'd bring this up with William and get him to meet Hector. A wave of guilt swept over her; she needed to ask the man she had fallen deeply in love with to put himself in harm's way for a still unconfirmed spy chase.

# CHAPTER TWELVE

*Date – 29 June 1942*
*Tour of Operations Count – Operation 36*
*Target Location – Bremen, Germany*
*Assigned Aircraft – Wellington Mk.III X.3538 AA-N*
*Take-off – 23:45*

William woke up early again; his third day in a row rising before six o'clock. He rolled over onto his back, but sprung up and he patted the bottom sheet, it felt damp and his skin clammy with the sweat still moistening his shoulders and upper chest. He remembered he'd woken up during the night at least twice, and didn't get back to sleep for long periods, so wasn't sure if he'd gotten close to five hours. He shuffled down to the ablution block; his reflection in one of the mirrors stopping him in his tracks; ashen coloured skin and blood shot eyes stared back at him. He grabbed the sides of the basin, dropped his head and let out a deep breath. Then he splashed a couple of handfuls of water onto his face to try to shake off his malaise. 'Please be tonight,' he whispered, 'I can't take much more of this.'

He looked around the Sergeants' Mess but didn't see any of his crewmates having breakfast. He was halfway through his bowl of porridge before Gordo came in. He grabbed a cup of tea and sat down with William with a sharp screech of his chair.

'You can't sleep either?' asked Gordo.

'Three nights in a row. I'm knackered,' replied William.

'Me too. You wake up with the shakes?' William nodded at Gordo's question. 'Christ Almighty. I always thought being down to one last run would be exciting.' He took a long pull on his cuppa, 'For the first time since back when we were still in single figures of ops done, the nerves are frayed to hell and stress levels off the bloody charts.'

'Doesn't help the last run was another thousand bomber raid. The flak put the frighteners up me,' said William.

'They seem to know when we're coming with the big numbers and throw everything they have at us. God, please let the last run be a gardening run. A nice, easy mine-laying op would see us right. You gonna eat that toast? Don't think I can hold down porridge,' Gordo said, pointing at William's tray.

William handed over the plate to Gordo and asked, 'You done your letter yet?'

'Nope. I didn't date the last one I did, so might reuse it. Nothing more to add from the last op. Don't want to think about it too much. You?' replied Gordo.

'Haven't done a new letter for a week or so. I'll do one for the family, but Darlene and I spent Saturday afternoon together and I gave her a note then. Don't know how much longer I can take being left on one run to go,' William pushed the half-full bowl away from him. 'Lost my appetite too.'

The door swung open with a loud thud, and heavy footsteps echoed through the room. Both men swivelled their heads to the source of the commotion.

'Good news, lads,' Tas almost shouted as he approached their table at double time. 'The bus is running tonight,' a wide smile broke across his face as he spoke. 'Nothing official yet. Weather still has to play ball, but one of the senior Erks told me they're on standby for op prep and bomb loading. Heard a rumour it's Bremen,' he finished his breathless update.

William and Gordo turned back to each other, both looking dejected. 'Not exactly the target we wanted but suppose gotta be happy the run is on. A chance to get the last bastard done,' said Gordo.

William nodded, 'Probably going to get heavy flak, like Thursday, but glad we aren't going back to Happy Valley. Small mercies, I suppose,' he added.

'Should get confirmation in the next couple of hours. Time for brekkie. Will be right back,' Tas strode off to the queue for food.

'How you feeling? Not sure if my stomach is knotted because of excitement or stress,' said Gordo.

'I think it's stress for me. Lord, I want it to be over. Next few hours are going to be tough. Might go for a lap or two around the base before the op briefing. Clear a few cobwebs out of the head. Want to join me?' asked William.

'You're right, Robbie. Probably good for both of us to have as much alone time as we can get. I might head to the library. See ya at the briefing, eh,' replied Gordo. The two men nodded and went their separate ways.

William was only a couple of steps out of the Mess when Joe Quin came round a corner and bumped into him.

'Sorry Guv. Didn't see … Oh, Robbie. Was off in my own little world,' Quin said.

'No worries, Joe. Good to see you. Haven't caught up since we had our chin wag. You take that leave? You tied the knot?' asked William.

'Absolutely. Was a wonderful day, and night.' Quin waved his left hand to show off his wedding ring, and gave William a cheeky smile.

'Delighted for you Quiney.' William gave him a warm handshake, 'Thinking about popping the question to my girl too. Waiting to finish my tour. Did you follow up with Olsen?'

The smile dropped from Quin, 'Tore strips off me. Made me feel guilty about how all you blokes have come halfway round the world to fight for Britain, and I want to give up. Gave me the LMF treatment. Threatened me with a court-martial. Last thing I want to do is end up in the brig now I've gotten married. I'm still a nervous wreck, but what am I to do? Lacking moral fibre. For fuck's sake, I've done over twenty runs, killed God knows how many Germans for them, and he tells me I've got no fight in me. Bastard.'

'Got word the bus is running tonight. Bremen,' said William.

'I'll go up tonight. Not really a choice now,' replied Quin.

'You'll be right. Bertram's a top pilot, and you've got my boy Reggie in the back looking after you.' William rubbed Quin's shoulder and smiled as they parted.

William looked out on the base and thought about his route; past the barracks, then the mechanical workshops, the main service hangars, the fuel tanks, then finally the aircraft stands. His pace and gait were slower and shorter than normal, reflecting his deliberations. Could it be true, that he was only twenty hours away from finishing his tour? Less than a full day from being able to go home, if he wanted. Being free to ask Darlene to marry him, and getting out of the physical and mental grinder of operations. Also being able to stop doing the mental gymnastics of the rights and wrongs of the operations.

He knew which one was now most important to him. Snippets of the last seven months flooded into his thoughts; the bailout on his first op, the flare fire over Lübeck, the constant stream of crews and aircraft not returning and crashing, Ray Tengrove not making it back, the night he and Ossie took flak shrapnel, the fear and stress of the thousand bomber raids, the hellish images of swirling firestorms sweeping over the target cities.

Visions he knew would stay with him to his last breath and would probably come back to him when he least expected and wanted them. He knew such was the lot of all who had been through the nightmare of war, and all those still to experience it. If he did make it through alive tonight, there'd be another young Kiwi lad to take his seat on the next raid, and others to take their spot. The conveyor belt would never stop.

Ever since he took the shrapnel and had a few days in hospital, Albert has been increasingly on his mind. The parallels between what he and his brother had been through were staring at him, blinking like the coastal lighthouses which helped guide them home. They'd both had their own near-death experiences, both fell in love with the Nurses who'd treated them, both questioned their commitment to the church, although his was minuscule in comparison to his brother, and both moved a long way from family for their callings. Were he and Albert really so different? Was Albert's decision so hard to understand and reconcile? Halfway through his return to the barracks, William came to the realisation he had to do all he could to have his brother back in the family fold.

Back in the barracks, William grabbed one of his family photos, took out his letter writing kit, his last "special letter" to use as a guide, and started writing to the family.

*29th June 1942*
*Dear Gary,*

*All my love to you and Sarah.*

*This is the most difficult letter I've ever had to write. It's the morning before what should be my last operation. So close to finishing my tour, I can taste it. Only a five-hour operation stands between me and freedom.*

*We think there's an op tonight, but if you have this letter, it means I haven't made it back. So close and yet so far. Never has that saying had so much meaning.*

*If we have gone down, there is always hope I've managed to bailout and I am a POW somewhere in Germany. We constantly get updates on the lads who are POWs, so until you hear otherwise, believe I'm still alive.*

*Getting this close to the finish line has forced me to think deeply about a few things. If I have come up short, I need to ask you to do something for me. It's five years since Albert and Abigail ran off, and they have been on my mind a lot recently. Where they are, what they are doing, have we got any nieces and nephews whose lives we aren't involved with? I'm absolutely positive we haven't made the right call in shunning them.*

*I need you to start making some enquiries about where they are. You'll need to keep Mother and Father in the dark. You know how she'll react. This isn't a request, more of a demand. Think of it as my dying wish. I know you may not want to, or you may feel unable to cross Mother's instructions.*

*This is where I'm going to repeat what I've written on previous final letters, which thankfully haven't needed to be sent. I demand this because if I have died, I don't want you to have lost two of your three brothers out of your life. The biggest and most chastening lesson of this war, for me, is life and family are too precious, and to knowingly and willingly lose people from the family is madness.*

*Thank you for being a wonderful brother. What a fantastic life and incredible memories we have had. You and the rest of the family have been in my thoughts on each op and will be again on tonight's flight.*

*Love now and forever,*
*William*

He reread the letter a couple more times, folded it up, slipped it into an envelope, popped Gary's address on it, then headed out to find the ground crew to hand over the letter.

*

The process of preparing for a raid was, by now, almost carried out by rote. Many of the men got to the point of doing it in a trance-like state. This evening, however, William paid particular attention to each aspect, every button, clip and clasp, and layer of clothing. His senses were at an extreme elevated level; his vision narrowed and highly focussed, the aroma of his leather jacket filled his nostrils, his fingers felt large and ultra-sensitive, making fastening the clips and buttons almost painful. First stage was long-johns, then his standard uniform, including shirt and tie, and finally he grabbed his old faithful leather flight jacket. He turned to his small chest of drawers, where his photographs were arranged in an arc in the middle; propped up on one of the frames was the photo he had of Darlene at The Cutter Inn. He picked it up and tried to straighten out the dog-eared corners and frayed edges. He then softly stroked Darlene's face and tucked the photo into the left breast pocket of his uniform.

As they left their room, Reggie put his hand on William's shoulder, 'Y'all be mighty careful tonight. Tell Ossie, nothing crazy. Y'all and Gordo gotta come back in one piece. Hear me, Billy-Bob?'

'Thanks, Reggie. Let's not think about it, eh mate? It's another run. Same as usual. Give Quin one of your bear hugs. He's having a rough time. I'll see you back here soon enough.' The big man pulled William into his chest, then gave him a firm slap on the back.

At the crew hut, William put on his overalls, pulled on his lined boots, the flight jacket, life jacket, then the harness for the parachute and mask. Last things were the silk inner gloves, thick leather outer gloves, helmet and the all-important operations briefcase.

A heavy silence settled over the Osborne crew, all weighed down, as if they were wearing the massive, electrically-heated flight suits of the gunners. The last vestiges of twilight dimly lit the men's faces as they stood outside the crew hut, waiting for the truck to take them to the aircraft. Feet shuffled, body weight shifted, and heavy sighs started to break the veil of calm. Tas nudged his way between William and Gordo, put his hands on their shoulders and gave them both a squeeze.

Boss and Ossie broke out of the line as soon as the truck shuddered to a stop. They unhooked the tailgate, jumped up into the back and offered their hands to the other three. Boss dug into the inside of his flight jacked, pulled out a pack of cigarettes and his lighter, popped a couple up out of the opening and offered them to William and Gordo, then Ossie and Tas. The flame of the Zippo lighter and resulting glow from the lit smokes illuminated their faces.

The unending noise emanating from the truck broke the silence on the trip out to the aircraft stands, then there was an unmistakeable belch from someone throwing up; one of the young pups on another crew had his head over the tailgate and his upper body heaved with multiple convulsions. The Osborne crew nodding together knowingly.

Gordo and William brought up the rear of the line of five men as they walked slowly to X3538. William liked the plane as it performed well; he was happy it'd take them up tonight. William smirked as he watched Gordo waddle in front of him. His oversized flight suit made him look like the Michelin Man. He stepped up to him and slapped him on the backside. 'Hurry up ya big lump. We'll miss the bus,' he said with a wide grin.

'Wouldn't be such a bad thing today,' Gordo replied, tapping William on the top of his helmet as they got to the aircraft.

'You get in. I want to give her a once-over. I did a quick tally up, and tonight will be the twenty-third run we've done with her. NUTS has been a bloody good plane for us,' said William to the crew, all of whom nodded at William's affection for X3538. He did a lap of the plane, stopping to pat different parts; the main fuselage, the propellers. He paid particular attention to the windows of the bomb aimer's bay, rubbing away some soot and buffing up the glass, 'Number twenty-three together, old girl. One last time. You'll get us through, won't you?' he asked in a soft, low voice.

As he returned to the ladder leading to the crew door, he stopped to say his usual prayer, 'Dear Lord, watch over us all tonight. Keep all the crews safe and return them home in one piece. Protect your flock one more time. Now I have someone to live for, guide me through the valley of death to be with her.' He crossed himself, kissed his hand and placed it on the belly of the aircraft.

The big Bristol Hercules engines fired up, with the usual cough and splutter, pouring exhaust fumes into the cabin. Ossie took them down to their allotted assemble point and waited for the order to taxi and take-off. William gave Ossie one last reminder of the initial phases of the flight plan, then the order to go came through. 'Crew, ready for take-off,' announced Ossie.

The plane shuddered, rattled and moaned as Ossie pulled it up into the night sky. The whole crew were quiet and subdued, all aware that with forty percent of the crew on their last run, a misplaced word or quip could upset the morale or jinx the flight.

William was deep in concentration, studying his maps and charts when Gordo came on the intercom, highly distressed, 'Lord Almighty. We've lost one behind us. They've gone straight into the deck from take-off. Oh, sweet Jesus. Robbie, it might have been Reggie. I think they were a couple behind us. Sorry mate.'

William ripped his mask off and jumped up to the observer's dome, to see a fireball rising into the dark night sky, 'No. No. No. Reggie. Quin.' He looked to the sky, 'Damn you to hell. What did I ask you a minute ago? This is what I get?' He slumped to the floor. Boss came over from the wireless position. He put his arm around William, pulled him up to his seat and whispered a reassuring word in his ear. William dropped his head, resting it on the desk and crossed himself. Back to business, come on now, there's a job still to do; he said to himself, the time for grieving will be later.

*

The run over to Bremen was smooth and quiet. Too quiet for William's liking. It was the smallest amount of flak they'd been through in about three months. The target zone was a few minutes away, so he took up his position in the bomb aimer's bay as Ossie took the plane down to bombing altitude; yes, business as usual, one last time. More death and destruction to drop. Reggie's words came back to him in his full Cajun drawl, 'Fuck 'em, Billy-Bob. Dey brung dis shit on demselves. We're God's vengeance.'

Ossie held the plane steady, 'We're on course. You should have the target within two minutes, Robbie,' he announced.

William picked up the bomb release trigger, looked through the sights, and checked the wind speed and drift. Landscape features matched the charts and maps of the area around the target came into view; almost there, all readings were within range. The drop coordinates and landmarks now matched, William hesitated for a couple of seconds; images of Darlene, Reggie, Ray and the London bomb sites flashed into vision. He shook his head to clear his sight, then pressed the trigger. 'Load one gone,' he said over the intercom. He reached over to the bomb selector unit, flicked the switch for load two, rechecked the sights, pressed the trigger, and repeated until the entire load was dropped. 'Bombs gone. Target area photographs about to be taken; Gordo, check for detonation. Let's go home,' William said to the crew. He lay there for a few seconds, rubbing his eyes and exhaling heavily, 'Job done,' he said to himself.

*

With the summer solstice just over a week ago, dawn came early, and was breaking as they approached Feltwell. The golden rays flooded the inside of the plane. 'Dear Lord. That is one magnificent sunrise,' Gordo said, as he got the full force of daybreak in the rear turret. William went up to the observer's dome and looked back to the east. A small bank of clouds sandwiched the sun to the horizon, causing some of the rays to become visible. The gilded light made the fields of crops glint and glow, and the ponds and drainage channels twinkle. Yes, indeed, a green and pleasant land, he thought. A land worth defending. A land, thanks in part to their efforts, which would not bow or be beaten. William smiled and nodded, 'Thanks for the welcome home, Britain. Happy to serve you on days like this,' he said quietly.

'Crew, prepare for landing,' Ossie instructed. A hush descended upon the plane. This was the last high-risk manoeuvre; they'd seen too many crashes and deaths on landing to take it for granted. William crossed himself one last time. The next three minutes seemed to last an hour; time did appear to be suspended. The tension was almost visible. Boss had his eyes closed and was mouthing 'Come on. Come on.'

The whole plane shook violently as the main wheels hit the runway harder than a usual Ossie landing. They bounced off the ground for a couple of seconds, then came down again. Ossie powered down slightly, allowing the tail to drop gently. He fully powered down, 'Sorry for the bump, lads. Safe and sound now. Welcome home.' There were a couple of woops from Tas and Gordo.

The deceleration pushed William forward, but he was shaking his clenched fists in delight, 'Thanks Ossie. A sensational piece of flying. Top stuff, mate,' he said over the intercom.

'A wizard prang to finish off your tour,' said Boss. A big gloved thumbs up came from around the partition from him. William grabbed Boss's hand and held it tightly.

All five men squinted in the growing sunlight as they stood in front of the aircraft. Deep, long and heavy handshakes with a few back slaps were exchanged all round. Gordo and William couldn't contain their smiles; they'd made it, difficult to believe and one of the smoothest ops ever to finish off their tour. Oh, the irony, thought William.

'By Jesus, lads, there's going to be some session at the Mess tonight,' shouted Tas, trying to be heard over the rumbling of the transport truck. 'Best you lot get some beauty sleep, 'cause I ain't going to let you bow out early on this one.' They all laughed and nodded as they handed around a couple of hip flasks.

At the Briefing Hall, Ossie and William recorded the operation details, including a successful bomb drop on the target. As soon as they were finished, William went over to the aircraft board and looked down the list. He wasn't holding out any hope, as it always seemed to be dashed in Bomber Command, and sure enough, next to the entry for Reggie and Quin's plane was: Crashed on T/O – All crew killed.

Ossie put a hand on his shoulder, 'So sorry, Robbie. This was meant to be a joyful day for you. This is terrible.'

'Thanks Ossie. You know Reggie and Betty are an item now, and he said a couple of days ago that because of her, he regretted signing back on and was going to ask if he could pull out. You didn't know Quin, but he got married a couple of weeks ago. Damn this war.' He turned to Ossie, his eyes puffy and red. 'Looks like another two of those visits needed.' Betty was quickly replaced by Darlene in his thoughts, 'I need to try to get hold of Darlene before she starts her shift. Thanks for the support, Ossie. See you a bit later.'

He jogged over to get on the phone at the barracks, but he knew he'd be lucky to get Darlene. 'Could I speak to Staff Nurse du Toit? Already gone? OK, thank you. Can I leave a message? Fabulous. Nice and short, please tell her William made it back safe and sound. On base and will call later. Thank you.' He exhaled and his shoulders dropped as he replaced the receiver.

William stood in the doorway of his room, staring at Reggie's bed; he couldn't cross the threshold, as if a force field kept him out, and rooted to the spot. A wave of guilt swept over him; why Reggie and not him?

The randomness of life and death in this war, and specifically in Bomber Command, was something he constantly struggled with. The difference between the two could be as minimal as taking off ten seconds earlier, or later, than you did, being in one part of the aircraft versus another. None of it made sense to him anymore, if it ever did.

He stepped into the room and a chill ran up his body. At Reggie's bed, William peeled from the wall a picture of Reggie and Betty; he hadn't been able to buy a frame yet. It was of them at the dance. It was like she had transformed him, instantaneously. Every spare minute he had in those past few days, he'd spent down at RAF Mildenhall with Betty. Only three nights ago, Reggie had snuck off base without a pass, and borrowed a villager's bicycle to keep a rendezvous with her. He remembered being woken up at three o'clock in the morning by Reggie clambering into their room through the window. William smiled broadly.

On the bedside table was a framed photograph of Reggie, his parents and his younger sister in front of the St Louis Cathedral in New Orleans. Big smiles on all four of them, with the three spires of the Cathedral towering above them.

Although they were both Catholic, William always was intrigued by the differences between their experiences; Reggie, from the French-influenced, deeply conservative southern American strand, and he from the Irish and English-leaning, slightly more liberal New Zealand thread.

There weren't any shades of grey in Reggie's views and the Old Testament loomed large in his consciousness. William, however, could appreciate both sides of an argument and he preferred the New Testament. It made for some interesting discussions, and some short ones when Reggie was adamant about a topic. Certainly, Albert's relationship and his decision to run off with Abby, got a swift verdict from Reggie; disgraceful was one of the more polite words he used. William had found himself defending, or at least rationalising Albert's actions, much to his own surprise.

He opened up Reggie's drawer; a Rosary, Bible, a packet of Lucky Strike cigarettes (he always had a couple of packs on the go – one on him and a back-up), a brooch in the shape of a rose (he presumed it was Betty's), a half-finished letter to his parents, his order papers confirming his re-signing for another tour, and a piece of shrapnel he kept as a good luck charm. It had hit his gun turret and wedged in the plane less than six inches from his head; again, the randomness of life and death. That was it. Mementoes of a straightforward man who lived an uncluttered life. He picked up the writing pad which had the embryonic letter to Reggie's parents. He prevaricated about reading it; was it an invasion of his privacy, something a good friend shouldn't do? It was only two paragraphs long, so he thought there couldn't be anything too earth-shattering in such a short piece.

*Saturday June 27th, 1942*
*Dear Mother and Father,*

*I do hope this note finds you in good health and all is well at home.*

*I have some big news for you. I have met a wonderful woman here and am going to ask her to marry me. Her name is Betty Hardwick, and she is a radio operator in the RAF Women's Auxiliary. This obviously will come as a shock to you both, especially as I was never one to step out with anyone for more than a few months. I wasn't expecting this to happen myself, but she has absolutely knocked me over. Who'd have thought I would have to come to the English countryside in the middle of a war to find love.*

*I already have my best man picked. He's my roommate Billy Robertson. I have talked about him in letters before. He's the dandy fella, all the way from New Zealand. We have been sharing a room since he arrived late last year. We were in the same flight crew for a few weeks but got split up. We've stayed friends ever since. Well, you have to really, if you are going to share a room. He's the brother*

*I always wanted. I now can't imagine my life without him around. I know he'll go back to New Zealand someday, and I'll either stay here with Betty or we'll return to New Orleans. Either way, he won't be nearby. That makes me sad. To have someone who means so much to you removed from your life will be difficult, I imagine. I'll need to find a way to keep him in my life.*

William stared out the window. The things men keep from each other; the depth of their true thoughts and feelings. Reggie could hardly have concealed this any better if he was a spy, trained in the art of secrecy. He was delighted to know Reggie better. He started to make a mental list of jobs to do; top of the list would be a visit with Betty, and a letter to Reggie's parents. He put his flight jacket back on, left the barracks walking towards the transport pool to borrow a vehicle to find Reggie's plane.

A couple of miles north of the base, he found the wreckage. William stopped the car short of the crash site. The morning sun glinted off the bare aluminium skeleton of the plane. He took in a deep breath to fortify himself as he approached the metal carcass. Even from fifty yards away, it was clear why there were no survivors.

He came to Reggie's rear turret position first; 'God, I hope he died on impact,' William whispered. Save for a few feet on the right-hand rear of the fuselage, the entire skin of the plane had been burnt off. Looking into the turret, his heart sank; it was completely black and charred, the metal bent and disfigured. He rested his head on one of the few intact glass panels.

As he continued his inspection, the state of the front of the plane made him freeze. From the wings to the front turret, there was not a piece of the fuselage intact or recognisable; it was twisted and molten metal. A combination of exploding fuel from full tanks, a complete bomb payload and munitions, had either ripped the plane apart or melted what was left. There was no cockpit, no nose, bomb-aimer's position, or front turret. The left-side engine was twisted and laying on its side. Quin and the rest of the crew never stood a chance. At least death would have been instantaneous.

You have to be thankful for small mercies. William crossed himself twice and whispered a prayer for the crew, before looking up to the sky, 'There for your grace goes each of us,' he said.

Back in their room, William took out a pad and started writing.

*Tuesday June 30th, 1942*
*Dear Mr and Mrs Dubois,*

*My name is William Robertson, and I am a good friend of your son, Reginald.*

*It is with infinite sadness I need to let you know that Reggie has died while on active duty with our squadron. I can't go into any great detail, but it was an accident related to a recent operation. I assume by now you have received official notification from the British War Office. Please forgive me if this letter reaches you before the War Office correspondence.*

*I have known Reggie for nearly a year, with us being crewmates late last year, then roommates for the past seven months. I am honoured to count Reggie as one of my best friends. We've been through a great deal together, including bailing out of a stricken aircraft (on my first operation) and falling in love almost simultaneously with two wonderful women we've met here in Britain.*

*I enclose a letter Reggie started to you only three days ago. Some of its contents will come as a surprise, as it did to myself, but certainly shows the character of Reggie. I always found him to be generous, loyal and full of life. I had hoped to be friends with him for the rest of our lives, swap stories of our adventures after the war, and come to visit our respective homes. Sadly, that now will never be. Although we are very different personalities, and from dramatically diverse backgrounds, we did share many things in common and were able to chat at length on any topic imaginable. His passion for life made him a force of nature and a foil to my stoicism. I will miss him with every fibre of my being.*

*I cannot begin to feel the level of grief you must be going through, and it will be of little comfort, but please know he was an outstanding member of our squadron, greatly admired and respected. We took him to our hearts, and he will always be an honorary 'Kiwi'.*

*Yours with my deepest sympathy,*
*Flight Sergeant William Robertson*
*75 New Zealand Squadron*
*RAF Bomber Command*

William took both letters, folded them in half, took the photograph of Reggie and Betty, placed it inside the letters and slipped them all into an envelope. He slumped onto his bed and fell asleep.

*

A series of heavy knocks on the door roused William from his deep slumber. 'Robbie. You awake mate? We're heading to the Mess for dinner in ten minutes,' yelled Tas.

Dinner? What, when? William thought to himself. He rubbed his eyes and looked at his watch – ten to five. More than five hours of sleep without stirring. 'Yeah, good as gold. I'll see you there,' his voice broken and raspy. William knew Tas would be leading the last raid booze-up for himself and Gordo. There'd be no hope in keeping up with Tas, but a big session ahead.

He straightened his shirt, re-did his tie, put on his regular service dress tunic, and grabbed his cap as he walked out the door. He only got as far as the barracks phone. He picked up the receiver and asked the base operator to be put through to the Ely Hospital. He got the hospital switchboard operator to connect him to Darlene's ward. The minutes of silence before she came to the phone seemed to drag on endlessly. He straightened up as soon as he heard her voice.

'Hello, Staff Nurse du Toit. How can I help you?' she asked.

'Darlene, it's William. I'm safe,' he almost shouted down the line. Silence greeted him. He heard a couple of sobs and deeper breaths, 'You still there, Honey?'

'Yes, yes, yes. Oh, William, I'm … Sorry, I've been beside myself all day. We knew there was an operation last night and we had a few wounded come in. I was praying for you all day,' she gulped in air between sentences.

'I left a message at the Nurses' Home. Obviously, you didn't get it, but I'm fine. Not a scratch on me. I'll make this quick, you're still on shift and the lads are waiting for me. I'll pick you up after work tomorrow. OK?' his voice ached with longing.

'Lord, please do. I'll count down the minutes. Love you,' she replied, now with joy in her voice.

'Love you, too. See you tomorrow.' William hung up and turned to walk out with a huge smile across his face.

The crew were in their usual spot in the Sergeants' Mess; far corner from the door, last table, next to the window. Five pints of bitter were on the table, but no food yet. As expected, the pint in front of Tas was half empty already. 'Robbie,' all four men shouted in unison. 'Was about to send out a search party,' added Boss.

'There you go lad. You're a couple of sips behind. You'll make it up,' said Tas.

Ossie stood up; the table quickly fell silent. 'Before we kick off the festivities for Gordo and Robbie, the first toast is to the Ragin' Cajun, Reginald Dubois, and the whole crew of X3333. The loose unit from Louisiana, the Cajun Kiwi. Here's to the larger than life legend. To Reggie. Rest in peace, big man.'

'Reggie,' the others clinked their glasses and took a hefty pull on the amber contents.

'Now, to Gordo and Robbie. Tough to say exactly what these two mean to us. The longest serving members of the Leggett and Osborne crews. Over twenty runs with me and some bloody hairy moments. Gordo, will we ever forget the flare fire over Lübeck? Nothing short of a miracle we didn't go down in a ball of flames or have to bailout. Robbie, looking after me when I took the shrapnel, and you almost lost a kidney as your reward. At least you got to spend a couple of days under the healing hands of Nurse du Toit,' Ossie winked as the others hooted and cat-whistled.

William shook his head and took another mouthful of beer. 'Seriously, most crews which stay stable all say they have the best lads, but honestly, you two blokes are some of the best in the business. The next run won't be the same without you. You've more than earned the privilege of getting out of the grinder. To Gordo and Robbie.' Tas and Boss joined in the salute. All five men took big gulps of beer.

Tas slammed down his glass, now empty, 'Another round,' he said getting up and heading to the bar.

'Thanks Ossie. Really appreciate it. Can't lie, lads, I'm bloody happy to be finished. I know it's shit for you to hear when you have a few more to go, but you're going to get through alright. I can feel it,' said Gordo.

'Cheers, Ossie. Likewise, lads. I know we shouldn't talk about it, Boss and Tas, you only have a couple to go and Ossie, about ten. You'll all make it. No doubt about it,' added William.

'Sup up, lads. You're falling behind,' said Tas as he placed a tray of five more pints on the table. 'Bottoms up you two,' he said, looking at Gordo and William, who obeyed the instruction.

William turned to Gordo, 'What's the story, Gordo? What's the plan for you?' he asked.

'Hoping to get home as soon as I can. With my time in Maritime Reconnaissance, I might be able to get back,' replied

Gordo. 'Thought about going into an instruction squadron and the brass are pressuring me to stay, but I've had a guts full. I'll try to get down to London one more time. Would like to see Anne again to check how she's getting on. Maybe Boo can give me a guided tour of London. I still haven't seen any of the sights. They'll kill me back home if I come back without seeing Buckingham Palace or Big Ben. Other than that, get on the first available troopship back. What about you, Robbie?'

'I'm going to stay. I've talked to the big wigs about a position. The squadron's going to get Stirling's soon and there's a new navigation system coming down the line too. They need experienced navigators to advise the young ones and work on flight plans. And ...' he trailed off, and Gordo cocked his head, 'Well, I want to stay close to Darlene for as long as I can,' William finished.

'Righto. Sounds serious. Should we get our dress uniforms dusted off for a special day?' asked Gordo, with a cheeky grin.

'Ease up, Gordo. Don't get ahead of yourself, but it might pay to make sure the moths haven't been at them,' William said with a warm smile.

'You bloody little beauty. Mum's the word, Robbie,' replied Gordo.

'After all the shit we've been through, it feels right to have some joy back,' said William.

'Know what you mean. I want to get back to the shaky isles as quickly as I can,' Gordo said. 'We've done more than our fair share, Robbie. Hell, how much luck have we had to still be alive and pretty much unscathed?' Gordo held his glass up for William to clink. 'I know I was a bit harsh with my views on the bombing strategy. Suppose it was a way to get through the runs, trying to justify the losses we got hit with.'

'Don't worry, Gordo. We all had to get numb to it. We've seen some of those poor bastards who let it get to them. Suppose it's a bit more confronting for me, as I was the one who had to flick the drop switch, seeing the target zones and all the fires. I talked to Pruno about this when he finished. Told him we had to try to smother this with lots of new, good memories. You get home as quick as you can. Imagine Gordo, it'll be heading into summer by the time you get there. Lazy days at the beach, fishing, and cold beers.'

'Stop, Robbie. Christ, I can see it now; shorts and a floppy hat, with a bloody monster snapper on the line,' replied Gordo.

'Oi, you two. Stop yakking and start drinking. You're falling behind.' Tas stood over them with a near empty glass.

# CHAPTER THIRTEEN

*1 July 1942*

Lying in bed, William was glad he'd told Darlene he'd see her after work. His head was still fuzzy and the inside of his mouth dry. He looked across at Reggie's empty, still made bed; sheets crisp and tightly tucked under the mattress, the single wool blanket neatly draped over the end of the bed. His internal voice told him not to forget to take Reggie's special letter for Betty and give it to Darlene today. He rubbed a tear from each eye.

He checked his watch, 'Bugger. Missed breakfast,' his raspy voice surprising him. Never mind, he'd go to the Mess to grab a cuppa and scone. Maybe the cooks would take pity and whip him up some eggs.

He eased himself up on one elbow, then swung his legs out of bed, careful not to move too quickly. His head still swooned and swam, so he grabbed his mattress to steady himself. 'Bloody Tas Morris. Booze hound,' he croaked. He slowly stood up, picked up his towel and toiletries bag and shuffled off to do his ablutions.

After a bath, shave and brushing his teeth, he felt more human. He opened his wardrobe and looked at his flight gear, never to be worn again for a live operation. It was hard to comprehend; thirty-six ops completed, now free from the horrors of a new run over enemy territory.

He put on his day uniform, but no long-johns, gloves, or his trusted leather flight jacket. As his hangover diminished, he felt light and unburdened for the first time since March, when raids were few and Darlene had relocated to Ely. March? It seemed like an eternity ago; a different season, almost ten different crewmates since then, over thirty fewer ops, before the thousand bomber raids, and a couple of major near-death experiences. He looked at himself in his small desk mirror; his skin looked and felt dry, there were small bags under his eyes and the beginnings of crow's-feet around the corners of his eyes. He knew he was gaunter and more creased than back then. A new chapter of life was about to start. A warm wave swept over him at the thought of seeing Darlene again and her being a more stable and regular part of his life. Leaving his room, his first stop was the motor pool to reserve a car, then to the Mess for sustenance.

*

She turned on her heels to pace out her tenth lap of the Nurses' Home foyer, as much in her wait for William, but also to check out her pant suit. She'd decided to add a splash of colour with a red and white striped blouse. Although tonight wasn't an official celebration, she wanted to make William's end of tour memorable. She added a ruby and gold brooch to her left lapel to set the ensemble off.

'Wow. You look stunning. What a great outfit.' Darlene spun around to face the entrance when she heard William's voice. They both broke into a jog as they came together and fell into a deep embrace and a passionate kiss.

'I can't believe it. You've actually finished and you're in one piece,' Darlene pulled back to look him up and down, while vigorously rubbing his arms. 'I haven't had much sleep the last couple of nights. Firstly, for the worry of if you'd make it back, then last night for the excitement of seeing you again.' She leaned in to kiss him again, as the body warmth between them built quickly.

She pulled him closer to her for a few more seconds, before they separated and went to his car.

Bob gave his usual warm welcome as they stepped into the pub, 'Dee and William. This is a surprise of a Wednesday.'

'Evening, Bob. Celebrating my end of tour. Definitely worth a drink,' replied William.

'Or two. Congratulations. You must be delighted. That's some achievement. The usual? They're on me,' Bob had a broad smile on his face as he started to pour the drinks.

'Thank you, too kind, Bob. Honestly, I don't know how you make a profit. So generous,' said Darlene.

'Don't worry. It's only the special and nice people I shout drinks for, and believe me, there's plenty of folks who don't get a freebie. Here you go. Snug tonight?'

Darlene and William gave a small shake of their heads together. 'We'll be fine here. Might take our Friday night table,' said Darlene as she took the lead and walked over to her crew's regular spot.

William pulled out Reggie's letter to Betty and placed it on the table in front of Darlene. 'Sorry to start off with bad news, but Reggie died the same night as my last op. Here's a letter he wrote to Betty. Can you give it to her? With her WAAF job, I presume she already knows, but it'd be good for her to get this.'

'Oh Lord, no. I hadn't heard. How did it happen? Shot down over Germany?' asked Darlene. She took William's hand and squeezed it.

'No. That's the kick in the teeth. Crashed on take-off. Barely got off the ground. We lost the whole crew,' William lightly spun his pint glass around as he spoke.

'William, I'm so sorry. Did you get to see him?'

He shook his head then took a sip of beer, 'By the time we got back, and I was able to get to the crash site, they'd removed the bodies. Wouldn't let me see him in the morgue. Funeral will be

Friday. Should have finished a few runs ago, but he signed up for a new tour. God, this war is getting more brutal, and I can't see it being over for a few more years yet.'

'I'll pop over to see Betty tomorrow. She'll be devastated,' Darlene added.

'I saw a half-finished letter to his parents. He was so smitten with Betty. He said he was going to ask her to get married. Best not tell her. It will only upset her more.'

'Good to know. Makes me doubly thankful you got through alright. Have you got your plans sorted?' she asked.

'I've finally made up my mind,' he said, holding Darlene's hands, 'I'm going to stay here and become a navigation advisor. I'll still be attached to 75 Squadron, helping with the roll-out of new aircraft.'

She threw her arms around his neck and showered him in kisses all over his face. She pulled back from him and he saw tears rolling down her face, 'Don't worry, these are happy tears,' she said. 'This is the best news ever.'

'I didn't want to plan too far ahead. Never a good idea in Bomber Command, but I've had some discussions with the squadron's brass, and they've committed to put me up for a promotion to Warrant Officer. I gave them the final decision this afternoon,' he added.

'Amazing. Oh my, I am beyond excited. Not having to leave Feltwell is a major bonus. What will you be doing?' asked Darlene.

'The squadron will be upgraded to Stirling's over the next few months and more crews will be formed, so they need experienced people to help with the flight planning and advising the really green navigators. I'm delighted with the job,' he replied.

'And so much safer. It means a lot,' added Darlene.

'I won't need to start straight away. Got a decent amount of end-of-tour leave due to me.' He took a long pull on his pint,

'I've been meaning to ask you about the photographs you had in your flight jacket,' said Darlene. William fidgeted in his chair and stared at his drink. She reached over and held his hand, 'It meant so much you had the pic of us at the pub. Have to say, I had a wee cry when I pulled it out of your pocket. I'm intrigued by the other one. Are they your brothers?'

'The four of us? Yeah, but how'd you know?' asked William.

'You're the spitting image of each other. Even the young one. Same nose, smile and chin. Four peas in a pod. You never told me you had a brother in the clergy. Very prestigious to have a sibling in the Church,' Darlene smiled as she spoke.

'It's complicated.' William sucked on his teeth and mulled over his reply. 'That's Albert. The eldest. He was a priest. Fully ordained, in fact. The picture is at Gary's wedding. He's the next oldest. Albert did the ceremony. Then,' he looked at the ceiling for a few seconds. Darlene squeezed his hand. 'Then he threw it all away and ran off to get married.'

Darlene rocked back and straightened up, 'He did what? Married? But, but, you're Catholic. That's not allowed, is it?' She took a strong pull on her gin and tonic.

'Exactly. It caused a huge rift in the family. Mother was devastated. He was ex-communicated immediately,' added William.

'Dear Lord. He must love her. Do you know her?' asked Darlene.

'No, not all. They met in the aftermath of a massive earthquake back home. Albert got severely injured and Abigail's a Nurse who got sent to his seminary to tend the wounded. By all accounts, he saw her and fell in love with her. Must have thought she was an angel sent to save him,' replied William.

'Oh, how beautiful. A proper forbidden love story. They ran away soon after?' asked Darlene.

'There's the kicker. Took them seven years. No one knows if they were seeing each other the whole time, or they happened to reconnect years later. He ended up as a teaching Father at a college. One day he was at school, the next he'd disappeared. High-tailed it off to Auckland and got hitched in 1937. No one in the family has made contact since. Mother black-listed them.' William exhaled, then took a large drink of ale.

'What? That's not right. They could have children by now. William, you're probably an uncle. You have to find him again. Do you know if they are still in Auckland? You must try to make contact when you eventually go back.' Darlene had fixed him in a strong stare.

'I was thinking about trying to track them down,' he shrugged his shoulders as he spoke.

'There's no thinking about it. You must. Surely this war has taught you to pull those you love close to you,' she added.

'Yes, yes. I know, you're right. I'd come to the same conclusion and promised myself. If it's only for me, I still have to do it.' Darlene smiled warmly and leaned in to hug him. He then tried to switch subjects. 'So, what's been happening with those two spies? You haven't told me anything about them for a couple of weeks.'

'Fortuitous you ask. Massive developments and at lightning pace,' Darlene leaned forward, broadened her shoulders, and gave William a full update on all her activities over the past couple of weeks.

'If they are spies, it won't take long before they start to connect the dots they are being watched. I need to take you to RAF Intelligence. We have an officer on base. We can see him today,' said William, his face enveloped in a fixed frown.

'Already done. Betty and I went to see the Intelligence Officer at Mildenhall. He reported to his HQ and a senior officer has taken on the case. Now I need a big favour from you.' William tilted his head and opened his palms to Darlene, inviting the question. 'Could you meet the officer at St Etheldreda's this Sunday for Mass? He wants to sight Milena and the man together. The officer's name is Flight Lieutenant Hector A'Court.'

'How does he know I go to St Etheldreda's?' asked William.

'I've met him a couple of times and given him all the details on what we've seen and found out.'

'Hell's bells, Darlene. You're up to your neck in this. If only half the stories we know about the Nazis is true, they'll kill you without a second thought if they think you've blown their operation. Tell me, you've left everything to this Intelligence Officer?'

'Yes, yes. That's why he wants to meet you at Mass, so I don't have go. And he's got some people looking out for me. It's fine.'

'What? Protection Officers? So, you are in danger? This is not exactly the sort of chat I thought we'd be having after I finished my tour. My head is spinning a bit. Do you need to go away, for your own protection? Can you go back to Exeter till this blows over?' William started rubbing his hands in tight and sharp motions.

'Honestly, Honey, it'll all be fine. Hector has it all under control,' replied Darlene.

'Hector? First name basis, is it? All he'll be interested in is snagging the spies. I wouldn't put too much truck on him looking after you,' snapped William.

'You're reading too much into it. Sorry I brought it up. Maybe I will have to go to Mass with him. Sounds like you don't want to help,' retorted Darlene.

'Not at all. If they're getting intel on local Bomber Command activities, it means me and my mates lives are potentially being put in greater danger. Hell, even on good nights, each run is like opening day of the duck shooting season and we're the bloody ducks. So, if they are feeding details to Nazi High Command, makes our ops more lethal. I want them caught as much as you, maybe more.'

'You're right, sorry.' Darlene reached out for William's hand and held it tight. 'That's what's been spurring me on, the thought they've got intel which has led to more casualties. Makes me sick when I think about it. So, you will meet Flight Lieutenant A'Court?'

'Of course, I will, but I'm serious about you going back to Exeter, maybe for a couple of weeks. As I said, I've got a whole month's end-of-tour leave coming up. We could go down together,' said William.

'Thank you so much. Meet him in the same place as we did a few weeks ago. Apparently, he has a photo of you, so knows what you look like. I'll think about Exeter. It does sound like a good idea. Can we talk about something else now? When's the rest of your crew going to finish their tours?'

*

*5 July 1942*

The Sunday morning sun had already warmed the air to the point where William took shelter under the shade of the large oak tree which overhung the church's boundary fence. His blue, wool RAF uniform soaked up the sun, making him perspire. The light coming through the branches and leaves dappled the ground around him. He was looking back down Egremont Street, towards the centre of Ely, and jumped when he heard a man's voice, close behind him.

'Flight Sergeant Robertson?' William turned to the man and nodded. 'I'm Flight Lieutenant A'Court,' said Hector.

William regarded Hector's RAF uniform and quickly recognised his epaulettes and gave him a salute, 'Yes, sir. Apologies, you gave me a bit of a jump. I was expecting you to come from town,' replied William.

'No need for the salute. Let's try not to bring attention to ourselves. I came in on the back roads from Mildenhall and parked on a side street. Thank you for agreeing to meet and chaperone me at St Etheldreda's. Much appreciated,' said Hector.

'We want to get this thing sorted out. It's been nearly two months since our concerns were roused. Seems a long time to have a couple of spies on the loose. Didn't those spies in Kent get caught after a few days?' asked William.

'Yes, it is longer than we would have liked, but you and Miss du Toit have done everything correctly. The ones who got picked up in Romney Marsh were rank amateurs. Idiots to be honest. These two do appear to be professional operators. The woman, and her family, have been deeply embedded in British life for close to fifteen years and the man must have excellent connections and training. If I make a positive identification today, we'll pick them up within the next week, you can be assured,' replied Hector.

'I'm concerned Darlene is now in harm's way, let alone what it's doing to her emotionally. She said you've put in some personal protection for her. It's got me worried, so I've suggested we get away soon. We're thinking about going down to Exeter. Darlene was at RAF Hospital Exeter, so has some friends there,' said William.

'Great idea. I commend your commitment to her safety and well-being. She's a lucky woman to be stepping out with you. The protection is a precaution. I don't expect anything to happen. Engaging with her, or anyone, in a confrontational way risks blowing their cover. If they have been operating for a couple of months, my guess is they are feeling comfortable and won't do anything to jeopardise it.' Hector checked his watch, 'Should we go in?'

William flicked back his left arm sleeve to confirm the time and nodded, 'There's a couple of areas which will give us a good view of the whole congregation. We can wait in the back of the church to see them come in. There's a secluded spot where we can watch the entrance. Follow me.'

Taking up a position in a cloister at the rear of the church, William and Hector scanned each parishioner as they entered; a mixture of Ely's long-time Catholic community, military personnel from all over Britain and the world, especially the Poles and French assigned to the RAF locally. All were dressed either in their "Sunday Best" or their military uniforms.

'Last time, they came in right before the start of Mass and slipped in near the back on the far side,' said William, pointing to the seats the two targets had sat on last time.

'I'm expecting the same. So far, they have kept to their processes. Doing their best to hide in plain sight. Not doing anything that stands out, nothing out of the ordinary, or things which are so different they might slip up trying to remember new practices,' replied Hector.

'Are you a regular church goer, Flight Lieutenant?' asked William.

'Not recently. Parents used to take us to the French Protestant Church in Soho Square down in London. I've drifted away, especially during the war,' replied Hector.

William nodded, 'Huguenot's? Must be tough to set foot in a Catholic Church, with all the historical implications. Hard to reconcile a benevolent God with what is going on, but war seems to be in the core nature of man. What I've seen has led to me asking some serious questions. Haven't got many answers yet.'

Both men checked their watches again; two minutes to ten. As William looked up, his body tensed and his jaw locked. He gave Hector a light tap on his forearm and nodded in the direction of a couple who had entered the church. They headed to the far side of the church, taking seats at the end of the third to last row. William led Hector to a couple of empty seats in the last row in the other bank of the pews. As William knew St Etheldreda's well, he chose the seats wisely to give Hector a strategic view of their targets.

William watched Hector as he studied the couple in quick, intense glances, making sure not to let his eyes linger too long on them. The constant up, down and kneeling of the Mass allowed him to steal more views than he expected. His jaw jutted out and he pursed his lips. After nearly ten minutes into the Mass, he turned to William and gave him a small nod and wink.

*

*6 July 1942*

Still in her uniform, Darlene slumped on her bed and rubbed her temples. If all the stress of the last couple of weeks wasn't enough, they'd lost one of their patients today. A young airman from Manchester had taken some flak shrapnel in the last thousand bomber raid. As sad as it was to lose a patient, they'd all been amazed at how long he'd survived. They were starting to think he might pull through. If this war had taught her anything, it was not to get your hopes up, set your expectations too high, or look too far into the future. Disappointment was lurking around most corners. Her eyes grew heavy, and her head went limp.

The ticking and clacking of her door handle being twisted woke her up with a start. She was struggling to focus on the door when a forceful voice came from down the hallway, 'Excuse me. What are you doing here? Men aren't allowed in the Home.' The door handle stopped jiggling and there was the sound of people running. The same voice sounded like it was outside her door, 'Halt, stay where you are. Shit.'

Darlene's heart felt like it was about to explode out of her chest as she slowly opened her door and looked down the hall to where the noise was now coming from, only to see a woman running away from her. She disappeared out of the exit door. By now a number of her Nurse colleagues had done the same as her, so the length of the hallway resembled a stable, where all the horses rush to the front of their stalls to investigate the noise. She contemplated joining the chase, but quickly remembered Hector's description of the mysterious man being "a nasty piece of work", so she decided to stay put for now.

About ten minutes later there was a knock on her door, followed by the woman's voice she'd heard earlier, 'Nurse du Toit? It's Corporal McCrea, I'm with the RAF Intelligence Branch. Can we talk?'

Darlene unlocked and opened the door; she straightened up and took a small step back at the familiar face, 'Corporal McCrea, come in.' The woman stepped into Darlene's room, closed and locked the door. 'We've met; you were at the university library,' added Darlene.

'Good memory. Yes, Flight Lieutenant A'Court got me to greet you the day you both met. Then he assigned me to watch out for you a few days ago. How are you? Not too shaken I hope?' asked McCrea.

'I'm fine, thanks. Was a bit scared and my heart was racing while all the commotion was going on. Thank you for being here. You are good at your job, as I had no idea you were here. What happened?' asked Darlene.

'We think it might have been the suspected spy. We can't be certain as we didn't get a good look at him and he managed to slip our chase. No need to worry. I think we gave him enough of a fright he won't be back. My colleague took a shot at him, missed though,' said McCrea.

'There are others? Hector really did pull out all the stops. It's reassuring,' added Darlene.

'We have a male NCO over in the hospital, who was watching the main entrance to this building. We think he came in through the back door. I'll get a couple of extra MPs to do some regular circuits from now on, but as I say, I think we scared him well enough. Don't think he expected a welcoming committee. If you are alright, I'll go back to my post. I'm in the stairwell at the other end of the hallway,' said McCrea.

'I'll be fine, especially now I know there's a few of you around. Thank you so much. Please pass on my thanks to your colleague,' replied Darlene.

As she closed the door on McCrea, Darlene decided the trip to Exeter was now a must. She and William would have to make definite plans, and fast.

*

*7 July 1942*

Darlene and William found Hector sipping a drink on the porch of The Cutter Inn. He was at the table Darlene had used last month. 'Nurse du Toit and Flight Sergeant Robertson. Thank you for coming. Would you like a drink? I got here early and it's such a lovely evening, I couldn't resist.' He stood up, shook his glass of whisky and water, making the ice tinkle. 'We can talk through a few things before we take a walk down the river path.'

'Thank you. Gin and tonic for me,' said Darlene.

'A half pint of Bass. Cheers,' added William.

'My pleasure. Please, grab a seat.' Hector turned and went into the pub.

They sat down and William took Darlene's hand and gently rubbed it, 'Who'd have thought one of our favourite spots would become a central part of a spy tale,' he said.

'This war keeps throwing up more and more surprises,' she replied, and gave William a warm smile.

'Here you are,' Hector placed the drinks on the table.

'You picked the same table I did when I watched Milena,' said Darlene.

'I can see why you did. Offers a perfect view of the whole path, without drawing attention to oneself. Blend into the pub crowd. Couldn't have picked a better spot. As I have told you before, you are somewhat of a natural at this. Here's cheers,' he said raising his glass to the middle of the three of them. The clink of glass on glass echoed across the deck. 'As we expected, and as per their process timetable you uncovered, Miss Dvořáček did attend Mass on Sunday with the man and acted exactly as they did when you both saw them.' Darlene and William nodded and sipped their drinks as they listened to Hector. 'I got a good look at the man, and he does match both the description you gave me and the one we had. So, a positive identification.'

William took a long pull on his beer, 'He looks like a right dodgy bugger. He oozes menace.'

Darlene felt her grip on her glass weaken and her hand started to shake. She quickly put the drink down and cupped her right hand into her left, hiding them under the table.

'Quite. We now have enough comfort and evidence to arrest both of them. If they keep to their process, their river path rendezvous and note drop should happen here this Saturday. I've already secured a couple of MPs and RAF Intelligence Branch Officers from Mildenhall and Lakenheath to assist. Nurse du Toit, could you talk through what you saw from here last month?' asked Hector.

'Um, yes, of course, Hector.' Darlene took in a deep breath and flattened out the front of her dress as she gathered her thoughts then recalled her afternoon in the same spot.

'Excellent. Thank you. You didn't see the man?' asked Hector.

Darlene shook her head, 'I waited a couple of minutes and had a good look around. There were a few people around but I didn't see him.'

'Maybe they are so confident in their process, he comes much later. Risky though, to leave an incriminating note out in the open for any length of time. You finished your drinks? Let's go down to the bridge.' All three of them stood simultaneously and stepped off the deck onto the river path.

They stopped at the bridge, next to the upside-down flowerpot. Hector stood with his hands on his hips and surveyed the area, up and down the river path, back into the pub.

'Here's the loose rock where she puts the notes,' added Darlene as she picked it up to show the opening.

'Right. Interesting area. Good in the respect we can get a great view of the whole area and set our men up at strategic locations, but bad in that it's very public and there's a number of ways in and out. See those gates leading to the houses, and I bet there's a path next to the rail bridge abutment,' Hector said as he pointed them out.

'We'll need two or three more men,' Hector continued. 'If I was our male target, I'd set myself up under the rail bridge, or over the river. Gives a much better total view, but the rail bridge allows you to quickly get to the drop point if something goes wrong. You didn't see anyone close to you the day you were in the pub together?'

Both Darlene and William shook their heads. 'It was rather quiet, if I recall correctly. Probably would have noticed someone like him. He is distinctive and out of the ordinary for around here,' said William

Hector rubbed his chin a few times. 'I think we'll set up with myself at the pub, one across the river, one on the path past the rail bridge, a couple around the houses past those gates, and two on Broad Street. Those two will pick up Milena once she's made the drop and on her way home. The rest of us will concentrate on the man. He'll be the real danger.'

'Oh, please be careful,' Darlene said quickly.

'Don't worry, we always are, but thanks for your concern. I think I have everything I need. I'll go to the town council to get some maps for planning,' added Hector.

'Given what's happened, we want to go away for a few days. I've got some friends in Exeter who we can stay with,' said Darlene.

'Yes, Flight Sergeant Robertson mentioned it on Sunday. I told him it's a good idea, at least until we have both of them in custody, and more important with what happened at the Nurses' Home yesterday. Wise to get you both out of town. I have suggestion for you. Do you know the town of Totnes?' asked Hector.

'I've heard of it. Seen it on the destination board for the Cornwall bound services at the Exeter train station. Haven't been there, though,' replied Darlene.

'Near Buckfast, isn't it? I bailed out near the Abbey on my first ever op. Which is what led to Darlene and I meeting. What happened at the Nurses' Home?' asked William.

'Oh, um, nothing major. We had an intruder. Some of my staff chased them off. They think it was a drunk local who's seeing one of the Nurses, and overstepped the mark,' Hector quickly came up with a plausible cover story to deflect William's angst. 'And yes, you're right about Totnes and Buckfast. It's about halfway between Exeter and Plymouth. Gorgeous town and an out-of-the-way place. A better place to go to keep a low profile. Staying here will be difficult to keep out of sight, and I fear Milena has too many connections in London to ensure that is safe for you. I have a contact at one of the nicest pubs in town, the Royal Seven Stars. They look after key personnel of ours regularly. I'll organise a couple of rooms for you both. We'll cover the cost. You got your train tickets yet?'

William shook his head to the question, 'Haven't got around to it yet. Was going to buy them as we went.'

'We'll take care of it and official travel passes as well. It'll be a full day of travel. Early morning train from here to Kings Cross, across to Paddington, then get the Penzance service. Once we're done here, let's go to the station booking office and get it all sorted out,' said Hector.

'Oh, thank you, Hector. Very generous,' said Darlene.

'The least we can do. Would you be able to leave tomorrow morning? Miss du Toit, I can get it signed off with your Matron, and Flight Sergeant, I can talk to your CO.'

'If you can get Matron to approve, I'll be ready to go tomorrow,' said Darlene.

'Thanks Sir. I'm fine. I'm officially on my end-of-tour leave, so am ready to go as soon as I pack a suitcase,' said William.

'Excellent. If you can organise it, might pay to get packed up and stay here in Ely tonight, so you and Miss du Toit can make an early start tomorrow,' added Hector.

'Bob has a couple of rooms at the Prince Albert. You can stay there,' added Darlene. William nodded at her suggestion.

'All agreed then. Thank you both for what you've done on this case. Without your diligence, who knows how long they would have operated undetected and how much damage they might have done. The country owes you a significant debt of gratitude. Best of luck with the trip south. I'll let you know how we get on with the arrest. Do you both have time to come down to the station to get the tickets?'

Darlene and William nodded at Hector's question. 'Wonderful. Let's go.' Hector gave both of them a warm handshake and smile as they turned and walked down the river path towards the Ely train station.

# Chapter Fourteen

*8 July 1942*
*Totnes, Devon*

The taxi pulled up to the entrance of the Royal Seven Stars Hotel, only three minutes after they'd left the train station. William offered an apology for wasting the driver's time on such a short drive, as he handed over some coins for the fare.

'Don't worry, Guv. Everyone does the same thing. You weren't to know. Better this way than lugging your suitcases around the streets. Have a nice stay,' said the driver.

Darlene and William regarded the building; at least three times larger than their beloved Prince Albert pub, with three storeys of early Georgian grandeur, five large sash windows on each floor looked out onto the street. Its entrance, set between windows two and three, disrupted the normal symmetrical look of Georgian architecture. It had a portico of two large pillars supporting a glass-enclosed sitting room. They nodded and smiled together.

William picked up both of their suitcases and they walked into the reception lobby, but they stopped, their mouths open. They were greeted with a glass topped atrium, the full height of the whole building, which flooded the lobby with late-afternoon summer light. A red carpeted stairway went straight up for the middle of the stone floored lobby to the first floor. The stairway was watched over by a series of mounted stags heads and heraldic plaques which lined the walls of the first floor. Doors on both sides of the lobby went into a saloon bar and public bar. To the right of the stairs was the door to reception.

'Oh, this looks lovely,' whispered Darlene.

Entering reception, oak wood panels and a lower roof swapped the impressive look of the lobby for a more cosy and hospitable feel. 'Good afternoon. Welcome to the Royal Seven Stars,' a warm voice filled the room.

'Thank you. What a fantastic place to greet us after a long trip,' replied William, as he regarded the receptionist; he guessed she was in her forties, dressed in a smart tweed jacket and white blouse.

'Where have you come from today?' she asked.

'Cambridgeshire. It's been a fair old journey,' replied Darlene.

'Nice part of England, especially Cambridge itself. Now how can I help you? You have a reservation?'

'Yes, should be two rooms under the name of Flight Sergeant William Robertson,' he said.

'Robertson, right,' her voice tailed off as she flipped through a box of indexed cards. 'Here we go. Yes, two premium double rooms, with a checkout of, hmm. Interesting,' the receptionist said.

'Is there a problem?' asked William.

'Oh, no problem, but there's no set checkout date. There's a note saying you will be staying for at least five days, but could be longer, and all charges to go back to the War Office in Whitehall. A never-ending holiday. How lovely. You must be important people. You a war hero, Flight Sergeant?' she asked.

William and Darlene exchanged a quick glance, 'Definitely not me. I'm a navigator for Bomber Command and this is my girlfriend, Darlene du Toit. She's a Nurse at one of the RAF hospitals,' he said.

'Well, you might not see yourselves as heroes, but you are in my book. Apologies, I haven't introduced myself. Joanna Wiggins, pleasure to meet you. And both from Australia?'

'New Zealand for William, and South Africa for me,' said Darlene.

'Apologies. Don't get too many of you here, so I can't pick the difference in accents. Now, here's your keys, rooms seven and eight. Round the back of the main stairs, take the door on the right, follow the hallway to the set of stairs and up on the first floor. Rooms are close to the stairs. Main dining room is on the ground floor at the front. We can slot you in for dinner this evening, if you'd like,' Joanna said with a broad, warm smile. 'Now, is this your first time to Totnes?' They both nodded. 'Alright. I'll sort out some ideas for things to see and a few day trips. Lots for you to see and do around here.'

Returning to their rooms after dinner, William and Darlene stopped outside her room. He took her hands in his, and leaned in to kiss her, but Darlene met him and switched the momentum of the embrace. She released her hands from his, enveloped him in a strong hug and pulled him into her. Their tongues intertwined as their kiss became more intense. The heat from their bodies increased and their breathing grew short and fast. She dug her fingers into his back and pulled him closer. He lifted his hands to cup and caress her breasts. She pulled away from him, let out a small sigh, flicked the door handle to her room and led him in.

*

*9 July 1942*

With breakfast finished, Darlene and William went back to the reception to find Joanna.

'Good morning. Sleep well?' Joanna asked, a warm smile breaking across her face.

'Very comfortable, thank you. Such a nice hotel,' replied Darlene.

'That's kind of you. Now, plans for your time here. There's loads to do. Anything you both really like or dislike?' Joanna took out a note pad and a pen.

'We're keen for anything. We both like history and nature. Neither of us have spent time around here before. I used to live in Exeter, but never got down this way,' said Darlene.

'I've been to Buckfast, but for less than a day,' added William. 'My plane crashed up on Dartmoor and I spent the night at the Abbey after I bailed out.'

'What? Last Christmas?' asked Joanna, with wide eyes. William nodded. 'That was huge news around here. I knew it, you are a war hero. How exciting. Alright, here's a few ideas. Totnes Castle is at the top of the town. It's a Norman-era castle. Take a riverboat down to Dartmouth. A lovely harbour town. Jump on the train to Plymouth to see the Mayflower Memorial and Museum. We can organise a car for you to explore Dartmoor and you can take in Buckfast Abbey. Paignton for a day at the beach. You can get a bus there. Torquay is restricted because of the war. Got a submarine base and an RAF training centre. Paignton is nicer anyway. Around town, we have many lovely tea rooms. My favourite is Grey's Dining Room, right at the top of town on High Street. A Devonshire High Tea to die for. Phew, that'll be enough to keep you going for about a week.' Joanna mockingly wiped her brow of imaginary sweat.

'We also wanted to have a day in Exeter to visit my friends. What about Cornwall? Is it too far for a day trip?' asked Darlene.

'Oh no. Penzance might be too much to bite off, but you could get the train to Par and then catch a bus to Fowey. Another delightful harbour town. There used to be a branch train from Lostwithiel, but it's been off and on since the start of the war. Heard it's going to be stopped again soon, so best to go to Par and take the bus. Exeter is easy enough; the train and bus are regular. I'll add them to the list. Fabulous, there you go,' she said, as she handed over the piece of paper to Darlene. 'Don't hesitate to ask about anything and enjoy exploring,' added Joanna.

'Thank you so much. Extremely helpful. I'm excited to get started. Shall we explore the town today? Try the Devonshire High Tea?' William asked Darlene.

'Let's get going,' replied Darlene.

They eased themselves into chairs at Grey's Dining Room, and both heaved a sigh.

'Listen to us. Anyone would think we're a couple of old codgers,' said Darlene, breaking into a laugh.

'Well, I reckon we've clocked up over three miles of walking, and it's a hilly town. The climb to the Castle had me sucking some wind,' said William.

'I'm ready for a nice cuppa and a scone,' added Darlene, as the waitress approached their table. 'Good afternoon. Two Devonshire high teas. Thank you.'

'Excellent. Whipped cream or clotted cream with your scones?' asked the young woman.

Darlene looked at William, and they both shrugged their shoulders, 'One of each, if it's not too much trouble,' she added. The waitress nodded, scribbled the order on her notepad and headed off to the kitchen. 'This place is the cutest,' Darlene said, as she inspected the cups and saucers on their table; pure white with bright green shamrocks around the middle.

Her eyes then darted around the tea rooms, 'Look at the far wall; all those gorgeous teapots.' She nodded to the display of ten ornate and colourful teapots set out on two shelves.

'I like the fireplace, behind you,' William pointed to the large, rough-stone fire hearth and surround. The mantelpiece was festooned with another six teapots, book-ended with large pewter tankards and old copper pots hung at the ends of the mantelpiece. In the mouth of the fireplace, an explosion of blue, purple, white and pink hydrangeas provided a stark contrast to the greys and browns of the stone and mortar.

'I love this town. Picturesque and quirky, and the people are lovely. I'm delighted Hector recommended it,' said Darlene.

'Yes, a great place to lie low, but with a lot to see and do,' replied William. 'So, we didn't really finish our chat about Flight Lieutenant A'Court.'

Darlene cocked her head at William, 'I thought we did. What do you mean?' she asked.

'You two seemed close, and I was a bit surprised by him suggesting and paying for this trip,' replied William.

'He has paid for both of us. He knows we're an item. Yes, we got close, but it was an intense situation, especially when he thought there was potential danger for us. He is a nice man, but he is married and …' her voice tailed off. William opened his hands to her. 'And, I love you.'

William was about to respond when the waitress returned with a large tray, laden with the high tea accoutrements; a smaller silver tray was placed in the middle of the table, containing a white porcelain teapot painted with pink flowers, a matching milk jug, a silver hot water pot and a silver-handled tea strainer. Next was a crystal platter with an ornate plinth, topped off with two fat scones, and dishes of butter, strawberry jam, whipped cream and clotted cream. Last was two side plates with knives, one of which was placed in front of Darlene, then William.

'Cream? How do you get that?' asked Darlene.

'The owner's brother has a dairy farm down the road. Keeps us well stocked regardless of ration limits. Sugar is in the bowl there. Enjoy,' said the waitress.

'Let me do the honours,' William said as he grabbed the teapot, held the lid in place and twirled the pot around twice both clockwise and anti-clockwise. He placed the strainer on top of Darlene's cup and poured in a brown elixir. The sweet aroma of freshly brewed tea filled the air between them. He repeated the same for his cup, then added a dash of milk and a single teaspoon of sugar.

'Thanks, Love. I'll do the scones,' replied Darlene. She placed a scone on each plate, cut them in half, and buttered the four round half-scones. 'Shall we mix and match the jam and cream? Jam then cream on two and cream then jam on the other two? See if there is a difference in taste.' She finished the preparation with the strawberry jam, whipped cream and clotted cream, cut them in two, so both of them had a piece of all four combinations. She handed a plate to William. 'Bon appétit, Love.' She had to shallow a mouthful of saliva as she anticipated her first bite.

'They look sensational, Hon. Loving the idea of a taste test.' He halved the slices, picked up a piece of jam then whipped cream topped scone and devoured it in one bite. Bringing his cup up to his lips, he blew on the tea a couple of times and took a mouthful. Next was the clotted cream and jam combination; again, gone in one bite.

'Verdict?' Darlene asked.

He held up a finger and nodded as he chewed a couple more times. 'Usually, I'm a cream on top, kind of bloke, but I have to admit the jam on top of the clotted cream is phenomenal. I'll try the reverse combo to be sure.'

'Right, let me try the one first,' she replied, as she picked up a quarter of the same combination and took a bite, leaving a dollop of jam and cream on the side of her cheek. William reached over and gently wiped the leftovers off her face. As quick as a spider grabbing its prey trapped in a web, she took his finger into her mouth, flicked her tongue over his finger, taking the sweet condiments into her mouth. She gave him a wink before releasing her grip on his finger. 'I think you're right. Clotted cream topped off with jam is amazing. I might be turned myself,' she said, licking her teeth and lips and giving him a warm smile.

*

*11 July 1942*
*Ely, Cambridgeshire*

Hector A'Court took up his position at The Cutter Inn, where Darlene had sat. A tall glass of soda water and a pint of ale sat on the table before him. He checked his watch; five past five. Earlier than Darlene had indicated the drop and pick up usually happens, but he didn't want to miss them if they decided to change their routine. The full arresting team had assembled at RAF Mildenhall earlier in the day, but taken multiple vehicles into Ely, and made their ways to their assigned spots individually. He could see his men; one down the path by the railway abutment and the other near the gate leading to the houses on Annesdale Street. He trusted Corporal McCrea and her partner were in place up on Broad Street and the last man was on Station Road.

He flicked open his copy of The Times and settled into what he expected to be a long waiting game. Soon, the chastening words of his Divisional Commanding Officer which had been swirling around his head since he left London for this apprehending mission, came back to him.

'A'Court, you better come back with a watertight case against this Dvořáček woman. I've had three members of the House of Lords bend my ear about her this week alone. If you can't make it stick, it'll be my and your career finished. I'm sure you understand, that can't happen,' bellowed the CO.

*

*Buckfast Abbey, Devon*

'I came down in a farmer's field a couple of miles up there and the aircraft hit the moor, about ten miles away,' William said, pointing to the hills of Dartmoor. 'Hobbled my way down the hill to the Abbey in the pitch black.'

William and Darlene, stood in front of Buckfast Abbey, as they took in the vista of the Abbey's grounds and the River Dart valley. A stand of trees, dense in their full summer leafy cloaks, lined the river at the back of the Abbey, and well-maintained out-buildings, gardens and lawns surrounded the majestic church. To the side of the main path, the orange and white flowers around a marble statue of the Blessed Virgin and Infant Jesus, danced lazily in the warm breeze, as if in a trance of worship to the stone deities.

'In the dead of winter, too. Must have been scary,' replied Darlene.

'Wasn't too bad. Apart from an over-zealous Home Guard lad who took a pot-shot at me. At least we made it back to Blighty. Could have easily gone down in France, or The Channel. Might have ended up in a German POW camp,' added William.

'Or dead, and we would never have met.' Darlene grabbed his arm and pulled him into her, 'Thank God that didn't happen.'

'Want to go in? I'll show you where I slept,' said William. Darlene nodded. They walked up to the arched doorway and were quickly enveloped in its twenty foot canopy. The dark oak doors were inlaid with swirls and curves of ornate ironwork. William strained as he used all his body weight to pull back one of the doors. He ushered Darlene in, and entered behind her, dipping his fingers in the basin of holy water and crossing himself.

'Oh, it's lovely. A lot brighter than the other old churches I've been into,' said Darlene craning her neck to take in the ceiling and archways running down the length of the building.

'Probably because it's not old. It was only completed four or five years ago, so it's bigger with more windows, better glass and more lights. Looks like it's been here for centuries, eh?' William pointed to the high-level windows and light fittings. 'I didn't get far. Collapsed on this pew right here.' He tapped the back of the last of the twelve rows of pews. 'Didn't wake up until the Brothers started Mass the next morning. Grab a seat.' Darlene shuffled along the pew and he joined her.

'Like you said, without the bailout and ending up here, I would never have met you. That night I thanked God for leading me here. One of his houses gave me sanctuary, then you gave me care. I've thought about those days often over the last couple of months. You're the one person who has given me the motivation to get through.' He slipped off the pew, crouched on one knee and took out a ring case from his jacket pocket, 'Darlene du Toit, would you make me the happiest man in the world and marry me?'

Darlene straightened up, her eyes widened, and mouth dropped open, as she placed both hands on her chest, 'Oh, William. What a wonderful surprise. Yes, yes, yes.' She put her arms around his neck and smothered his face with a shower of small kisses. She pulled back as William took out the ring and slid it onto her ring finger.

*

*Ely, Cambridgeshire*

The pint of ale only had dregs left in it, the second glass of soda water was completely empty, and he was two pages away from finishing his third read-through of the newspaper. Hector checked his watch for the hundredth time; ten minutes since Milena had made the drop and flipped over the flowerpot. There was still no sign of her contact. Had he and this crew been spotted? Had the man been spooked? He hadn't heard any noise or commotion from up on Broad Street. Was that good or bad? Had McCrea arrested Milena without issue, or had she given McCrea the slip?

Hector exhaled deeply; a vision of his CO going apoplectic at a failed mission flashing through his mind. A line of sweat dribbled down the small of his back.

He went to grab the pint glass when he saw a man in a dark suit pass by the railway abutment. Hector's body tensed up so violently, his leg kicked the table, causing the glasses to wobble and hit each other. 'Christ, settle down,' he whispered.

He held the paper up so he could still peer over the top if the page and take in the whole towpath. The dark suited man slowed his pace as he approached the bridge. He stopped and leaned against the stonework, scanning up and down the towpath a couple of times then reached behind himself. Hector squinted and focussed on the man's hands. He saw a piece of paper in his left hand, which was then stuffed in his trouser pocket. The man pushed off the bridge, flicked flowerpot upside down and started walking towards the cut through to Annesdale Street. As Hector rose from the pub table, his backup MPs started moving toward the target.

'We're on,' he whispered.

# CHAPTER FIFTEEN

*13 July 1942*

William held the door to the breakfast room for Darlene when Joanna called out, 'Flight Sergeant Robertson. You have a telegram.' William turned to see her walking towards him, waving a brown envelope.

'Thank you,' he said, as he showed Darlene the Post Office Telegram. 'Interesting. No one knows we're here, except for Flight Lieutenant A'Court. I didn't tell anyone.'

'Come on, open it. He might have news about Milena,' replied Darlene.

William flicked the flap up, took out the single page, held it between them both and read the message;

*OPERATION SUCCESSFUL*
*STAND EASY = HECTOR*

He flipped it over a couple of times, 'Hmm. Short and sweet.' He turned to Darlene, 'Looks like it's over.'

'Oh, Lord, I hope so,' said Darlene. They fell into each other's arms. 'Thank you so much for standing by me.' Her breathing got shallower, and tears started to well up.

He pulled back to see her face, 'No thanks needed. Was never an option not to. You've smashed a spy ring. Not many people will ever be able to say that.'

'It couldn't have worked without you. It would have been easy to say I was loopy,' she said.

'Come on, let's have some brekkie and plan a fun day. It's nice not to have it hanging over you,' said William, guiding Darlene to an empty table.

After they had sat down, Darlene reached for William's hand, 'It feels like a dark, heavy cloud has lifted,' she said softly.

'Almost like a fresh start. All the stress and pressure has evaporated. You're my war hero.' William stroked her hand and gave her a wide smile.

'Shush. Took you, Betty, Hector and all his personnel to pull it off. It's an incredible feeling. Time for breakfast, I say. What about today? What say we do the day trip to Cornwall. What was the town Joanna mentioned?' asked Darlene.

'Fowey. Great idea. Weather looks good, too. Let's do it.' The waiter come to their table and interrupted their conversation. 'Two breakfasts of Weetabix, toast and tea, please. Thank you,' said William.

*

The bus from Par rumbled and rattled down narrow, hedgerow-lined country lanes on its way to Fowey. William and Darlene snuggled together in the back seat; half through affection and half protecting themselves from the jumps and bumps of the journey. Their eyes were glued to the coastal rural views; fields of oats, flocks of sheep, small herds of dairy cows and glimpses of the sea through the gaps in the hedges.

The road went from a gradual slope to a full downhill descent. The hedgerows gave way to high stone walls. Eventually the outlook opened up again as quaint, terraced Georgian houses became more numerous. The road became narrower and narrower, and the bus slowed to a crawl.

Darlene looked at William with wide eyes and clenched teeth as the buildings closed in on the bus. She looked from the window to see the footpath had disappeared and, at one point, thought she could reach out and touch the buildings. The bus took a hard left, then a tight chicane and stopped abruptly, 'Fowey town centre,' shouted the driver, as he opened the door.

Darlene and William emerged and took in the view of a stone church which greeted them. The tiny lanes of the town were busy with people, the odd vehicle and some horses and carts.

'Oh, Lord. This place is gorgeous. It will be fun to explore. Where to first?' Darlene asked with a broad smile.

'I saw the sea down one of those lanes back there. There was a pub on the corner too. Could be worth a look for lunch.' He grabbed Darlene's hand and they crossed the street to seek out the harbour. A short stroll of about one-hundred yards along a narrow lane opened up to the harbour; blue-green water, a green forested shoreline on the other side of the harbour and a bright blue sky welcomed them.

They walked to the edge of the waterfront and took in the view. A light breeze came up the estuary from the sea, ruffling Darlene's hair and causing the flotilla of fishing boats, rowboats, tenders and pleasure craft to bob on the water. They scanned the estuary, from the main Fowey River to their left and down to the headlands protecting the harbour from the English Channel.

Darlene grabbed William's upper arm and gave it an excited squeeze, 'Wow, stunning. You can picture this being a setting for "Kidnapped". I can imagine smugglers stashing their bounty in the nooks and crannies on the far shore, then coming over here for their tankard of ale. Have you read Daphne du Maurier's new novel, "Frenchman's Creek"?' William shook his head. 'You should, this view brings it to life.'

'It's beautiful. You can feel the history of the place. You're right, you can picture the place swarming with fishermen, pirates and smugglers. Shall we take a wander up the main street?' William suggested.

Strolling along another lane they passed a couple of small warehouses and some fishing and sailing supply shops with window displays of nets, ropes, knots and heavy, wet weather gear. They turned onto Forte Street and were greeted by a bakery proudly displaying a wide range of Cornish Pasties, cakes and scones. The narrow street had a small footpath on only one side, barely two-yards wide.

The shops on the other side of the street had their doorsteps right on the street itself. The absence of traffic allowed the locals to meander along the thoroughfare, safe in the knowledge they wouldn't have to dodge cars or trucks. It added to the relaxed atmosphere of the whole town. Fish mongers, bakeries, maritime supplies and pubs dominated the shopfronts. Every few yards, laneways opened up back to the foreshore and jetties, festooned with buoys, fishing nets and lobster pots.

They strolled around the streets until they came back to the church and their starting point. 'The pub I saw is nearby,' said William. Around the next corner they saw The Ship Inn. The small façade was covered with hanging baskets and flower boxes, their flowers exploding with vibrant colours; purples, blues, oranges, reds and yellows. A selection of maritime signal flags decorated the large sash window.

Walking into the pub, William had to duck. Although there was a foot to spare to the ceiling, the small main bar area made him feel claustrophobic. 'Grab the table next to the front window. Can I get you a G and T? I'll find out what the lunch options are.' He found the bar dominated by a burly, broad-shouldered bartender.

'Alright, shag?' the man said.

William leaned in and turned an ear at the strong Cornish accent, 'Um, good, thank you. Could I have a gin and tonic and a pint of bitter, please. What's a good local one?'

'St Austell is as good as any, me bewty. Yee not from round here, eh?' the bartender asked as he grabbed a glass and started pulling the pint.

'Good as gold, thanks. No, I'm a New Zealander and my girlfriend is from South Africa. We're with the RAF up in Cambridgeshire. Down here on leave.'

'Arrr, then. Welcome to Fowey. Here ye go. Two bob, thanks' said the bartender as he handed over the drinks.

'Thank you. What's on for lunch?' asked William.

'Fish 'n chips. It's haddock, fresh this morning. Mussels 'n clams in a cream broth. Leak 'n potato soup. And we have pasties,' replied the bartender.

The bartender served them their lunches on two large plates. William held up his drink, 'Cheers, Love. Here's to the best spy-catcher I know.'

Darlene clinked her glass against William's. 'To that cloud lifting,' she added, then turned to the bartender, 'We've got a couple of hours before the bus back to Par. What would you recommend for the afternoon?' asked Darlene.

'Arrr now, yee have walked round town?' the bartender asked, to nods from Darlene and William. 'If yee din not mind a wander, take a look at St Catherine's Castle. Take the Esplanade all dee way down, past Readymoney Cove and up dee path. Lovely.' He gave them a warm smile as he went back to the bar.

'I hope you understood. A lot escaped me,' said Darlene to William.

On the headland of the Fowey River estuary, the dense woods on both side of the path coming up from Readymoney Cove, thinned to reveal St Catherine's Castle. A blast of sea air rushed up the cliff and hit them as they stopped and took in the structure; a two level, half-round turret, dark grey stone, crumbling and covered with vines, creepers and moss.

They were plunged into a dark, damp and dank environment as they entered the turret itself; the building was a shell, with no floor between levels and no roof. Small shafts of light from small windows on the upper level failed miserably to illuminate the space. The dark green growth of moss reached to about three feet up the walls. Wild grasses and weeds peeped out of the walls and the window recesses.

'Spooky,' said Darlene, as she craned her neck to take in as much of the structure as she could while holding onto William's arm.

'It's seen better days,' replied William. 'Look how thick the walls are?' He crouched into one of the archways over a window, and was almost swallowed by the void.

'Amazing to think it's been here for four hundred years and it's still solid. Notwithstanding no floors or roof,' added Darlene.

Emerging from the turret, they stopped as they took in a far more modern second tier of the site. Down a forty-odd step staircase they saw a gun emplacement adorned with two shiny units and a concrete pillbox.

'Definitely out of place,' said Darlene.

'Anti-aircraft guns. Our version of those bastard 88s we face when on ops.' William shook his head as visions of dense flak fields over their German targets came back to him. 'Incredible something from the 1500s can still be used today. Best we stay up here.'

'Look, over there. That's a good place to take in the view,' Darlene pointed to a railing on the far side of the turret. 'Stunning. It takes in the whole harbour. Gives you a great view of the village on the other side of the harbour.' She pointed to a small group of houses, lit up by the sun.

'I can see now why they built it here; it's strategically placed,' replied William, as he put his arm around Darlene's waist and pulled her close to him.

'Always thinking about the military implications.' She gently poked him in the ribs.

'Sorry. Yes, I need to lift my head and break out of operational thoughts,' he replied. He turned to face Darlene, 'Actually, I've been thinking a bit over the last couple of days. Why don't we get married while we're down here?'

'What? Here in Fowey? Today?' Darlene's voice went up a couple of octaves.

'No, no. I mean sometime during our stay in Totnes. Now I've done my tour, and your spies have been nicked, we're free of those big things which held us back,' said William.

'Wow. Engaged on Friday and married within the week? That's a lot to wrap my head around,' said Darlene.

'But we met in December and have been stepping out since March. There are loads of couples who have got married less than six months after meeting. With all we've been through and seen, the death, suffering and loss, shouldn't we have our chance of happiness, and start as soon as possible?'

'True. I've heard of many Nurses, WAAF's and ATS'ers who have married quickly at small ceremonies. You wouldn't want any of your mates there?' asked Darlene.

'Pruno has gone into a transport squadron, but living back in Kings Lynn. Gordo's still to make up his mind whether to demob and go home, or go into a training squadron. Ossie, Tas and Boss still have a few runs to go, so they may have a run on the day we plan. And poor Reggie's gone. We could do the ceremony in Totnes, call this whole trip our honeymoon, then throw a knee's up at the Prince Albert at our leisure when we get back,' said William.

'I would like to have Betty and Miriam there, but with Reggie gone, maybe it would be adding to Betty's heartbreak. It's not rubbing her nose in it, but it could be construed as a bit heartless.' She put her arms around his neck and fixed him with an intense gaze, 'Yes, Flight Sergeant Robertson. Let's do it.' She leaned in and they kissed deeply, as the sun emerged from behind a cloud and bathed them in a glow of warm light.

*

*16 July 1942*

The Totnes Justice of the Peace and Town Clerk shuffled their feet, shifted their weight from side to side and engaged in idle chit-chat. William stood in an at-ease position in his RAF dress uniform, staring at the door leading into the Totnes Guildhall's Mayor's Parlour, where the three men waited. He picked some fluff off his uniform tunic, and gave himself a nod for bringing his long-length, four-button jacket and his best pair of trousers. He hadn't expected things to progress this fast, but he was happy he had been prepared for the best outcome. He took a quick glance at his watch; six minutes past one. He wouldn't call it late, as tradition did call for the bride to keep the groom waiting for a short time. The other two men followed William's lead and looked at their watches.

A heavy, metallic clunk pulled all three men's eyes to the door; first into the room was Joanna from the Royal Seven Stars, in a shin-length burgundy dress, with three-quarter length sleeves and a round neck. She carried a small bouquet of carnations, begonias and fuchsias. A couple of yards behind her, came Darlene, in her "for best" powder-blue, tailored skirt suit; the one her grandmother had given to her when she left South Africa to come to Britain.

She carried a similar bouquet to Joanna, but nearly double the size. On her head, she wore a flower fascinator, with a large white rose as its centrepiece. William exhaled, then a wide smile broke across his face. As she took her place next to him, he leaned in, 'You are so beautiful. I'm so happy,' he said. She gave him a wink and a big smile.

'Good afternoon folks and welcome to the Totnes Guildhall for this wedding between Flight Sergeant William Robertson and Staff Nurse Darlene du Toit,' said the Justice of the Peace as he started the wedding ceremony.

*

'It's been a whirlwind,' said Joanna. 'Eight days ago, I welcomed you to the hotel, and now I'm helping you celebrate your wedding. This war certainly has created some odd situations.' She was putting the finishing touches to a small screened-off area in the dining room at the hotel, where Darlene and William's wedding dinner function was to be held. 'I know it won't be much of a party, but my hubby will join us, and the JP said he'd pop in soon. I've primed the chef to do a special dinner and my friend at Grey's Dining Room has done a fab little wedding cake for free. It's their thank you for going there so often. We'll make it memorable for you.' She gave them both a broad, warm smile as she pulled out the chairs from the table.

'We can't thank you enough, Joanna. You've gone above and beyond in the last couple of days,' Darlene opened her arms and enveloped Joanna in a strong hug. 'I don't know what we would have done without you.'

'Shush now. It's an absolute pleasure. You've been such lovely guests. Anyway, who doesn't love a wedding, regardless of how big or small? We have a treat for you. Hubby had a hunt around the cellar and found a few bottles of French bubbles we had from before the war. Let me do the honours.'

'So kind, but I'm not sure we can afford French wine.' Worry lines formed on William's forehead as he spoke.

'Don't worry, it's on us. Consider the drinks tonight as our wedding present. We'll add dinner to the bill going to the War Office. They won't mind. Anyway, I'm presuming you'll need only one room for the rest of your stay. We won't tell them you've only been using one room since the first day,' Joanna gave them an exaggerated wink. Darlene felt her temperature rise as her face turned red, and William looked at his feet. Joanna went to a small drinks trolley and picked up a bottle of champagne; a loud pop echoed around the room as she opened the bottle. The satisfying glug, glug sound of the wine being poured into their glasses brought smiles from Darlene and William.

'Oh my. I'm sure I've never had French champagne,' said William.

'We have some nice sparkling wines from the Stellenbosch region, but I don't think I've ever had a French one either. Isn't this fabulous,' Darlene wore a cheeky grin.

'To you Mrs Robertson. Thank you for making me the happiest man in the world today,' said William, holding up his glass.

'Mr Robertson. The love of my life,' Darlene replied. The tinkle of their crystal glasses filled the room.

*

*24 July 1942*

Darlene and William walked into the snug to find Bob teetering on a chair, as he reached up to pin the last of the decorations to the wall.

'Christ. Bob. Be careful,' yelled William, as he lurched to grab the chair and support Bob's precarious stance.

'Thanks, William. Had it under control. What do ya think? Worthy of the wedding celebration of two great kids?' Bob threw his arms open to the room, with a smile and a twinkle in his eye.

The guests of honour regarded the room; an eclectic mix of wedding, birthday and Christmas decorations festooned the snug. Tinsel, rosettes, "good luck" horseshoes and a couple of vases of fresh flowers gave the intimate space sparkle.

'It's gorgeous, Bob. You've done a sterling job. We love it,' said Darlene. She threw her arms around his neck and gave him a long kiss on his cheek.

The big man's face went bright red, 'Least we could do. You two are ruddy legends round here, after those spies were nicked. Didn't like Milena from day one. As for the bloke? Christ, he gave me the creeps. Anyways, food will be here in a few minutes. I'd better get ready for that. I'll open the big hatch to get access to the bar for drinks. Bloody hell. First guests are here already.'

William and Darlene turned to the door to see Ossie, Gordo, Boss and Tas. 'Lads. Come in,' William yelled, opening his arms. The five men embraced warmly. 'Come over. Hon, you remember the crew from the dance? Arthur Osborne, our skipper, Paul Bosson, Wireless Operator, Kerry Morris, or Tas, our Front Gunner, and my great mate, Gordon Newdick, our Rear Gunner. Lads, my amazing wife, Darlene.' They did their introductions. 'Tas and Boss, well done on finishing. God, I can't tell you how relieved I am you got through.'

'Not as much as us, Robbie. She's an odd feeling, eh,' stated Boss. 'I'm off to one of the heavy bomber conversion units. Looking forward to working on the big boys.'

'I'm wating on my discharge papers to head home. My dad has taken a turn for the worse and can't run the farm anymore, so I've put in a request to go back,' said Tas.

'Thank goodness you're still here, Gordo. Would have bet good money you'd have been on your way home,' said William.

'The brass got their way, and I'm staying to become an instructor. They've thrown in a promotion to Warrant Officer. Still to find out where I'm going. They've narrowed it down to Abingdon or Torquay,' replied Gordo.

'Torquay? That's close to where we were in Totnes. You'd love there,' said Darlene.

'Yeah, it sounds nice, but there's more flying opportunities at Abingdon. I'll be told next week,' replied Gordo.

'Now to get Ossie through, then all six of the old Leggett crew will be done, unscathed. What, seven to go, Skip? asked Tas.

Ossie nodded, then turned to William, 'Robbie, can't stay long. I need to get back to base by twenty-hundred. Got a training flight.

More newbies to initiate now these two mongrels' have done their tours and bailed on me.' He gave Tas and Boss a wide smile and a wink.

'No worries, Ossie. So happy you could make it. Means so much to me. You'll have a shandy, though?' asked William.

'Hell's bells, Robbie. She's a bloody dry argument, mate. A bloke could die of thirst,' said Tas, as he looked over to the bar.

'Sorry, lads. Bob, can you sort them out?' William ushered the men over to the landlord. Bob had already poured Darlene and William their usual, and he handed them over as he took the crew's order.

'Pace yourself, girl. Could be a long night,' Betty said as she led in the Friday night drinks crew. Miriam, Stan and Harold followed her in. Darlene enveloped Betty in a deep, long hug. Both women had watery eyes when they pulled back.

'Thanks for popping over the other day,' said Betty, holding Darlene's hands, 'I'm so happy for you. Definitely missing Reggie, but day by day it gets easier. Tonight is about you two. Look at you, you're glowing.'

'As long as we keep talking, we'll get through it together,' replied Darlene.

'You know 75 Squadron is moving to Mildenhall next month? We'll be able to spend loads more time together,' said Betty. 'I'm so happy for you, and to get married in Devon. Oh, bliss.' Betty gave Darlene another warm hug, 'Now, where's the punch bowl?'

'Congratulations, Dee,' said Stan. 'Bloody brilliant. I saw you and William at the train station the other day and knew something was up. You both looked like you were floating through the station. Seemed very much in love,' said Stan.

'Thank you, Stan. Yes, we have been in our own little world for the past week. Back to reality now. Looking forward to restarting our Friday night catch-ups,' replied Darlene.

'The super spy-catcher,' said Harold, 'Have to apologise. I didn't believe you about Milena. Maybe I was blinded by her, but your suspicions were bang on.'

'Not needed. We all played our part. You kept schtum and didn't let on we knew about her. Could have all gone wrong if we hadn't stuck together,' replied Darlene.

'You missed all the commotion. We've had reporters from all over in here. A bloke from The Times came up from London, too. They interviewed us, but mainly they wanted to talk to you,' added Stan.

'They haven't tracked you down, have they?' asked Harold.

'Not yet, but there were dozens of messages at the Nurses' Home when I got back. I might talk to the local paper, eventually. Thanks for coming tonight, you two. Looks like Bob has got your drinks lined up. Preferential treatment for regulars,' Darlene pointed to the bar.

'Dee, you little minx. Running off to Devon to get hitched without telling us.' Miriam threw her arms wide and hugged Darlene.

'Was all a bit of a whirl. Head was spinning for most of it. So glad you came, Mer. How are you doing?' asked Darlene

Miriam pulled her aside, away from the others, 'I want to thank you for not telling anyone about Milena and me. I don't know what I was thinking. She had me wrapped round her finger. The ATS would sack me if they found out. Crikey, they might have court-martialled me,' said Miriam.

'There was no way I was going to spill the beans,' replied Darlene. 'We're mates. Have to look out for each other. I knew Milena was a manipulator. She's an attractive woman too. Easy to fall for her,' replied Darlene.

'My preferences don't bother you?' asked Miriam.

'Makes absolutely no difference to me. If I was so inclined, I might have been interested,' Darlene gave her a wink and a warm smile.

The screech of the snug door pulled Darlene's head away from Miriam. Her mouth fell open and eyes grew wide at a couple who walked in.

'Congratulations, Darlene. Looks like you made the most of the trip to Totnes.' Hector A'Court smiled widely as he stepped close to her. 'Did William not tell you he invited me?' he asked.

'He got in touch? Um, no, but I'm delighted you came.' She looked towards Hector's partner.

'Let me introduce my wife. Valerie, and this is Darlene du Toit, apologies, Robertson. The famous spy-catching Nurse I told you about.' He opened his arms to bring the two women together.

Darlene offered her hand to Valerie and regarded her; as expected, stunningly good-looking, fine features, bright blond hair and a finely-tailored skirt suit. Darlene motioned to William. 'Hon, Hector and Valerie A'Court. You didn't tell me they were coming.'

'Thought it would be a nice surprise,' William gave her a kiss on her cheek before greeting the guests, 'Valerie, pleasure to meet you. Flight Lieutenant. Great to see you again.' He passed a couple of glasses of punch to the A'Courts.

'Please, call me Hector. With all we've been through and tonight's celebration, we can drop the formalities,' replied Hector.

'Wonderful to finally meet you both,' Valerie added, with a light French accent. 'Hector has told me so much about you. Incredible what you managed to uncover,' she said to Darlene.

'Wasn't too hard. I was in the right place at the right time, and did some digging,' Darlene blushed at Valerie's compliment.

'How did the arrests go?' asked William. 'We've been wondering since your telegram. Wasn't exactly heavy on details.'

'Relatively smooth in the end. Sorry, but had to be brief in an open telegram. The two of them kept to their process. Creatures of habit, thankfully. Milena did her drop, walked back to town. You remember Corporal McCrea?' Darlene nodded to Hector's question, 'She and an MP arrested Milena as soon as she hit Broad

Street. Didn't make a peep. Came peacefully. Unfortunately, her partner didn't do the same.'

Both Darlene and William cocked their heads and raised their eyebrows. 'No one was hurt?' asked Darlene.

'Only him, but it was a bit hairy. He picked up the note from the bridge, then went to leave via a cut-through path to Victoria Street. We were a bit light on personnel there. Was up to me and one MP to get him. He pulled a knife and was going for a pistol too. He managed to cut through my jacket before the MP smacked him across the head with a billy club,' he said, patting his ribs.

'Bloody hell, Hector. You're alright?' asked William.

'Good as gold, old boy. Although my favourite herring-bone suit jacket is stuffed. I was expecting it, so took evasive action. They are both in court next week. With all the background we had on them, the evidence you both provided and nicking them in possession of the note, they haven't got a hope. Wouldn't have happened without you.' Hector raised his glass to them, 'Congratulations to my favourite spy-catchers.'

# CHAPTER SIXTEEN

*3 May 1943*

The sun's heat seeped into his blue uniform, warming his body to its core. William turned his face to the sky, to let the rays caress his skin. A small smile broke across his face; 'God, I love England in the springtime,' he whispered. The rattle and clunk of a large vehicle made him open his eyes, but he had to blink a couple of times to adjust to the bright light. He got up from the bus stop bench and watched the passengers disembark; Darlene was one of the last to step out of the bus. He enveloped her in a deep hug and a quick kiss.

'How was your day?' he asked as they walked onto the base, showing their identification cards to the MPs in the guard house of RAF Mildenhall.

'Thanks for coming to meet me. Tough, to be honest. We had a few lads come in from those recent ops to Dortmund and Dusseldorf. Lost one today. Hate it when we can't save them. The rest of them should pull through. How about you?'

'No training flights today, but had a morning class. There's a big op coming up soon, so worked on the navigation plans for the run. Such a lovely afternoon. You want to do a lap of the base?' he asked.

'Great idea. Been cooped indoors up all day; would love to be out in the sunshine. You're distracted. What's on your mind?' She poked him in the ribs.

'Can't get anything past you. Got called into the Wing Commander's office this afternoon,' he replied.

'Oh dear. Nothing too serious?' she asked.

'Quite significant, actually. The top brass thinks the tide of the war has turned in our favour. The Russians are pushing the Germans back. Stalingrad was a huge defeat for the Nazis. We've got them on the run in North Africa, and the Yanks have stopped the Japanese advance in the Pacific. Handed them a big defeat at a place called Guadalcanal,' he said.

'Betty and Miriam reckon it could be all over by the end of next year. At least in Europe,' added Darlene.

'That's what the bosses think too. Cutting to the chase, they ordered me to return home, to join the navigation instruction programme for a new reconnaissance squadron. I'm off to Liverpool, sail to New Zealand via New York, then I'll fly up to Fiji, where the squadron is stationed. Finally, off to The Solomon Islands once training is done,' he said.

Darlene stopped quickly and turned to William, her face a couple of shades paler than a minute ago, 'Fiji? In the middle of the Pacific? When?'

William took both her hands in his, 'Yes, can't get much different than here. Will take me almost a month to get home, so they want me to leave within the next two or three weeks.'

'The next couple of weeks? You'll be away for our anniversary. William, this is such a shock. Is there any chance I can follow? There must be openings for Nurses.' Darlene's voice raised a couple of octaves.

'I know. It cuts me up too. I asked if I could go later in June, but the bulk of planes are arriving in June and July. They've already got the first delivery and started training in Auckland, so they want me there as quickly as possible. They also offered me a promotion to Flying Officer before I head up to Fiji. A full Commissioned Officer rank. I asked them about bringing you over. They couldn't make a commitment on the spot, but would push your case. Without doubt, they'll need Nurses both on the frontline and back in New

Zealand.' He cupped his hands around her face, wiping a tear off her cheek with his thumb.

'There's not much chance of them pulling back, is there?' she asked.

'It's the military, in wartime and it was an order, so not likely to change, and no chance of me refusing. Unless I want to get court-martialled.'

'Darling, there's no way I want that. You're an honourable man, and obviously extremely good at what you do. Otherwise, they would have asked someone else to go. God, I'm bouncing between sadness and the anger of losing you, especially so close to our anniversary, and pride they have chosen you. It's this whole war in a nutshell, isn't it?' William cocked his head at her question. 'It's torn the world apart, yet it's allowed us to find each other. We're only one couple. Must be so many others like us. It takes away so much, but has some shafts of light here and there.'

'I can't stand the thought of leaving you, but it's a chance of getting home earlier and in a much safer place. Here we're still only two-hundred miles away from the Nazis, living on a bomber base. Fiji is over a thousand miles from the frontline,' he tried to reassure Darlene.

'Let's find a way to make this work,' she said. 'I'll talk to Matron tomorrow to see how I can get transferred to New Zealand. We'll simply have to celebrate our anniversary early.' They leaned in and hugged deeply. They continued their stroll around the base, arm in arm, their faces turned up to the sun. 'I can lean on Betty for a bit of support while you're gone,' she said.

'It's great you have Betty. I don't know anyone in Auckland. Apart from Albert,' he said.

'But you'll have a chance to track down your brother. That'd be wonderful,' Darlene's voice lifted as she spoke.

'Albert and Abigail have crossed my mind. Not much to go on to find them, but if I'm in Auckland for more than a couple of days,

I'll give it crack.' William let out a deep sigh, 'I have no idea what I'd say, if I did find him.'

'Don't worry. It'll come. Main thing is finding him. You want him back in your life. I want to know all your family, not some selected few. Their story is beautiful. I'd love to get to know them both.' Darlene grabbed William's upper arm and pulled herself close to him, resting her head on his shoulder.

*

A heavy silence hung over Darlene and William as they stood, hand-in-hand, at the edge of the station platform, oblivious to the service personnel and railways staff around them. Nearly a dozen other airmen from 75 Squadron who'd finished their operational tours were boarding the train, for the trip to Liverpool; the first leg in their journey home. The hum of banter between the men and the noise of the steam train added to the couple's sadness.

The sound of running feet pulled their gaze away. 'Thank God, you're still here,' Betty said, breathlessly, 'Thought I was going to miss you.' She enveloped the couple in a hug.

'Thanks for coming. Means a lot,' said William.

Betty turned to Darlene, who had started to wipe away tears, 'Come on girl. You'll be on your way to New Zealand too, soon enough.' She pulled out a handkerchief and dabbed Darlene's cheeks. 'Upside is we get more time together.'

'You're such a dote, Betty. I don't know what I'd do without you. She turned back and hugged William, 'You telegram me whenever you can, alright?'

'Absolutely, Hon. The wireless officer will be sick of the sight of me by the end of the trip,' he replied.

A high-pitched whistle came from one of the railway staff. 'Prepare to board,' he shouted

'No, no, no. Not yet,' whispered Darlene. Tears filled her eyes again.

'I love you, so much. I'll write and telegram the whole time. Less than three months till you come over. You've got your transfer confirmed now. Love you,' he pulled her in for a deep, long embrace. They transferred tears to each other's cheeks, then he slowly pulled away.

*

*21 June 1943*
*Auckland, New Zealand*

Taking an open spot on the railing, William turned up the collar on his old leather flight jacket, as a keen southerly breeze swirled around the ship. The bite of the Southern Hemisphere winter had grown sharper over the past week. The stop in Rarotonga had given them a taste of summer; seventy degrees felt different on the skin in the tropical Cook Islands than in temperate climes.

However, the route down to New Zealand was a stark reminder of the seasonal change. The cool, but calm waters of the Hauraki Gulf and Waitemata Harbour had provided a welcome haven from the extreme, rough edge of the South Pacific, which churned, hissed and spat almost non-stop from a day out of Rarotonga.

The entire voyage had left him perturbed. To any outside observer, it should have been a wonderful journey. First and foremost, he had left the European theatre of war to return home; away from the meat grinder of Bomber Command to the safe haven of New Zealand and eventually a training gig in the benign environs of Fiji.

They had sailed via New York, arguably, the greatest city in the "New World". They'd taken in the Caribbean Sea and the Panama Canal and its engineering marvels. Except for the last few days, the entire trip was in summer or tropical and sub-tropical weather.

There were more than one hundred and fifty Royal New Zealand Air Force personnel on the ship, a few of whom he'd instructed, so there were men to yarn and chat with over a beer. Lastly, the *Akaroa* itself was a fine ship. It was more utilitarian in its wartime role, but it was still a comfortable cruiser of the high seas.

*

Exhilaration and awe had swept over him as they passed through the Verrazzano Narrows where he was able to see the Statue of Liberty and the Manhattan skyline. Dizzy excitement was palpable throughout the airmen when they disembarked for the day. His comrades appeared evenly split between heading to see the vivacity of Times Square, the majesty of the Empire State Building, or finding the nearest bar, or to be entranced by the wiles of ladies of Manhattan.

William did a quick walk around the main sights of Midtown, then headed south to immerse himself in the nooks and crannies of Greenwich Village. He stopped outside the Village Vanguard on Seventh Avenue, and rued the fact they had a curfew. He wished he could have taken in an evening show.

He tried to satisfy his desire for a real New York experience with a massive lunch at a local diner. No rationing in the USA meant a meal of gargantuan proportions; a Reuben sandwich, fries and coleslaw, washed down with Coca-Cola and a bottomless cup of coffee. He immediately became acquainted with the concept of a doggy-bag.

Although New York was far removed from any sort of the normal life he'd experienced, the freedom from the immediate threat of the war, full shops and bustling streets filled him with a longing for the end of the conflict. Physically, it was like the relief he felt when he took off his heavy flight gear following a raid. How quickly he'd been conditioned to the pressure, anxiety, food scarcity and horrors of war in Britain. He felt lighter in step as he made his way back to the docks.

*

The elation of the New York stopover was replaced with sadness when they reached Nassau. Memories of Reggie swamped William; his booming voice, his lyrical Louisianan accent, his impenetrable Cajun slang, his unrelenting positivity and unquestioning friendship. Coming into the same port Reggie had sailed into on his fishing boat, filled him with pain. A small smile broke across his face as he pictured Reggie jumping off the boat to stride into British military offices, demanding to join the war effort.

'Top poulain, Reginald Louis Dubois the third,' William whispered, as he saluted.

*

The sun had started to set as the *Akaroa* docked at Queens Wharf; William stuck his hands deep in his pockets as the temperature dropped with the disappearing sun. He scanned the quayside, estimating only a couple of hundred people, as they waved, cheered, and cried, desperately searching the mass of faces on the ship for their loved ones.

A few New Zealand, British and American flags added some colour. Definitely lower levels of adulation than he'd expected, with about eighty percent of the passengers being returning New Zealand servicemen. After four years of war, William anticipated he'd feel more elation on reaching home. It was a scene and range of emotions he'd dreamt of, rehearsed in his mind so many times since he left in late 1940; he was positive of how it would play out. Now he was here, seeing the people, streets, hills and sky of his homeland, he felt relieved, rather than elated.

With Darlene still many weeks away from arriving, he didn't have the excitement of seeing his love again amongst the faces on the wharf. Visions flew across his mind's eye: the bailing out over Devon on his first op, having pints with Reggie in the Sergeants' Mess, holding Ossie on the Essen raid, the first time he saw Darlene from his hospital bed.

His thoughts moved to Albert and his family: Would he still be at work? Was he still a teacher? Had his children finished school for the day? Did Abby pick them up, or was she back working as a nurse? He had a thousand-and-one questions running around his head. All of them would have to wait until they met. If they met. He knew he had a lot of detective work ahead. He had less than ten days to find Albert and Abby, before he was shipped off to Fiji.

*

William found a quiet corner in the Sergeants' Mess at the RNZAF Hobsonville Base, set down his seven-ounce glass of beer on the side table, lit a cigarette and settled into the armchair to study the Auckland phone book. All he had to reference against was their names and an address in Mount Eden that Gary told him was on a Christmas card envelope from back in 1939. A quick scan down the Robertson's came up with no matches on Albert, Al, Abigail, A, or A & A with a Mount Eden address.

There were only two Robertson's in Mount Eden; one was Henry and the other Peter. The first clue was a dead end. He opened a fresh flight logbook and started copying potential listings. An hour later, all the Robertson entries had been reviewed with a few potential leads:

One listing of an Albert Robertson
Four listings of A Robertson
One listing of A & A Robertson

Only six phone numbers and addresses. Slim pickings. William let out a sigh and his shoulders dropped a couple of inches. Not a lot to go on and something told him none of the numbers would lead to Albert and Abby. It wouldn't surprise him if they have an unlisted number.

He took a long pull on his beer and winched when the sugary liquid hit his tongue. Had he gotten so used to British ales that Kiwi beer was such a shock to his taste buds? He thought about calling but when he checked the time it was after nine o'clock, too late to be making random calls to people he didn't know. He closed his notebook and picked up his glass, took a depth breath and drained the rest of its contents.

*

The next day, he tackled the first name on the list. 'Hello. Could I speak to Albert Robertson?' William's voice was hesitant and soft.

'This is he. How can I help you?' came the reply.

The voice was raspy, and definitely older than his brother William thought this person would have to be in their seventies or late sixties at a push. 'Forgive the intrusion. My name is William Robertson and I'm looking for my brother Albert. You're not from Wanganui originally, are you?

'Sorry my boy. Auckland born and bred. No brother called William. Mine were Michael and Peter. Both dead now though,' replied the man.

'Thank you, sir. Apologies for disturbing you.' William drew the call to a close as quickly as he could.

*

With all the phone book leads resulting in dead ends, it was time for alternate plans. Start with what he had – an address from the

Christmas card of 1939. A couple of days later, when he managed to get time off, he grabbed a car from the pool and headed into town. Although the road in was the main north and south route between Auckland and Northland, because of the Waitemata Harbour's reach and all the rivers, creeks and tidal mud flats, the road meandered for miles both west and south before it turned east to head into the city.

Time enough for William to run through ideas of what to say; one for Albert and Abby and one for someone else, if they had moved on. After two years of thinking about this scenario, he wasn't sure if his words would be adequate, appropriate or meaningful. Would they actually need to say anything? Would seeing each other again be enough? There would be a time and place for in-depth analysis of what happened, and forgiveness requested (and hopefully given) on both sides, but for the first meeting, would words be required?

As he turned the Austin 8 onto the street, his heartbeat quickened, his knuckles turned white as he gripped the steering wheel a little tighter. Beads of sweat formed on his temples; he rolled the window down and the sharp winter air hit him like a cold wave on the beach. He parked outside the house; a cute early 1900s single storey villa, painted in brilliant white, with forest green windowsills, porch railings and front door.

The house was framed on one side by an oak, its branches virtually naked of leaves, leaving its craggy trunk fully exposed; on the other side was an evergreen pohutukawa. There was no outward sign of life, or activity, around the property. William drummed his fingers on top of the steering wheel for a few minutes while staring at the house, 'Nothing's going to happen while you're sitting here, Robbie,' he said out loud. He grabbed his blue RNZAF hat off the passenger seat, put it on with a firm slap, opened the car door and strode across the street.

A woman in her thirties answered his knock. She was holding a toddler in her arms and another child ran up the hall and clung to her leg. The woman had a Rita Hayworth-like, blond hairstyle and wore a light blue knee-length dress with a brown belt. William knew Abby was in her thirties and had at least one school-aged child, so this person might, or might not, be Abigail Robertson.

'Good morning, ma'am. Warrant Officer William Robertson. Please excuse the intrusion. I'm looking for an Albert and Abigail Robertson, and this is the last address I have for them.'

'Not us, sorry. We've only been here ten months and didn't know the previous tenants,' the woman replied.

'They didn't leave a forwarding address?' William questioned.

She shook her head, but then raised her voice, 'Duncan might know. Our postie.' She pointed to a mailman across the street as she spoke.

'Thank you, ma'am. You've been most helpful. I won't delay you any longer. Have a good day.' William touched the peak of his hat, stepped off the porch and hurried across the street. 'Excuse me, sir. Have you been the postie here for a few years?'

'Yeah, mate. Mount Eden's been my patch for nearly ten years. Can I help you with something?' asked the postman.

'Hopefully. Do you remember a couple who used to live there? Albert and Abigail Robertson are their names,' William said pointing at the house.

'Sure do. Really nice family.' William's eyes grew wider and a small smile broke across his face as the mailman spoke. 'Lived there nearly five years. Moved over Epsom, Royal Oak way; Raurenga Avenue, I think. Had two lovely little girls by the time they left.'

'Raurenga Avenue, you reckon,' William nodded and replied almost to himself.

'Yeah. Can't remember the number though and Epsom ain't my patch. Sorry, mate. I should ask why you want to know.'

'Yes, of course. I should have introduced myself earlier. Warrant Officer William Robertson. Albert's my brother. We lost contact a few years back and now I'm back from the war, I wanted to say g'day.' This stranger didn't need to know all the intimate details.

'Good as gold. I can see the resemblance. Eyes and nose especially. Hope you track them down. Like I said, a terrific couple. Now, if you'll excuse me, I gotta get back to me rounds. Oh, almost forgot; he's a big-wig in one of the food companies. Might help you connect the dots,' he said, walking away, digging into his mailbag.

'Cheers. Great lead. What a stroke of luck,' William said out loud as he got into his car. Now for the last couple of lines of enquiry to complete the picture.

At the Town Hall Records Office, William thumbed through the pages of the 1940 electoral roll. After the morning's success, disappointment returned; the entries for Albert and Abby both listed their address as Mount Eden, not Epsom. The clerk told him the roll for the 1943 general election wouldn't be completed for at least another month. William closed the large volume with a forceful thud, causing a look of distain from the clerk. William waved his hand and mouthed 'sorry'.

His last option required a small amount of book research, but would also entail a fair bit of footwork; attend the main Sunday Mass of every Catholic Church in the central Auckland suburbs from Ponsonby, through Grey Lynn, Sandringham, Mount Eden, Newmarket to Parnell. The list had only four churches; he would start with Our Lady of the Sacred Heart on Banff Avenue in Epsom.

On the drive back to Hobsonville, William ran through all the new information; a reasonably up-to-date partial address, they had at least two daughters, Al worked for a food company, and a list of churches the family might attend – if they were still practising Catholics.

He tapped the steering wheel in exhilaration, as short of having a certified address or phone number, this was more than he had expected to have at the start of the day. With a bit more luck, he might track them down within a couple of Sundays. Getting closer to the end result filled him with excitement and trepidation, in equal measure.

Sleep that night didn't come easily; his mind ran at a thousand miles an hour, thinking of the potential scenarios which might play out over the next couple of weeks. Would he meet them at their house, at church, at Albert's work? Would neutral territory be best, or would the privacy of their place would be advisable.

*

He waited until he was one of the last in the church to approach the priest. 'Hello Father. I enjoyed Mass. Thank you,' William shook the priest's hand as he spoke.

'The pleasure is all ours. Delighted to have service personnel join us. Where are you based?' asked the clergyman.

'I was in Britain for over two years. Was with Bomber Command, but now stationed at Hobsonville and about to go up to Fiji. I'll be heading up there in a week or two,' added William.

'Oh, Bomber Command. I've heard it's a tough assignment, on many fronts. Hobsonville? A long drive in. Thank you for making the effort.'

'It's good to be able to go to Mass again, Father. I'm actually after some help. Does an Albert or Abigail Robertson attend Our Lady?' asked William.

'Why yes, Abigail comes most Sundays with the girls. Don't see much of Albert though. In fact, you've just missed them. Hold on. They're still on the street. Down there, near the corner,' said the priest, pointing down the road. 'That's Abigail in the mink shawl, Belinda is in the purple dress and Sybil is wearing blue. You want me to call them back?' asked the priest.

'No, no, no. I don't want to hold them up. In fact, I need to get moving back to base. I'll see them next week.' William craned his neck to get a better look at the three of them. 'You wouldn't happen to know where Albert works? he asked.

'He's with Butland Industries. You know the Chesdale Cheese folks. On the Great South Road in Penrose. He's a scientist of some kind,' replied the priest.

'Thanks, Father. Much appreciated. I'll see you at Mass next Sunday.' William had a spring in his step as he walked back to his car.

*

'You two get changed, then head to the kitchen and start washing some potatoes for the roast. Good girls,' said Abigail, as she ushered Belinda and Sybil to their room. She opened the living room door and was hit by a wave of warmth emanating from the fireplace. Her eyes darted from side to side, scanning the room.

Albert looked up from his armchair, as he read the Sunday papers. His pipe was delicately hanging from the right side of his mouth, a thin column of smoke rose from the pipe, adding a sweet tinge to the whole smoky environment. 'Hello, Love. How was Mass?' he asked.

Abby didn't answer. Instead, she strode over to the sideboard and picked up one of the picture frames arranged on top. 'I knew it.' She tapped the photograph with an index finger.

'What are you on about? What picture is that?' asked Al, as he folded the newspaper and took the pipe out of his mouth.

Abby sat on the arm of Al's chair, put her left arm around him, snuggled in close and showed him the photograph, 'Hon, it's William. He's here. I'm absolutely positive. This is from Christmas 1936, right? The last time your whole family was together?'

Al took the picture frame then looked at Abby, 'William? No, it can't be. Where'd you see him?'

'At Mass. It definitely was him. I saw this man come in, wearing an Air Force uniform and he sat at the back, scanning the assembly the whole time. I instantly had a "I've seen him before" feeling; the Robertson eyes, nose and mouth, all identical to you. Then it hit me during the sermon it was the William from all these pictures,' Abby waved her hand towards the rest of the photographs on the sideboard. 'He looks older, thinner and more drawn than this, but I suppose the war's done that to him, but absolutely it was him,' she said tapping the image of William in the photo with her fingernail.

'I'm struggling to believe it. If it was him, why here, why now? I had no idea he was in the Air Force,' Al bit down on his pipe as he spoke. The fire popped and spat out sparks into the screen.

'You weren't to know he was in the services. We haven't had any contact with either side of our families since we got married. Not a single reply to any of our letters, birthday or Christmas cards. Being in the Air Force makes sense. He's the right age to have enlisted and you've always said he was obsessed with airplanes. My big question; is he looking for us?' asked Abby.

'Is he, or is it a coincidence?'

'Come on, Hon. No such thing as a pure coincidence. Especially like this. He has to be looking for us. If he's there next Sunday, I'll introduce myself.' Abby lifted herself off the chair's arm and put the picture back on the sideboard. 'We'll have him over for Sunday roast.'

*

The facade of the Butland's building cast a long shadow over the car parks close to the front door. William shivered at the instant drop in temperature as he pulled into the shaded visitors parking slot. He held the car door tightly as he opened it, but a strong gust almost pulled it from his grasp. The winds which chopped up the waters of the Waitemata Harbour, forcing the abandonment of Catalina operations, were making their presence felt in south Auckland.

'Good afternoon,' he said to the receptionist, as he shook off the cold. 'I'm looking for Albert Robertson. I believe he works here.'

'Yes, he does, but unfortunately he isn't in today. He's down in the Waikato visiting the dairy factory of one of our suppliers. He'll be back in tomorrow. Do you want to leave him a message?' asked the receptionist.

'No, that's fine. I'll see him soon enough. Thank you for your assistance.' He started to walk out, but turned around, 'Out of interest, what does Albert do?'

'He's Deputy Head of Food Research. They say he's one of our best scientists.'

'My word, impressive. Good to know. You wouldn't know his address?' asked William.

'Only the Personnel Department has it, and they don't usually give it out. Sorry.' The receptionist pulled down her glasses and gave William a narrow stare.

'Yes, fair enough. Thank you for all your help. Good day.' He nodded to the receptionist as he opened the front door and battled the wind to get back into the car.

*

Abby took up a strategic position at the back of the Our Lady of the Sacred Heart church, which gave her the perfect position to scan the whole congregation and all the parishioners as they came in for Sunday Mass. She nodded and waved to each person and family members who came in. She pulled her sleeve up and her glove down to check her watch; seven to ten. Her right foot started an uncontrolled gentle tapping the floor. Her head dropped as she let out a small sigh and flipped through the Mass booklet. Thoughts started swimming around her mind; was introducing herself the right idea? Was it actually him? Was he actually looking for the family? Was this merely a coincidence and was today a fool's errand? As her courage wavered, a flash of blue caught her eye. She turned around to look at the man in the uniform. She'd seen the same man last week, and was struck by the resemblance to all the Robertson boys in the photographs. She felt her ears heat up and tingles shot down her arms, numbing her fingertips. 'Don't get cold feet now,' she whispered. She took a deep breath, before exhaling slowly, then stood up and walked towards the man.

She sat down next to him and offered her hand, 'Good morning. William Robertson, isn't it? This may shock you, but I'm your sister-in-law. Abigail Robertson. Pleasure to meet you.' She gave William a warm smile.

William's face lost a couple of shades of colour and his mouth dropped open for a few seconds, before he could speak, 'Dear Lord. How did you know? I'm sorry, yes I am. Forgive me, this has knocked me off kilter.'

'To be expected. All you Robertson boys are the spitting image of each other. I saw you last week and double-checked against Albert's family pictures. Are you looking for us?' she asked.

William nodded and a smile broke across his face as he remembered his brothers, 'Yes, I have been. I got back from Britain about ten days ago and have been inching closer to finding you since I arrived.'

'Exactly what I told Albert, but he was a bit sceptical. Mainly that you were here, rather than you were trying to track us down. I have to say I'm glad you're here. Albert has missed you not being in our lives. You do want to reconnect? I'm not wishing on a false hope?' Abby grabbed hold of William's hand when she asked the question.

'Oh, Abigail, I do, I do.' He squeezed her hand in return. 'I can't live with the idea of not having my older brother in my life. The last few years brought home to me how foolish we've been in shunning you all. The war has sharpened my views.'

'I can't tell you how happy this will make Albert. So, you'll join us for Sunday dinner? I've saved up most of our rations this week,' she said.

'Wonderful, thank you. The girls will be there?' William asked.

'Oh, yes. I gave them the day off Mass and they're getting the veggies ready. I had expected to meet you in the hope you'd come over,' said Abigail.

'Seems like you had this rendezvous better planned than I did.' The rising congregation signalled the start of Mass and their conversation quickly ended.

William opened the car door for Abigail, then jumped in the driver's side. 'Easy to drive from here. Right at the end of the street, first left down Manukau Road, then second left after Cornwall Park,' instructed Abigail, as she watched William swing the car into the street. 'You're married?' she asked, nodding at his wedding ring.

'To a Nurse, no less,' he replied, nodding vigorously.

'Well now. How about that. You knew I am a Nurse too? What's her name? Is she here?' she asked excitedly.

'Absolutely. It's not lost on me the parallel. Her name is Darlene du Toit. From South Africa. She's due here in a month or two.' His voice dropped as he spoke the last sentence.

'It must be tough, but now we're reconnected, she'll have family to look after her when she arrives. I'll be keen to learn all about how you two met and courted.' She looked at his hands gripped tightly around the steering wheel; his knuckles drained of blood and his jaw jutting out. 'Don't worry, William. Albert will be so happy to see you again.' She put her hand on his and gave him a smile.

William turned the car onto Raurenga Avenue and took in a deep breath. He felt a bead of sweat trickle down his back.

'Second last on the right, number fifty-nine. You can pull into the driveway,' Abby said. Parking the car, William couldn't let go of the steering wheel. 'Come on. Let's start making new family memories,' she said.

As he walked up the path, William felt his legs grow weak and tears blurred his vision.

Albert opened the door, stepped into the porch and waited for William to reach him, then took his brother into a deep, powerful and emotional hug.

*

# Acknowledgements

In memory of my great uncle and aunt, Jim and Daphne Robinson, who provided the inspiration for Find Your North Star.

To Ray and Lindy Robinson, Lyneve Robinson and John and Dorothy Osborne, thank you for your support, positivity and seemingly endless troves of information, especially about Jim and Arthur's time in 75 New Zealand Squadron. It's been a pleasure bringing their stories to life.

To the terrific group of professionals who have helped edit the manuscript: Jane Gulliford Lowes, The Oxford Editors, Donna Blaber and my uncle John Babington. Your knowledge, expertise and keen eyes have ensured the novel is the best it could be.

A big thank you to the wonderfully friendly and helpful members of the New Zealand Bomber Command Association. You've been incredibly supportive and a wealth of knowledge.

Finally, to the crewmates, families and descendants of the Leggett and Osborne crews and all other crews of 75 New Zealand Squadron during World War II. This book is dedicated to you and the memory of all who served in Bomber Command.